DARK DREAMERS

CHRISTINE FEEHAN

MARJORIE M. LIU

LEISURE BOOKS NEW YORK CITY

A LEISURE BOOK®

September 2006

Published by

Dorchester Publishing Co., Inc.
200 Madison Avenue
New York, NY 10016

ISBN 0-8439-5687-9

The name "Leisure Books" and the stylized "L" with design are trademarks of Dorchester Publishing Co., Inc.

Printed in the United States of America.

Visit us on the web at www.dorchesterpub.com.

TABLE OF CONTENTS

DARK DREAM

by

Christine Feehan

PROLOGUE

The night was black, the moon and stars blotted out by ominous swirling clouds gathering overhead. Threads of shiny black obsidian spun and whirled in a kind of fury, yet the wind was still. Small animals huddled in their dens, beneath rocks and fallen logs, scenting the mood of the land.

Mists floated eerily out of the forest, clinging to the tree trunks so that they seemed to rise up out the fog. Long, wide bands of shimmering white. Swirling prisms of glittering opaque colors. Gliding across the sky, weaving in and out of the overhead canopy, a large owl circled the great stone house built into the high cliffs. A second owl, then a third appeared, silently making lazy circles above the branches and the rambling house. A lone wolf, quite large, with a shaggy black coat and glittering eyes, loped out of the trees into the clearing.

Out of the darkness, on the balcony of the rock house,

3

a figure glided forward, looking out into the night. He opened his arms wide in a welcoming gesture. At once the wind began to move, a soft, gentle breeze. Insects took up their nightly chorus. Branches swayed and danced. The mist thickened and shimmered, forming many figures in the eerie night. The owls settled, one on the ground, two on the balcony railing, shape-shifting as they did, the feathers melting into skin, wings expanding into arms. The wolf was contorting even as it leaped onto the porch, shifting easily on the run so that a man landed, solid and whole.

"Welcome." The voice was beautiful, melodious, a sorcerer's weapon. Vladimir Dubrinsky, Prince of the Carpathian people, watched in sorrow as his loyal kindred materialized from the mist, from the raptors and wolves, into strong, handsome warriors. Fighters every one. Loyal men. True. Selfless. These were his volunteers. These were the men he was sending to their death. He was sentencing each of them to centuries of unbearable loneliness, of unrelenting bleakness. They would live out their long lives until each moment was beyond endurance. They would be far from home, far from their kin, far from the soothing, healing soil of their homeland. They would know no hope, have nothing but their honor to aid them in the coming centuries.

His heart was so heavy, Vladimir thought it would break in two. Warmth seeped into the cold of his body, and he felt her stirring in his mind. Sarantha. His lifemate. Of course she would share this moment, his darkest hour, as he sent these young men to their horrendous fate.

4

They gathered around him, silent, their faces serious—good faces, handsome, sensual, strong. The unblinking, steady eyes of confident men, men who were tried and true, men who had seen hundreds of battles. So many of his best. The wrenching in Vladimir's body was physical, a fierce burning in his heart and soul. Deep. Pitiless. These men deserved so much more than the ugly life he must give them. He took a breath, let it out slowly. He had the great and terrible gift of precognition. He saw the desperate plight of his people. He had no real choice and could only trust in God to be merciful as he could not afford to be.

"I thank all of you. You have not been commanded but have come voluntarily, the guardians of our people. Each of you has made the choice to give up your chance at life to ensure that our people are safe, that other species in the world are safe. You humble me with your generosity, and I am honored to call you my brethren, my kin."

There was complete silence. The Prince's sorrow weighed like a stone in his heart, and, sharing his mind, the warriors caught a glimpse of the enormity of his pain. The wind moved gently through the crowd, ruffled hair with the touch of a father's hand, gently, lovingly, brushed a shoulder, an arm.

His voice, when it came again, was achingly beautiful. "I have seen the fall of our people. Our women grow fewer. We do not know why female children are not born to our couples, but fewer are conceived than ever before, and even fewer live. It is becoming much more difficult to keep our children alive, male or female. The

5

scarcity of our women has grown to crisis point. Our males are turning vampire, and the evil is spreading across the land faster than our hunters can keep up. Before, in lands far from us, the lycanthroscope and the Jaguar race were strong enough to keep these monsters under control, but their numbers have dwindled and they cannot stem the tide. Our world is changing, and we must meet the new problems head on."

He stopped, once again looking over their faces. Loyalty and honor ran deep in their blood. He knew each of them by name, knew each of their strengths and weaknesses. They should have been the future of his species, but he was sending them to walk a solitary path of unrelenting hardship.

"All of you must know these things I am about to tell you. Each of you weigh your decision one last time before you are assigned a land to guard. Where you are going there are none of our women. Your lives will consist of hunting and destroying the vampire in the lands where I send you. There will be none of your countrymen to aid you, to be companions, other than those I send with you. There will be no healing Carpathian soil to offer comfort when you are wounded in your battles. Each kill will bring you closer to the edge of the worst possible fate. The demon within will rage and fight you for control. You will be obliged to hang on as long as you are able, and then, before it is too late, before the demon finds and claims you, you must terminate your life. Plagues and hardships will sweep these lands, wars are inevitable, and I have seen my own death and the death of our women and children. The death of mortals and immortals alike."

That brought the first stirring among the men, a protest unspoken but rather of the mind, a collective objection that swept through their linked minds. Vladimir held up his hand. "There will be much sorrow before our time is finished. Those coming after us will be without hope, without the knowledge, even, of what our world has been and what a lifemate is to us. Theirs will be a much more difficult existence. We must do all that we can to ensure that mortals and immortals alike are as safe as possible." His eyes moved over their faces, settled on two that looked alike.

Lucian and Gabriel. Twins. Children of his own second in command. Already they were working tirelessly to remove all that was evil from their world. "I knew that you would volunteer. The danger to our homeland and our people is as great as the danger to the outside world. I must ask that you stay here where the fight will be brother against brother and friend against friend. Without you to guard our people, we will fall. You must stay here, in these lands, and guard our soil until such time as you perceive you are needed elsewhere."

Neither twin attempted to argue with the Prince. His word was law, and it was a measure of his people's respect and love that they obeyed him without question. Lucian and Gabriel exchanged one long look. If they spoke on their private mental path, they didn't share their thoughts with any other. They simply nodded their heads in unison, in agreement with their Prince's decision.

The Prince turned, his black eyes piercing, probing,

searching the hearts and minds of his warriors. "In the jungles and forests of far-off lands the great Jaguar have begun to decline. The Jaguar are a powerful people with many gifts, great psychic talents, but they are solitary creatures. The men find and mate with the women then leave them and the young to fend for themselves. The Jaguar men are secretive, refusing to come out of the jungles and mingle with humans. They prefer that the superstitious revere them as deities. The women have naturally turned to those who would love them and care for them, see them as the treasures they are. They have, for some time, been mating with human men and living as humans. Their bloodlines have been weakened; fewer and fewer exist in their true form. Within a hundred years, perhaps two hundred, this race will cease to exist. They lose their women because they know not what is precious and important. We have lost ours through nature itself." The black eyes moved over a tall, handsome warrior, one whose father had fought beside the Prince for centuries and had died at the hands of a master vampire.

The warrior was tall and straight with wide shoulders and flowing black hair. A true and relentless hunter, one of so many he would be sentencing to an ugly existence this night. This fighter had been proven many times over in battle, was loyal and unswerving in his duties. He would be one of the few sent out alone, while the others would go in groups or pairs to aid one another. Vlad sighed heavily and forced himself to give the orders. He leaned respectfully toward the warrior he was addressing, but spoke loudly enough for all to hear.

"You will go to this land and rid the world of the monsters our males have chosen to become. You must avoid all confrontation with the Jaguar. Their species, as ours must, will either find a way to join the world or become extinct like so many others before us. You will not engage them in battle. Leave them to their own devices. Avoid the werewolf as best you can. They are, like us, struggling to survive in a changing world. I give you my blessing, the love and thanks of our people, and may God go with you into the night, into your new land. You must embrace this land, make it your own, make it your home.

"After I have gone, my son will take my place. He will be young and inexperienced, and he will find it difficult to rule our people in troubled times. I will not tell him of those I have sent out into the world as guardians. He cannot rely on those much older than he. He must have complete faith in his ability to guide our people on his own. Remember who you are and what you are: guardians of our people. You stand, the last line of defense to keep innocent blood from being spilled."

Vladimir looked directly into the gaze of the young warrior. "Do you take this task of your own free will? You must decide. None will think the less of any who wish to remain. The war here will also be long and difficult."

The warrior's eyes were steady on the Prince. Slowly he nodded acceptance of his fate. In that moment his life was changed for all time. He would live in a foreign land without the hope of love or family. Without emotion or color, without light to illuminate the unrelenting darkness. He would never know a lifemate, but would spend his entire existence hunting and destroying the undead.

CHAPTER ONE

Present Day

The streets were filthy and smelled of decay and waste. The dreary drizzle of rain could not possibly dispel the offensive odor. Trash littered the entrances to rundown, crumbling buildings. Ragged shelters of cardboard and tin were stacked in every alleyway, every conceivable place, tiny cubicles for bodies with nowhere else to go. Rats scurried through the garbage cans and gutters, prowled through the basements and walls. Falcon moved through the shadows silently, watchful, aware of the seething life in the underbelly of the city. This was where the dregs of humanity lived, the homeless, the drunks, the predators who preyed on the helpless and unwary. He knew that eyes were watching him as he made his way along the streets, slipping from shadow to shadow. They couldn't make him out, his body fluid, blending, a part of the night. It was a scene that had been played out a thousand times, in a thousand places. He was weary of the predictability of human nature.

Falcon was making his way back to his homeland. For far too many centuries he had been utterly alone. He had grown in power, had grown in strength. The beast within him had grown in strength and power also, roaring for release continually, demanding blood. Demanding the kill. Demanding just once, for one moment, to *feel*. He wanted to go home, to feel the soil soak into his pores, to look upon the Prince of his people and know he had fulfilled his word of honor. Know that the sacrifices he had made had counted for something. He had heard the rumors of a new hope for his people.

Falcon accepted that it was too late for him, but he wanted to know, before his life was over, that there was hope for other males, that his life had counted for something. He wanted to see with his own eyes the Prince's lifemate, a human woman who had been successfully converted. He had seen too much death, too much evil. Before ending his existence, he needed to look upon something pure and good and see the reason he had battled for so many long centuries.

His eyes glittered with a strange red flame, shining in the night as he moved silently through the filthy streets. Falcon was uncertain whether he would make it back to his homeland, but he was determined to try. He had waited far too long, was already bordering on madness. He had little time left, for the darkness had nearly consumed his soul. He could feel the danger with every step he took. Not emanating from the dirty streets and shadowed buildings, but from deep within his own body.

He heard a sound, like the soft shuffle of feet. Falcon continued walking, praying as he did so for the salvation of his own soul. He had need of sustenance and he was at his most vulnerable. The beast was roaring with eagerness, claws barely sheathed. Within his mouth his fangs began to lengthen in anticipation. He was careful now to hunt among the guilty, not wanting innocent blood should he be unable to turn away from the dark call to his soul. The sound alerted him again, this time many soft feet, many whispering voices. A conspiracy of children. They came running toward him from the three-story hulk of a building, a swarm of them, rushing toward him like a plague of bees. They called out for food, for money.

The children surrounded him, a half dozen of them, all sizes, their tiny hands slipping under his cloak and cleverly into his pockets as they patted him, their voices pleading and begging. The young ones. Children. His species rarely could keep their sons and daughters alive beyond the first year. So few made it, and yet these children, as precious as they were, had no one to cherish them. Three were female with enormous, sad eyes. They wore torn, ragged clothing and had dirt smeared across bruised little faces. He could hear the fear in their pounding hearts as they begged for food, for money, for any little scrap. Each expected blows and rebuffs from him and was ready to dodge away at the first sign of aggression.

Falcon patted a head gently and murmured a soft

word of regret. He had no need of the wealth he had acquired during his long lifetime. This would have been the place for it, yet he had brought nothing with him. He slept in the ground and hunted live prey. He had no need of money where he was going. The children all seemed to be talking at once, an assault on his ears, when a low whistle stopped them abruptly. There was instant silence. The children whirled around and simply melted into the shadows, into the recesses of the dilapidated and condemned buildings as if they had never been.

The whistle was very low, very soft, yet he heard it clearly through the rain and darkness. It carried on the wind straight to his ears. The sound was intriguing. The tone seemed to be pitched just for him. A warning, perhaps, for the children, but for him it was a temptation, a seduction of his senses. It threw him, that soft little whistle. It intrigued him. It drew his attention as nothing had in the past several hundred years. He could almost see the notes dancing in the rain-wet air. The sound slipped past his guard and found its way into his body, like an arrow aimed straight for his heart.

Another noise intruded. This time it was the tread of boots. He knew what was coming now, the thugs of the street. The bullies who believed they owned the turf, and anyone who dared to walk in their territory had to pay a price. They were looking at the cut of his clothes, the fit of his silk shirt beneath the richly lined cape, and they were drawn into his trap just as he'd known they would be. It was always the same. In every land. Every city. Every decade. There were always the packs who ran together bent on destruction or wanting the right to take what did not belong to them. The incisors in his mouth once more began to lengthen.

His heart was beating faster than normal, a phenomenon that intrigued him. His heart was always the same, rock steady. He controlled it casually, easily, as he controlled every aspect of his body, but the racing of his heart now was unusual, and anything different was welcome. These men, taking their places to surround him, would not die at his hands this night. They would escape from the ultimate predator and his soul would remain intact because of two things: that soft whistle and his accelerated heartbeat.

An odd, misshapen figure emerged from a doorway straight in front of him. "Run for it, mister." The voice was low, husky, the warning clear. The strange, lumpy shape immediately melted back and blended into some hidden cranny.

Falcon stopped walking. Everything in him went completely, utterly still. He had not seen color in nearly two thousand years, yet he was staring at an appalling shade of red paint peeling from the remnants of a building. It was impossible, not real. Perhaps he was losing his mind as well as his soul. No one had told him that a preliminary to losing his soul was to see in color. The undead would have bragged of such a feat. He took a step toward the building where the owner of that voice had disappeared.

It was too late. The robbers were spreading out in a loose semicircle around him. They were large, many of them displaying weapons to intimidate. He saw the gleam of a knife, a long-handled club. They wanted him scared and ready to hand over his wallet. It wouldn't end there. He had witnessed this same scenario too many times not to know what to expect. Any other time he would have been a beast whirling in their midst, feeding on them until the aching hunger was assuaged. Tonight was different. It was nearly disorienting. Instead of seeing bland gray, Falcon could see them in vivid color, blue and purple shirts, one an atrocious orange.

Everything seemed vivid. His hearing was even more acute than usual. The dazzling raindrops were threads of glittering silver. Falcon inhaled the night, taking in the scents, separating each until he found the one he was looking for. That slight misshapen figure was not a male, but a female. And that woman had already changed his life for all time.

The men were close now, the leader calling out to him, "Throw me your wallet." There was no pretending, no preliminary. They were going to get straight down to the business of robbing, of murdering. Falcon raised his head slowly until his fiery gaze met the leader's cocky stare. The man's smile faltered, then died. He could see the demon rising, the red flames flickering deep in the depths of Falcon's eyes.

Without warning, the misshapen figure was in front of Falcon, reaching for his hand, dragging at him. "Run, you idiot, run now." She was tugging at his hand, attempting to drag him closer to the darkened buildings. Urgency. Fear. The fear was for him, for his safety. His heart turned over.

The voice was melodic, pitched to wrap itself around his heart. Need slammed into his body, into his soul.

Deep and hard and urgent. It roared through his bloodstream with the force of a freight train. He couldn't see her face or her body, he had no idea what she looked like, or even her age, but his soul was crying out for hers.

"You again." The leader of the street gang turned his attention away from the stranger and toward the woman. "I told you to stay outta here!" His voice was harsh and filled with threat. He took a menacing step toward her.

The last thing Falcon expected was for the woman to attack. "Run," she hissed again and launched herself at the leader. She went in low and mean, sweeping his legs out from under him so that the man landed on his backside. She kicked him hard, using the edge of her foot to get rid of his knife. The man howled in pain when she connected with his wrist, and the knife went spinning out of his hand. She kicked the knife again, sending it skittering over the sidewalk into the gutter.

Then she was gone, running swiftly into the darkened alleyway, melting into the shadows. Her footfalls were light, almost inaudible even to Falcon's acute hearing. He didn't want to lose sight of her, but the rest of the men were closing in. The leader was swearing loudly, vowing to tear out the woman's heart, screaming at his friends to kill the tourist.

Falcon waited silently for them to approach, swinging bats and lead pipes at him from several directions. He moved with preternatural speed, his hand catching a lead pipe, ripping it out of astonished hands, and deliberately bending it into a circle. It took no effort on his part and no more than a second. He draped it around the pipe wielder's head like a necklace. He shoved the man with casual strength, sent him flying against the wall of a building some ten feet away. The circle of attackers was more wary now, afraid to close in on him. Even the leader had gone silent, still clutching his injured hand.

Falcon was distracted, his mind on the mysterious woman who had risked her life to rescue him. He had no time for battle, and his hunger was gnawing at him. He let it find him, consume him, the beast rising so that the red haze was in his mind and the flames flickered hungrily in the depths of his eyes. He turned his head slowly and smiled, his fangs showing as he sprang. He heard the frenzied screams as if from a distance, felt the flailing of arms as he grabbed the first of his prey. It was almost too much trouble to wave his hand and command silence, to keep the group under control. Hearts were pounding out a frantic rhythm, beating so loudly the threat of heart attack was very real, yet he couldn't find the mercy in him to take the time to shield their minds.

He bent his head and drank deeply. The rush was fast and addictive, the adrenaline-laced blood giving him a kind of false high. He sensed he was in danger, that the darkness was enveloping him, but he couldn't seem to find the discipline to stop himself.

It was a small sound that alerted him, and that alone told him just how far gone he really was. He should have sensed her presence immediately. She had come back for him, come back to aid him. He looked at her, his black eyes moving over her face hungrily. Blazing with urgent need. Red flames flickering. Possession stamped there.

"What are you?" The woman's soft voice brought him back to the reality of what he was doing. She gasped in shock. She stood only feet from him, staring at him with large, haunted eyes. "What are you?" She asked it again, and this time the note of fear registered deep in his heart.

Falcon lifted his head, and a trickle of blood seeped down his prey's neck. He saw himself through her eyes. Fangs, wild hair, only red flames in his otherwise empty eyes. He looked a beast, a monster to her. He held out his hand, needing to touch her, to reassure her, to thank her for stopping him before it was too late.

Sara Marten stepped backward, shaking her head, her eyes on the blood running down Nordov's neck to stain his absurdly orange shirt. Then she whirled around and ran for her life. Ran as if a demon were hunting her. And he was. She knew it. The knowledge was locked deep within her soul. It wasn't the first time she had seen such a monster. Before, she had managed to elude the creature, but this time was very different. She had been inexplicably drawn to this one. She had gone back to be sure he got away from the night gang. She *needed* to see that he was safe. Something inside her demanded that she save him.

Sara raced through the darkened entryway into the abandoned apartment building. The walls were crumbling, the roof caving in. She knew every bolt hole, every escape hatch. She would need them all. Those black eyes had been empty, devoid of all feeling until the . . . thing . . . had looked at her. She recognized possession when she saw it. Desire. His eyes had leaped to life.

Burning with an intensity she had never seen before. Burning for her as if he had marked her for himself. As his prey.

The children would be safe now, deep in the bowels of the sewer. Sara had to save herself if she was going to continue to be of any assistance to them. She jumped over a pile of rubble and ducked through a narrow opening that took her to a stairwell. She took the stairs two at a time, going up to the next story. There was a hole in the wall that enabled her to take a shortcut through two apartments, push through a broken door and out onto a balcony where she caught the lowest rung of the ladder and dragged it down.

Sara went up the rungs with the ease of much practice. She had scoped out a hundred escape routes before she had ever started working in the streets, knowing it would be an essential part of her life. Practicing running each route, shaving off seconds, a minute, finding shortcuts through the buildings and alleyways, Sara had learned the secret passageways of the underworld. Now she was up on the roof, running swiftly, not even pausing before launching herself onto the roof of the next building. She moved across that one and skirted around a pile of decaying matter to jump to a third roof.

She landed on her feet, already running for the stairs. She didn't bother with the ladder, but slid down the poles to the first story and ducked inside a broken window. A man lolling on a broken-down couch looked up from his drug-induced fog and stared at her. Sara waved as she hopped over his outstretched legs. She was forced to avoid two other bodies sprawled on the floor.

Scrambling over them, she was out the door and running across the hall to the opposite apartment. The door was hanging on its hinges. She went through it fast, avoiding the occupants as she crossed the floor to the window.

Sara had to slow down to climb through the broken glass. The splintered remains caught at her clothes, so that she struggled a moment, her heart pounding and her lungs screaming for air. She was forced to use precious seconds to drag her jacket free. The splinters scraped across her hand, shearing off skin, but she thrust her way outside into the open air and the drizzling rain. She took a deep, calming breath, allowing the rain to run down her face, to cleanse the tiny beads of sweat from her skin.

Suddenly she went very still, every muscle locked, frozen. A terrible shiver went down her spine. He was on the move. Tracking her. She *felt* him moving, fast and unrelenting. She had left no trail through the buildings, she was fast and quiet, yet he wasn't even slowed down by the twists and turns. He was tracking her unerringly. She knew it. Somehow despite the unfamiliar terrain, the crumbling complex of shattered buildings, the small holes and shortcuts, he was on her trail. Unswerving, undeterred, and absolutely certain he would find her.

Sara tasted fear in her mouth. She had always managed to escape. This was no different. She had brains, skills; she knew the area and he didn't. She wiped her forehead grimly with the sleeve of her jacket, suddenly wondering if he could smell her in the midst of the decay and ruin. The thought was horrifying. She had seen what his kind could do. She had seen the broken, drained bodies, white and still, wearing a mask of horror.

Sara pushed the memories away, determined not to give in to fear and panic. That way lay disaster. She set off again, moving quickly, working harder at keeping her footfalls light, her breathing soft and controlled. She ran fast through a narrow corridor between two buildings, ducked around the corner, and slipped through a tear in the chain-link fence. Her jacket was bulky, and it took precious seconds to force her way through the small opening. Her pursuer was large. He'd never be able to make it through that space; he would have to go around the entire complex.

She ran into the street, racing now with long, open strides, arms pumping, heart beating loudly, wildly. Aching. She didn't understand why she should feel such grief welling up, but it was there all the same.

The narrow, ugly streets widened until she was on the fringes of normal society. She was still in the older part of the city. She didn't slow down, but cut through parking lots, ducked around stores, and made her way unerringly uptown. Modern buildings loomed large, stretching into the night sky. Her lungs were burning, forcing her to slow to a jog. She was safe now. The lights of the city were beginning to appear, bright and welcoming. There was more traffic as she neared the residential areas. She continued jogging on her path.

The terrible tension was beginning to leave her body now, so that she could think, could go over the details of what she had seen. Not his face; it had been in the shadows. Everything about him had seemed shadowed and

22

vague. Except his eyes. Those black, flame-filled eyes. He was very dangerous, and he had looked at her. Marked her. Desired her in some way. She could hear her own footsteps beating out a rhythm to match the pounding of her heart as she hurried through the streets, fear beating at her. From somewhere came the impression of a call, a wild yearning, an aching promise, turbulent and primitive so that it seemed to match the frantic drumbeat of her heart. It came, not from outside herself but rather from within; not even from inside her head but welling up from her very soul.

Sara forced her body to continue forward, moving through the streets and parking lots, through the twists and turns of familiar neighborhoods until she reached her own house. It was a small cottage, nestled back away from the rest of the homes, shrouded with large bushes and trees that gave her a semblance of privacy in the populous city. Sara opened her door with shaking hands and staggered inside.

She dropped her soggy jacket on the entryway floor. She had sewn several bulky pillows into the overlarge jacket so that it would be impossible to tell what she looked like. Her hair was pressed tight on her head, hidden beneath her misshapen hat. She flung the hairpins carelessly onto the countertop as she hurried to her bathroom. She was shaking uncontrollably; her legs were nearly unable to hold her up.

Sara tore off her wet, sweaty clothes and turned on the hot water full blast. She sat in the shower stall, hugging herself, trying to wipe away the memories she had blocked from her mind for so many years. She had been a teenager when she had first encountered the monster. She had looked at him, and he had seen her. She had been the one to draw that beast to her family. She was responsible, and she would never be able to absolve herself of the terrible weight of her guilt.

Sara could feel the tears on her face, mingling with the water pouring over her body. It was wrong to cower in the shower like a child. She knew it did no good. Someone had to face the monsters of the world and do something about them. It was a luxury to sit and cry, to wallow in her own self-pity and fear. She owed her family more than that, much more. Back then, she had hidden like the child she was, listening to the screams, the pleas, seeing the blood seeping under the door, and still she hadn't gone out to face the monster. She had hidden herself, pressing her hands to her ears, but she could never block out the sounds. She would hear them for eternity.

Slowly she forced her muscles under control, forced them to work once again, to support her weight as she drew herself reluctantly to her feet. She washed the fear from her body along with the sweat from running. It felt as if she had been running most of her life. She lived in the shadows, knew the darkness well. Sara shampooed her thick hair, running her fingers through the strands in an attempt to untangle them. The hot water was helping her overcome her weakness. She waited until she could breathe again before she stepped out of the stall to wrap a thick towel around herself.

She stared at herself in the mirror. She was all enormous eyes. So dark a blue they were violet as if two vivid pansies had been pressed into her face. Her hand was throbbing, and she looked at it with surprise. The skin was shredded from the top of her hand to her wrist; just looking at it made it sting. She wrapped it in a towel and padded barefoot into her bedroom. Dragging on draw-string pants and a tank top, she made her way to the kitchen and prepared a cup of tea.

The age-old ritual allowed a semblance of peace to seep into her world again and make it right. She was alive. She was breathing. There were still the children who needed her desperately, and the plans she had been making for so long. She was almost through the red tape, almost able to realize her dream. Monsters were everywhere, in every country, every city, every walk of life. She lived among the rich, and she found the mon-sters there. She walked among the poor, and they were there. She knew that now. She could live with the knowl-edge, but she was determined to save the ones she could.

Sara raked a hand through her cap of thick chestnut hair, spiking the ends, wanting it to dry. With her teacup in hand, she wandered back outside onto her tiny porch, to sit in the swing, a luxury she couldn't pass up. The sound of the rain was reassuring, the breeze on her face welcome. She sipped the tea cautiously, allowing the stillness in her to overcome the pounding fear, to retake each of her memories, solidly closing the doors on them one by one. She had learned there were some things best left alone, memories that need never be looked at again.

She stared absently out into the dazzling rain. The drops fell softly, melodically onto the leaves of the bushes and shimmered silver in the night air. The sound of water had always been soothing to her. She loved the ocean, lakes, rivers, anywhere there was a body of water. The rain softened the noises of the streets, lessened the harsh sounds of traffic, creating the illusion of being far away from the heart of the city. Illusions like that kept her sane.

Sara sighed and set her teacup on the edge of the porch, rising to pace across its small confines. She would never sleep this night; she knew she would sit in her swing, wrapped in a blanket, and watch the night fade to dawn. Her family was too close, despite the careful closing off of her memories. They were ghosts, haunting her world. She would give them this night and allow them to fade.

Sara stared out into the night, into the darker shadows of the trees. The images captured in those gray spaces always intrigued her. When the shadows merged, what was there? She stared at the wavering shadows and suddenly stiffened. There was someone—no, *something* in those shadows, gray, like the darkness, watching her. Motionless. Completely still. She saw the eyes then. Unblinking. Relentless. Black with bright red flames. Those eyes were fixed on her, marking her.

Sara whirled around, springing for the door, her heart nearly stopping. The thing moved with incredible speed, landing on the porch before she could even touch the door. The distance separating them had been nearly forty feet, but he was that fast, managing to seize her with his strong hands. Sara felt the breath slam out of her as her body impacted with his. Without hesitating, she brought her fist up into his throat, jabbing hard as she stepped back to kick his kneecap. Only she didn't connect. Her fist went harmlessly by his head, and he dragged her against him, easily pinning both of her wrists in one large hand. He smelled wild, dangerous, and his body was as hard as a tree trunk.

Her attacker thrust open the door to her home, her sanctuary, and dragged her inside, kicking the door closed to prevent discovery. Sara fought wildly, kicking and bucking, despite the fact that he held her nearly helpless. He was stronger than anyone she had ever encountered. She had the hopeless feeling that he was barely aware of her struggles. She was losing her strength fast, her breath coming in sobs. It was painful to fight him; her body felt battered and bruised. He made a sound of impatience and simply took her to the floor. His body trapped hers beneath it, holding her still with enormous strength, so that she was left staring up into the face of a devil . . . or an angel.

CHAPTER TWO

Sara went perfectly still beneath him, staring up into that face. For one long moment time stopped. The terror receded slowly, to be replaced by haunted wonder. "I know you," she whispered in amazement.

She twisted her wrist almost absently, gently, asking for release. Falcon allowed her hands to slip free of his grip. She touched his face tentatively with two fingertips. An artist's careful stroke. She moved her fingers over his face as if she were blind and the memory of him was etched into her soul rather than in her sight.

There were tears swimming in her eyes, tangling on her long lashes. Her breath caught in her throat. Her trembling hands went to his hair, tunneled through the dark thickness, lovingly, tenderly. She held the silken strands in her fists, bunching the heavy fall of hair in her hands. "I know you. I do." Her voice was a soft measure of complete wonder.

She did know him, every angle and plane of his features. Those black, haunting eyes, the wealth of blue-black hair falling to his shoulders. He had been her only companion since she was fifteen. Every night she slept with him, every day she carried him with her. His face, his words. She knew his soul as intimately as she knew her own. *She knew him. Dark angel. Her dark dream.* She knew his beautiful, haunting words, which revealed a soul naked and vulnerable, and so achingly alone.

Falcon was completely enthralled, caught by the love in her eyes, the sheer intensity of it. She glowed with happiness she didn't even try to hide from him. Her body had gone from wild struggling to complete stillness. But now there was a subtle difference. She was wholly feminine, soft and inviting. Each stroke of her fingertips over his face sent curling heat straight to his soul.

Just as quickly her expression changed to confusion, to fright. To guilt. Along with sheer terror he could sense determination. Falcon felt the buildup of aggression in her body and caught her hands before she could hurt herself. He leaned close to her, capturing her gaze with his own. "Be calm; we will sort this out. I know I frightened you, and for that I apologize." Deliberately he lowered his voice so that it was a soft, rich tapestry of notes designed to soothe, to lull, to ensnare. "You cannot win a battle of strength between us, so do not waste your energy." His head lowered further so that he rested, for one brief moment, his brow against hers. "Listen to the sound of my heart beating. Let your heart follow the lead of mine."

His voice was one of unparalleled beauty. She found she *wanted* to succumb to his dark power. His grip was extraordinarily gentle, tender even; he held her with exquisite care. Her awareness of his enormous strength, combined with his gentleness, sent strange flames licking along her skin. She was trapped for all time in the fathomless depths of his eyes. There was no end there, just a free fall she couldn't pull out of. Her heart did follow his, slowing until it was beating with the exact same rhythm.

Sara had a will of iron, honed in the fires of trauma, and yet she couldn't pull free of that dark, hypnotic gaze, even though a part of her recognized she was under an unnatural black-magic spell. Her body trembled slightly as he lifted his head, as he brought her hand to his eye level to inspect the shredded skin. "Allow me to heal this for you," he said softly. His accent gave his voice a sensual twist she seemed to feel right down to her toes. "I knew you had injured yourself in your flight." He had smelled the scent of her blood in the night air. It had called to him, beckoned him through the darkness like the brightest of beacons.

His black eyes burning into hers, Falcon slowly brought Sara's hand to the warmth of his mouth. At the first touch of his breath on her skin, Sara's eyes widened in shock. Warmth. Heat. It was sensual intimacy beyond her experience, and all he had done was breathe on her. His tongue stroked a healing, soothing caress along the back of her hand. Black velvet, moist and sensual. Her entire body clenched, went liquid beneath him. Her breath caught in her throat. To her utter astonishment, the stinging disappeared as rough velvet trailed along each laceration to leave a tingling awareness behind. The black eyes drifted over her face, intense, burning. *Intimate.* "Better?" he asked softly.

Sara stared at him helplessly for an eternity, lost in his eyes. She forced air through her lungs and nodded her head slowly. "Please let me up."

Falcon shifted his body almost reluctantly, easing his weight from hers, retaining possession of her wrist so he could pull her to her feet in one smooth, effortless tug as he rose fluidly. Sara had planned out each move in her head, clearly and concisely. Her free hand swept up the knife hidden in the pocket of her sodden jacket, which lay beside her. As he lifted her, she jack-knifed, catching his legs between hers in a scissors motion, rolling to bring him down and beneath her. He continued the roll, once more on top. She tried to plunge the knife straight through his heart, but every cell in her body was shrieking a protest and her muscles refused to obey. Sara determinedly closed her eyes. She could not look at his beloved face when she destroyed him. But she would destroy him.

His hand gripped hers, prevented all movement. They were frozen together, his leg carelessly pinning her thighs to the floor. Sara was in a far more precarious position than before, this time with the knife between them. "Open your eyes," he commanded softly.

His voice melted her body so it was soft and yielding like honey. She wanted to cry out a protest. His voice matched his angel face, hiding the demon in him. Stubbornly she shook her head. "I won't see you like that."

"How do you see me?" He asked it curiously. "How do you know my face?" He knew her. Her heart. Her soul. He had known nothing of her face or her body. Not even her mind. He had done her the courtesy of not invading her thoughts, but if she persisted in trying to kill him, he would have no choice.

"You're a monster without equal. I've seen your kind, and I won't be fooled by the face you've chosen to wear. It's an illusion like everything else about you." She kept her eyes squeezed tight. She couldn't bear to be lost in his black gaze again. She couldn't bear to look upon the face she had loved for so long. "If you are going to kill me, just do it; get it over with." There was resignation in her voice.

"Why do you think I would want to harm you?" His fingers moved gently around her hand. "Let go of the knife, *piccola*. I cannot have you hurting yourself in any way. You cannot fight me; there is no way to do so. What is between us is inevitable. Let go of the weapon, be calm, and let us sort this out."

Sara slowly allowed her fingers to open. She didn't want the knife anyway. She already knew she could never plunge it into his heart. Her mind might have been willing but her heart would never allow such an atrocity. Her unwillingness made no sense. She had so carefully prepared for just such a moment, *but the monster wore the face of her dark angel.* How could she *ever* have prepared for such an unlikely event?

"What is your name?" Falcon removed the knife from her trembling fingers, snapped the blade easily with pressure from his thumb, and tossed it across the room. His

33

palm slid over her hand with a gentle stroke to ease the tension from her.

"Sara. Sara Marten." She steeled herself to look into his beautiful face. The face of a man perfectly sculpted by time and honor and integrity. A mask unsurpassed in artistic beauty.

"I am called Falcon."

Her eyes flew open at his revelation. She recognized his name. *I am Falcon and I will never know you, but I have left this gift behind for you, a gift of the heart.* She shook her head in agitation. "That can't be." Her eyes searched his face, tears glittering in them again. "That can't be," she repeated. "Am I losing my mind?" It was possible, perhaps even inevitable. She hadn't considered such a possibility.

His hands framed her face. "You believe me to be the undead. The vampire. You have seen such a creature." He made it a statement, a raw fact. Of course she had. She would never have attacked him otherwise. He felt the sudden thud of his heart, fear rising to terror. In all his centuries of existence, he had never known such an emotion before. She had been alone, unprotected, and she had met the most evil of all creatures, *nosferatu.*

She nodded slowly, watching him carefully. "I have escaped him many times. I nearly managed to kill him once."

Sara felt his great body tremble at her words. "You tried such a thing? The vampire is one of the most dangerous creatures on the face of this earth." There was a wealth of reprimand in his voice. "Perhaps you should tell me the entire story."

Sara blinked at him. "I want to get up." She felt very vulnerable lying pinned to the floor beneath him, at a great disadvantage looking up into his beloved face.

He sighed softly. "Sara." Just the way he said her name curled her toes. He breathed the syllables. Whispered it between exasperated indulgence and purring warning. Made it sound silky and scented and sexy. Everything that she was not. "I do not want to have to restrain you again. It frightens you, and I do not wish to continue to see such fear in your beautiful eyes when you look upon me." He wanted to see that loving, tender look, that helpless wonder spilling from her bright gaze as it had when she first recognized his face.

"Please, I want to know what's going on. I'm not going to do anything." Sara wished she didn't sound so apologetic. She was lying on the floor of her home with a perfect stranger pinning her down, a stranger she had seen drinking the blood of a human being. A rotten human being, but still . . . *drinking blood.* She had seen the evidence with her own eyes. How could he explain that away?

Falcon stood up, his body poetry in motion. Sara had to admire the smooth, easy way he moved, a casual rippling of muscles. Once again she was standing, her body in the shadow of his, close, so that she could feel his body heat. The air vibrated with his power. His fingers were wrapped loosely, like a bracelet, around her wrist, giving her no opportunity to escape.

Sara moved delicately away from him, needing a small space to herself. To think. To breathe. To be Sara and not part of a Dark Dream. Her Dark Dream.

"Tell me how you met the vampire." He said the words calmly, but the menace in his voice sent a shiver down her spine.

Sara did not want to face those memories. "I don't know if I can tell you," she said truthfully and tilted her head to look into his eyes.

At once his gaze locked with hers, and she felt that curious falling sensation again. Comfort. Security. Protection from the howling ghosts of her past.

His fingers tightened around her wrist, gently, almost a caress, his thumb sliding tenderly over her sensitive skin. He tugged her back to him with the same gentleness that often seemed to accompany his movements. He moved slowly, as if afraid to frighten her. As if he knew her reluctance, and what he was asking of her. "I do not wish to intrude, but if it will be easier, I can read the memories in your mind without your having to speak of them aloud."

There was only the sound of the rain on the roof. The tears in her mind. The screams of her mother and father and brother echoing in her ears. Sara stood rigid, in shock, her face white and still. Her eyes were larger than ever, two shimmering violet jewels, wide and frightened. She swallowed twice and resolutely pulled her gaze from his to look at his broad chest. "My parents were professors at the university. In the summer, they would always go to some exotic, fantastically named place, to a dig. I was fifteen; it sounded very romantic." Her voice was low, a complete monotone. "I begged to go, and they took my brother Robert and me with them." Guilt. Grief. It swamped her.

She was silent a long time, so long he thought she might not be able to continue. Sara didn't take her gaze from his chest. She recited the words as if she'd memorized them from a textbook, a classic horror story. "I loved it, of course. It was everything I expected it to be and more. My brother and I could explore to our hearts' content and we went everywhere. Even down into the tunnels our parents had forbidden to us. We were determined to find our own treasure." Robert had dreamed of golden chalices. But something else had called to Sara. Called and beckoned, thudded in her heart until she was obsessed.

Falcon felt the fine tremor that ran through her body and instinctively drew her closer to him, so that the heat of his body seeped into the cold of hers. His hand went to the nape of her neck, his fingers soothing the tension in her muscles. "You do not have to continue, Sara. This is too distressing for you."

She shook her head. "I found the box, you see. I knew it was there. A beautiful, hand-carved box wrapped in carefully cured skins. Inside was a diary." She lifted her face then, to lock her eyes with his. To judge his reaction.

His black eyes drifted possessively over her face. Devoured her. *Lifemate.* The word swirled in the air between them. From his mind to hers. It was burned into their minds for all eternity.

"It was yours, wasn't it?" She made it a soft accusation. She continued to stare at him until faint color crept up her neck and flushed her cheeks. "But it can't be. That box, that diary, is at least fifteen hundred years old. More. It was checked out and authenticated. If that was yours, if you wrote the diary, than you would have to be . . ." She trailed off, shaking her head. "It can't be." She rubbed at her throbbing temples. "It can't be," she whispered again.

"Listen to my heartbeat, Sara. Listen to the breath going in and out of my lungs. Your body recognizes mine. You are my true lifemate."

For my beloved lifemate, my heart and my soul. This is my gift to you. She closed her eyes for a moment. How many times had she read those words?

She wouldn't faint. She stood swaying in front of him, his fingers, a bracelet around her wrist, holding them together. "You are telling me you wrote the diary."

He drew her even closer until her body rested against his. She didn't seem to notice he was holding her up. "Tell me about the vampire."

She shook her head, yet she obeyed. "He was there one night after I found the box. I was translating the diary, the scrolls and scrolls of letters, and I felt him there. I couldn't see anything, but it was there, a presence. Wholly evil. I thought it was the curse. The workmen had been muttering about curses and how so many men died digging up what was best left alone. They had found a man dead in the tunnel the night before, drained of blood. I heard the workers tell my father it had been so for many years. When things were taken from the digs, it would come. In the night. And that night, I knew it was there. I ran into my father's room, but the room was empty, so I went to the tunnels to find him, to warn him. I saw it then. It was killing another worker. And it looked up and saw me."

Sara choked back a sob and pressed her fingertips harder into her temples. "I felt him in my head, telling me to come to him. His voice was terrible, gravelly, and I knew he would hunt me. I didn't know why, but I knew it wasn't over. I ran. I was lucky; workmen began pouring into the tunnels, and I escaped in all the confusion. My father took us into the city. We stayed there for two days before it found us. It came at night. I was in the laundry closet, still trying to translate the diary with a flashlight. I felt him. I felt him and knew he had come for me. I hid. Instead of warning my father, I hid there in a pile of blankets. Then I heard my parents and brother screaming, and I hid with my hands pressed over my ears. He was whispering to me to come to him. I thought if I went he might not kill them. But I couldn't move. I couldn't move, not even when blood ran under the door. It was black in the night, not red."

Falcon's arms folded her close, held her tightly. He could feel the grief radiating from her, a guilt too terrible to be borne. Tears locked forever in her heart and mind. A child witnessing the brutal killing of her family by a monster unsurpassed in evil. His lips brushed a single caress onto her thick cap of sable hair. "I am not vampire, Sara. I am a hunter, a destroyer of the undead. I have spent several lifetimes far from my homeland and my people, seeking just such creatures. I am not the vampire who destroyed your family."

"How do I know what you are or aren't? I saw you take that man's blood." She pulled away from him in a quick, restless movement, wholly feminine.

"I did not kill him," he answered simply. "The vampire kills his prey. I do not."

Sara raked a trembling hand through the short spikes of her silky hair. She felt completely drained. She paced restlessly across the room to her small kitchen and poured herself another cup of tea. Falcon filled her home with his presence. It was difficult to keep from staring at him. She watched him move through her home, touching her things with reverent fingers. He glided silently, almost as if he floated inches above the floor. She knew the moment he discovered it. She padded into the bedroom to lean her hip against the doorway, just watching him as she sipped her tea. It warmed her insides and helped to stop her shivering.

"Do you like it?" There was a sudden shyness in her voice.

Falcon stared at the small table beside the bed where a beautifully sculpted bust of his own face stared at him. Every detail. Every line. His dark, hooded eyes, the long fall of his hair. His strong jaw and patrician nose. It was more than the fact that she had gotten every single detail perfect, it was *how* she saw him. Noble. Old World. Through the eyes of love. "You did this?" He could barely manage to get the words past the strange lump blocking his throat. *My Dark Angel, lifemate to Sara.* The inscription was in fine calligraphy, each letter a stroke of art, a caress of love, every bit as beautiful as the bust.

"Yes." She continued to watch him closely, pleased with his reaction. "I did it from memory. When I touch things, old things in particular, I can sometimes connect with events or things from the past that linger in the object. It sounds weird." She shrugged her shoulders. "I can't explain how it happens, it just does. When I touched the diary, I knew it was meant for me. Not just anyone, not any other woman. It was written for me. When I translated the words from an ancient language, I could see a face. There was a desk, a small wooden one, and a man sat there and wrote. He turned and looked at me with such loneliness in his eyes, I knew I had to find him. His pain could hardly be borne, that terrible black emptiness. I see that same loneliness in your eyes. It is your face I saw. Your eyes. I understand emptiness."

"Then you know you are my other half." The words were spoken in a low voice, made husky by Falcon's attempt to keep unfamiliar emotions under control. His eyes met hers across the room. One of his hands rested on the top of the bust, his fingers finding the exact groove in a wave of the hair that she had caressed thousands of times.

Once again, Sara had the curious sensation of falling into the depths of his eyes. There was such an intimacy about his touching her familiar things. It had been nearly fifteen years since she had really been close to another person. She was hunted, and she never forgot it for a single moment. Anyone close to her would be in danger. She lived alone, changed her address often, traveled frequently, and continually changed her patterns of behavior. But the monster had followed her. Twice, when she had read of a serial killer stalking a city she was in, she had actively hunted the beast, determined to rid herself of her enemy, but she had never managed to find his lair.

She could talk to no one of her encounter; no one would believe her. It was widely believed that a madman had murdered her family. And the local workers had been convinced it was the curse. Sara had inherited her parents' estate, a considerable fortune, so she had been lucky enough to travel extensively, always staying one step ahead of her pursuer.

"Sara." Falcon said her name softly, bringing her back to him.

The rain pounded on the roof now. The wind slammed into the windows, whistling loudly as if in warning. Sara raised the teacup to her lips and drank, her eyes still locked with his. Carefully she placed the cup in the saucer and set it on a table. "How is it you can exist for so long a time?"

Falcon noticed she was keeping a certain distance from him, noticed her pale skin and trembling mouth. She had a beautiful mouth, but she was at the breaking point and he didn't dare think about her mouth, or the lush curves of her body. She needed him desperately, and he was determined to push aside the clawing, roaring beast and provide her with solace and peace. With protection.

"Our species have existed since the beginning of time, although we grow close to extinction. We have great gifts. We are able to control storms, to shape-shift, to soar as great winged owls and run with our brethren, the wolves. Our longevity is both gift and curse. It is not easy to watch the passing of mortals, of ages. It is a terrible thing to live without hope, in a black endless void."

42

Sara heard the words and did her best to comprehend what he was saying. Soar as great winged owls. She would love to fly high above the earth and be free of the weight of her guilt. She rubbed her temple again, frowning in concentration. "Why do you take blood if you are not a vampire?"

"You have a headache." He said it as if it were his most important concern. "Allow me to help you."

Sara blinked and he was standing close to her, his body heat immediately sweeping over her cold skin. She could feel the arc of electricity jumping from his body to hers. The chemistry between them was so strong it terrified her. She thought of moving away, but he was already reaching for her. His hands framed her face, his fingers caressing, gentle. Her heart turned over, a funny somersault that left her breathless. His fingertips moved to her temples.

His touch was soothing, yet sent heat curling low and wicked, making butterfly wings flutter in the pit of her stomach. She felt his stillness, his breath moving through his body, through her body. She waited in an agony of suspense, waited while his hands moved over her face, his thumb caressing her full lower lip. She felt him then, his presence in her mind, sharing her brain, her thoughts, the horror of her memories, her guilt. . . . Sara gave a small cry of protest, jerked away from him, not wanting him to see the stains forever blotting her soul.

"Sara, no." He said it softly, his hands refusing to relinquish her. "I am the darkness and you are the light. You did nothing wrong. You could not have saved your family; he would have murdered them in front of you."

"I should have died with them instead of cowering in a closet." She blurted out her confession, the truth of her terrible sin.

"He would not have killed you." He said the words very softly, his voice pitched low so that it moved over her skin like a velvet caress. "Remain quiet for just a moment and allow me to take away your headache."

She stayed very still, curious as to what would happen, afraid for her sanity. She had seen him drink blood, his fangs in the neck of a man, the flames of hell burning in the depths of his eyes, yet when he touched her, she felt as if she belonged to him. She *wanted* to belong to him. Every cell in her body cried out for him. Needed him. *Beloved Dark Angel.* Was he the angel of death coming to claim her? She was ready to go with him, she would go, but she wanted to complete her plans. Leave something good behind, something decent and right.

She heard words, an ancient tongue chanting far away in her mind. Beautiful, lilting words as old as time. Words of power and peace. Inside her head, not from outside herself. His voice was soft and misty like the early morning, and somehow the healing chant made her headache float away on a passing cloud.

Sara reached up to touch his face, his beloved familiar face. "I'm so afraid you aren't real," she confessed. *Falcon. Lifemate to Sara.*

Falcon's heart turned over, melted completely. He pulled her close to his body, gently so as not to frighten her. He trembled with his need of her, as he framed her face with his hands, holding her still while he slowly bent his dark head toward hers. She was lost in the fathomless depths of his eyes. The burning desire. The intensity of need. The aching loneliness.

Sara closed her eyes right before his mouth took possession of hers. And the earth moved beneath her feet. Her heart thudded out a rhythm of fear. She was lost for eternity in that dark embrace.

CHAPTER THREE

Falcon pulled her closer still, until every muscle of his body was imprinted on the softness of hers. His mouth moved over hers, hot silk, while molten lava flowed through her bloodstream. The entire universe shifted and moved, and Sara gave herself up completely to his seeking kiss. Her body melted, soft and pliant, instantly belonging to him.

His mouth was addictive. Sara made her own demands, her arms creeping up around his neck to cradle him close. She wanted to feel him, his body strong and hard pressed tightly to hers. Real, not an elusive dream. She couldn't get enough of his mouth, hot and needy and so hungry for her. Sara didn't think of herself as being a sensual person, but with him she had no inhibitions. She moved her body restlessly against his, wanting him to touch her, *needing* him to touch her.

There was a strange roaring in her ears. She knew no

thoughts, only the feel of his hard body against hers, only the sheer pleasure of his mouth taking possession of her so urgently. She gave herself up completely to the sensations of heat and flame. The rush of liquid fire running in her veins, pooling low in her body.

He shifted her closer, his mouth retaining possession, his tongue dueling with hers as his hand cupped her breast, his thumb stroking her nipple through the thin material of her shirt. Sara gasped at the exquisite pleasure. She hadn't expected company and she wore nothing beneath the little tank top. His thumb nudged a strap from her shoulder, a simple thing, but wickedly sexy.

His mouth left hers to blaze a path of fire along her neck. His tongue swirled over her pulse. She heard her own soft cry of need mingle with his groan of pleasure. Teeth scraped gently, erotically, over her pulse, back and forth while her body went up in flames and every cell cried out for his possession. His teeth nipped, his tongue eased the ache. His arms were hard bands, trapping her close so that she could feel the heavy thickness of him, an urgent demand, tight against her.

A shudder shook Falcon's body. Something dark and dangerous raised its head. His needs were swamping him, edging out his implacable control. The beast roared and demanded its lifemate. The scent of her washed away every semblance of civilization so that for one moment he was pure animal, every instinct alive and darkly primitive.

Sara sensed the change in him instantly, sensed the danger as his teeth touched her skin. The sensation was erotic, the need in her nearly as great as the need in him.

Fraternizing with the enemy. The words came out of nowhere. With a low cry of self-recrimination, Sara dragged herself out of his arms. She had *seen* him take blood, his fangs buried deep in a human neck. It didn't matter how familiar he looked; he wasn't human, and he was very, very dangerous.

Falcon allowed her to move away from him. He watched her carefully as he struggled for control. His fangs receded in his mouth, but his body was a hard, unrelenting ache. "If I planned on harming you, Sara, why would I wait? You are the safest human being on the face of this planet, because you are the one I would give my life to protect."

I am Falcon and I will never know you, but I have left this gift behind for you, a gift of the heart.

Sara closed her eyes tightly, pressed a hand to her trembling mouth. She could taste him, feel him; she *wanted* him. How could she be such a traitor to her family? The ghosts in her mind wailed loudly, condemning her. Their condemnation didn't stop her body from throbbing with need, or stop the heat moving through her blood like molten lava.

"I felt you," she accused, the tremors running through her body a result of his lethal kiss more than fear of his lethal fangs. She had almost wanted him to pierce her. For one moment her heart had been still as if it had waited all eternity for something only he could give her. "You were so close to taking my blood."

"But I am not human, Sara," he replied softly, gently, his dark eyes holding a thousand secrets. His head was unbowed, unshamed by his dark cravings. He was a strong, powerful being, a man of honor. "Taking blood is natural to me, and you are my other half. I am sorry I frightened you. You would have found it erotic, not distasteful, and you would not have come to any harm."

She hadn't been afraid of him. She had been afraid of herself. Afraid she would want him so much the wails of her family would fade from her mind and she would never find a way to bring their killer to justice. Afraid the monster would find a way to destroy Falcon if she gave in to her own desires. Afraid to reach for something she had no real knowledge of. Afraid it would be sinfully and wonderfully erotic.

For my beloved lifemate, my heart and my soul. This is my gift to you. It was his beautiful words that had captured her heart for all time. Her soul did cry out for his. It didn't matter that she had seen those red flames of madness in his eyes. In spite of the danger, his words bound them together with thousands of tiny threads.

"How is it you came to be here in Romania? You are American, are you not?" She was very nervous, and Falcon wanted to find a safe subject, something that would ease the sexual tension between them. He needed a respite from the urgent demands of his body every bit as much as Sara needed her space. He was touching her mind lightly, could hear the echoes of her family demanding justice.

Sara could have listened to his voice forever. In awe, she touched her mouth, which was still tingling from the pressure of his. He had such a perfect mouth and such a killer kiss. She closed her eyes briefly and savored the taste of him still on her tongue. She knew what he was doing, distracting her from the overwhelming sexual tension, from her own very justified fears. But she was grateful to him for it. "I'm American," she admitted. "I was born in San Francisco, but we moved around a lot. I spent a great deal of time in Boston. Have you ever been there?" Her breath was still fighting to find its way into her lungs and she dragged in air, only to take the scent of him deep within her body.

"I have never traveled to the United States but I hope that we will do so in the future. We can travel to my homeland together and see my Prince and his lifemate before we travel to your country." Falcon deliberately slowed his heart and lungs, taking the lead to get their bodies, both raging for release, back under control.

"A Prince? You want me to go with you to meet your Prince?" In spite of everything, Sara found herself smiling. She couldn't imagine herself meeting a Prince. The entire evening seemed something out of a fantasy, a dark dream she was caught in.

"Mikhail Dubrinsky is our Prince. I knew his father, Vladimir, before him, but I have not had the privilege of meeting Mikhail in many years." Not for over a thousand years. "Tell me how you came to be here, Sara," he prompted softly. The Prince was not entirely a safe subject. If Sara began thinking too much about what he was, she would immediately leap to the correct conclusion that Mikhail, the Prince of his people, was also of Falcon's species. Human, yet not human. It was the last thing he wanted her to dwell on.

"I saw a television special about children in Romania being left in orphanages. It was heartrending. I have a huge trust fund, far more money than I'll ever use. I knew I had to come here and help them if I could. I couldn't get the picture of those poor babies out of my mind. It took great planning to get over to this country and to establish myself here. I was able to find this house and start making connections."

She traced the paths of the raindrops on the window with her fingertip. Something in the way she did it made his body tighten to the point of pain. She was intensely provocative without knowing it. Her voice was soft in the night, a melancholy melody accompanied by the sounds of the storm outside. Every word that emerged from her beautiful mouth, the way her body moved, the way her fingertips traced the raindrops entranced him until he could think of nothing else. Until his body ached and his soul cried out and the demon in him struggled for supremacy.

"I worked for a while in the orphanages, and it seemed an endless task—not enough medical supplies, not enough people to care for and comfort the babies. Some were so sick it was impossible to help them. I thought there was little hope of really helping. I was trying to establish connections to move adoption proceedings along quicker when I met a woman, someone who, like me, had seen the television special and had come here to help. She introduced me to a man who showed me the sewer children." Sara pushed at her gleaming sable hair until it tumbled in spiky curls and waves all over her head. The light glinted off each strand, making Falcon long to touch the silky whorls. There was a terrible pounding in his head, a relentless hammering in his body.

"The children you whistled a warning to tonight." He tried not think about how enticing she looked when she was disheveled. It was all he could do not to tunnel his hands deep in the thick softness and find her mouth again with his. She paced restlessly across the room, her lush curves drawing his dark gaze like a magnet. The thin tank top was ivory, and her nipples were dark and inviting beneath the sheath of silk. The breath seemed to leave his body all at once, and he was hard and hot and uncomfortable with a need bordering on desperation.

"Well, of course those were only a few of them. They are excellent little pickpockets." Sara flashed a grin at him before turning to stare once again out the window into the pouring rain. "I tried to get them to turn in earlier, before dark, because it's even more dangerous on the street at night, but if they don't bring back a certain amount, they can be in terrible trouble." She sighed softly. "They have a minicity underground. It's a dangerous life; the older ones rule the younger and they have to band together to stay safe. It isn't easy winning their confidence or even helping them. Anything you give them could easily get them killed. Someone might murder them for a decent shirt." She turned to look over her shoulder at him. "I can't stay in one place too long, so I knew I could never really help the children the way they needed."

There was a sense of sadness clinging to her, yet she was not looking for pity. Sara accepted her life with quiet dignity. She made her choices and lived with them. She stood there with the window behind her, the rain falling softly, framing her like a picture. Falcon wanted to enfold her in his arms and hold her for eternity.

"Tell me about the children." He glided silently to the narrow table where she kept a row of fragrant candles. He could see clearly in the darkness, but Sara needed the artificial light of her lamps. If they needed lights, he preferred the glow of candlelight. Candlelight had a way of blurring the edges of shadows, blending light into dark. He would be able to talk of necessary things to Sara in the muted light, to talk of their future and what it would mean to each of them.

"I found seven children who have interesting talents. It isn't easy or comfortable to be different, and I realized it was my difference that drew that horrible monster to me. I knew when I touched those children that they would also draw him to them. I know I can't save all the orphans, but I'm determined to save those seven. I've been setting up a system to get money to the woman aiding the children in the sewers, but I want a home for my seven. I know I won't be able to be with them always, at least not until I find a way to get rid of the monster hunting me, but at least I can establish them in a home with money and education and someone trustworthy to see to their needs."

"The vampire will only be interested in the female children with psychic talents. The boys will be expendable; in fact, he will view them as rivals. It will be best to move them as quickly as possible to safety. We can go the mountains of my homeland and establish a home for the children there. They will be cherished and protected by many of our people." Falcon spoke softly, matter-of-factly, wanting her to accept the things he told her without delving too deeply into them yet. He was astonished that she already knew about vampires, and that she could be so calm about what was happening between them. Falcon didn't feel calm. His entire being was in a meltdown.

Her heart pounded out a rhythm of fear at the casual way he acknowledged that her conclusions were correct. The vampire would go after her children, and she had inadvertently placed them directly in his path.

She watched curiously as Falcon stared at the candles. The fingers of his right hand swirled slightly and the entire row of candles leaped to life. Sara laughed softly. "Magic. You really are magic, aren't you?" Her beloved sorcerer, her dark angel of dreams.

He turned to look at her, his black eyes drifting over her face. He moved then, unable to keep from touching her, his hands framing her face. "You are the one who is magic, Sara," he said, his voice a whisper of seduction in the night. "Everything about you is pure magic." Her courage, her compassion. Her sheer determination. Her unexpected laughter in the face of what she was up against. *Monster without equal.* And worse, Falcon was beginning to suspect that her enemy was one of the most feared of the vampires, a true ancient.

"I've told you about me. Tell me about you, about how you can be as old as you are, how you came to write the diary." More than anything else, she wanted the story of the diary. Her book. The words he had written for her, the words that had poured out of his soul into hers and filled her with love and longing and need. She wanted to forget reality and lean into him, taking possession of his perfect mouth.

Sara needed to know how his words could have crossed the barrier of time to find her. Why had she been drawn into the darkness of those ancient tunnels? How had she known precisely where to find the hand-carved box? What was there about Sara Marten that drew creatures like him to her? *What had drawn one of them to her family?*

"Sara." He breathed her name into the room, a whisper of velvet, of temptation. The rain was soft on the rooftop, and his lifemate was only a scant few inches from him, tempting him with her lush curves and beautiful mouth and enormous violet eyes.

Reluctantly he allowed his hands to fall away from her face. He forced his gaze from her mouth when he needed the feel of it again so desperately. "We are very close to the Carpathian Mountains. It is wild still, where we will go, but your plan to establish a house for the children will be best realized there. Few vampires dare to defy the Prince of our people on our own lands." He wanted her to accept his words. To know he meant to be with her and help her with whatever she needed to make her happy. If she wanted a house filled with orphans, he would be at her side and he would love and protect the children with her.

Sara took several steps backward. Afraid. Not so much of the man exuding danger and power, filling her home with his presence, filling her soul with peace and her mind with confusion. She was afraid of herself. Of her reaction to him. Afraid of her terrible aching need of him. He was offering her a life and hope. She had not envisioned either for herself. Not once in the last fifteen years. She pressed her body close to the wall, almost paralyzed with fear.

Falcon remained motionless, recognizing she was fighting her own attraction to him, the fierce chemistry that existed between them. The call of their souls to one another. The beast in him was strong, a hideous thing he was struggling to control. He needed his anchor, his lifemate. He must, for both of their sakes, complete the ritual. She was a strong woman who needed to find her own way to him. He wanted to allow her that freedom, yet they had so little time. He knew the beast was growing stronger, and his new, overwhelming emotions only added to his burden of control.

Sara smiled suddenly, an unexpected humor in her eyes. "We have this strange thing between us. I can't explain it. I feel your struggle. You need to tell me something but you are very reluctant to do so. The funny thing about it is that there is no real expression on your face and I can't read your body language, either. I just know there's something important you aren't telling me and you're very worried about it. I'm not a shrinking violet. I believe in vampires, for lack of a better word to call such creatures. I don't know what you are, but I believe you aren't human. I haven't made up my mind whether you are one of them; I'm afraid I'm blinded by some fantasy I've woven about you."

Falcon's dark eyes went black with hunger. For a moment he could only stare at her, his desire so strong he couldn't think clearly. It roared through him with the force of a freight train, shaking the foundations of his control.

"I am very close to turning. The males of our race are predators. With the passing of the years, we lose all ability to feel, even to see in color. We have no emotions. We have only our honor and the memories of what we felt to hold us through the long centuries. Those of us who must hunt the vampire and bring him to justice are taking lives. That adds to the burden of our existence. Each kill spreads the darkness on our souls until we are consumed. I have existed for nearly two thousand years, and my time has long since past. I was making my way home to end my existence before I could become the very thing I have hunted so relentlessly." He told her the truth starkly, without embellishment.

Sara touched her mouth, her eyes never leaving his face. "You feel. You could never fake that kiss." There was a wealth of awe in her voice.

Falcon felt his body relax, the tension draining from him at her tone. "When we find a lifemate, she restores our ability to feel emotion. You are my lifemate, Sara. I feel everything. I see in color. My body needs yours, and my soul needs you desperately. You are my anchor, the one being, the only being who can keep the darkness in me leashed."

She had read his diary; the things he was telling her were not new concepts. She was light to his darkness. His other half. It had been a beautiful fantasy, a dream. Now she was facing the reality, and it was overwhelming. This man standing so vulnerable in front of her was a powerful predator, close to becoming the very thing he hunted.

Sara believed him. She felt the darkness clinging to him. She felt the predator in him with unsheathed claws and waiting fangs. She had glimpsed the fires of hell in his eyes. Her violet eyes met his without flinching.

"Well, Sara." He said it very softly. "Are you going to save me?"

The rain poured onto the roof of her home, the sound a sensual rhythm that beat through her body in time to the drumming of her heart. She couldn't pull her gaze away from his. "Tell me how to save you, Falcon." Because every word he'd spoken was truth. She felt it, *knew* it instinctively.

"Without binding us with the ritual words, I am without hope. Once I speak them to my true lifemate, we are bound together for all eternity. It is much like the human marriage ceremony, yet more."

She knew the ancient words. He had said them to her, had *whispered* them to her a thousand times in the middle of the night. Beautiful words. *I claim you as my lifemate. I belong to you. I offer my life for you. I give to you my protection, my allegiance, my heart, my soul, and my body. I take into my keeping the same that is yours. Your life, happiness, and welfare will be cherished and placed above my own for all time. You are my lifemate, bound to me for all eternity and always in my care.*

She had stumbled over the translation for a long time, wanting each word perfect in its beauty, with the exact meaning he had intended. The words that had gone from his heart to hers. "And we would be considered married?"

"You are my lifemate; there will never be another. We would be bound, Sara, truly bound. We would need the touch of our minds, the coming together of our bodies often. I could not be without you, nor you without me."

She recognized that there was no compulsion in his voice. He was not trying to influence her, yet she felt the impact of his words deep inside her. Sara lifted her chin, trying to see into his soul. "Without binding us, you would really become like that monster who killed my family?"

"I struggle with the darkness every moment of my existence," he admitted softly. A jagged bolt of lightning lit the night sky and for one moment threw his face into harsh relief. She could see his struggle etched plainly there, a certain cruelty about his sensual mouth, the lines and planes and angles of his face, the black emptiness of his eyes. Then once again the darkness descended, muted by the glow of the candles. Once again he was beautiful, the exact face in her dreams. Her own dark angel. "I have no other choice but to end my life. That was my intention as I made my way to my homeland. I was already dead, but you breathed life back into my shattered soul. Now you are here, a miracle, standing in front of me, and I ask you again: Are you willing to save my life, my soul, Sara? Because once the words are said between us, there is no going back, they cannot be unsaid. You need to know that. I cannot unsay them. And I would not let you go. I know I am not that strong. Are you strong enough to share your life with me?"

She wanted to say no, she didn't know him, a stranger who came to her straight from taking a man's blood. But she did know him. She knew his innermost thoughts. She had read every word of his diary. He was so alone, so completely, utterly alone, and she knew, more than most, what it was like to be alone. She could never walk away from him. He had been there for her all those long, empty nights. All those long, endless nights when the ghosts of her family had wailed for vengeance, for justice. He had been there with her. His words. His face.

Sara put her hand on his arm, her fingers curling around his forearm. "You have to know I will not abandon the children. And there is my enemy. He will come. He always finds me. I never stay in one place too long."

"I am a hunter of the undead, Sara," he reminded, but the words meant little to him. He was only aware of her touch, the scent of her, the way she was looking at him. Her *consent*. He was waiting. His entire being was waiting. Even the wind and rain seemed to hesitate. "Sara." He said it softly, the aching need, the terrible hunger, evident in his voice.

Closing her eyes, wanting the dream, she heard her own voice in the stillness of the room. "Yes."

Falcon felt a surge of elation. He drew her against him, buried his face in the softness of her neck. His body trembled from the sheer relief of her commitment to him. He could hardly believe the enormity of his find, of being united with his lifemate in the last days of his existence. He kissed her soft, trembling mouth, lifted his head to look into her eyes. "I claim you as my lifemate."

The words broke out of him, soared from his soul. "I belong to you. I offer my life for you. I give to you my protection, my allegiance, my heart, my soul, and my body. I take into my keeping the same that is yours. Your life, happiness, and welfare will be cherished and placed above my own for all time. You are my lifemate, bound to me for all eternity and always in my care." He buried his face once more against her soft skin, breathed in her scent. Beneath his mouth her pulse beckoned, her life force calling to him, tempting. So very tempting.

She felt the difference at once, a strange wrenching in her body. Her aching heart and soul, so empty before, were suddenly whole, complete. The feeling filled her with elation; it terrified her at the same time. It couldn't be her imagination. She *knew* there was a difference.

Before she could be afraid of the consequences of her commitment, Sara felt his lips, velvet soft, move over her skin. His touch drove out all thought, and she gave herself willingly into his keeping. His arms held her closer still to his heart, within the shelter of his body. His teeth scraped lightly, an erotic touch that sent a shiver down her spine. His tongue swirled lazily, a tiny point of flame she felt raging through her bloodstream. Of their own volition, her arms reached up to cradle his head. She was no young girl afraid of her own sexuality; she was a grown woman who had waited long for her lover. She wanted the feel of his mouth and hands. She wanted everything he was willing to give her.

His hands moved over her, pushing aside the thin barrier of her top to take in her skin. She was softer than

anything he had ever imagined. He whispered a powerful command; his teeth sank deep, and whips of lightning lashed through his body to hers. White-hot heat.
Blue fire. She was sweet and spicy, a taste of heaven. He
wanted her, every inch of her. He needed to bury his
body deep within her, to find his safe haven, his refuge.
He had fed well, and it was a good thing, or he never
would have found the will to curb his strength. It took
every ounce of control to stop himself from indulging
wildly. He took only enough for an exchange. He would
be able to touch her mind, to reassure her. That would
be absolutely necessary for their comfort and safety.

He slashed his own chest, pressed her mouth to his
ancient, powerful blood, and softly commanded her
obedience. She moved sensuously against him, driving
him closer and closer to the edge of his control. He
wanted her, needed her, and the moment he knew she
had taken enough for the exchange, he whispered his
command to stop feeding. He closed the wound carefully and took possession of her mouth, sweeping his
tongue along hers, dueling and dancing, so that, as she
emerged from the enthrallment, there was only the
strength of his arms, the heat of his body, and the seduction of his mouth.

Without warning, the storm increased in intensity,
battering at the windowsills. Bolts of lightning slammed
into the ground with such force, the ground shook.
Sara's little cottage trembled, the walls shaking omi-
nously. Thunder roared so that it filled the spaces in the
house, a deafening sound. Sara tore herself out of his

arms, clapped her hands over her ears, and stared in horror out into the fury of the squall. She gasped as another bolt of lightning sizzled across the sky in writhing ropes of energy. Thunder crashed directly overhead, wrenching a soft, frightened cry from her throat.

CHAPTER FOUR

Before another sound could escape from Sara, Falcon's hand covered her mouth gently in warning. Sara didn't need his caution; she already knew. Her enemy had found her once again. "You have to get out of here," she hissed softly against his palm.

Falcon bent his head so that his mouth was touching her ear. "I am a hunter of the undead, Sara. I do not run from them." The taste of her was still in his mouth, in his mind. She was a part of him, inseparable now.

She tipped her head back to stare up at him, wincing as the wind howled and shrieked with enough force to cause small tornadoes in the street and yard, throwing loose paper, leaves, and twigs into the air in a rush of anger. "Are you any good at killing these things?" She asked it with a hint of disbelief. There was a challenge in her voice. "I need to know the truth."

For the first time that he could remember, Falcon felt like smiling. It was unexpected in the midst of the vampire's arrival, but the doubt in her voice made him want to laugh. "He is sending out his threat ahead of him. You have angered him. You have a built-in shield, a rare thing. He cannot find you when he scans, so he is looking for an awareness, a surge of fear that will tell him you know who he is. That is how he tracks you. I will send my answer to him so he is aware that you are under my protection."

"No!" She caught his arm with suddenly tense fingers. "This is it, our chance. If he doesn't know about you, then he will come for me. We can lay a trap for him."

"I do not need to use you as bait." His voice was very mild, but there was a hint of some unnamed emotion that made her shiver. Falcon was unfailingly gentle with her, his tone always soft and low, his touch tender. But there was something deep inside him that was terribly dangerous and very dark.

Sara found herself shivering, but she tightened her hold on him, afraid that if he went into the raging storm he would be lost to her. "It's the best way. He'll come for me; he always comes for me." Already her bond with Falcon was so strong, she couldn't bear the thought of something happening to him. She must protect him from the terrible thing that had destroyed her family.

"Not tonight. Tonight I'll go after him." Falcon put her from him gently. He could clearly see her fears and her fierce need to be sure that he was safe. She had no concept of what he was, of the thousands of battles he had fought with these very monsters: Carpathian males who had waited too long, or who had chosen to give up their souls for the fleeting momentary pleasure of the kill. His brethren.

Sara caught his arm. "No, don't go out there." There was a catch in her voice. "I don't want to be alone tonight. I know he's here, and for the first time, I'm not alone."

He leaned down to capture her soft mouth with his. At once there was that melting sensation, the promise of silken heat and ecstasy he had never dared to dream about. "You are worried about my safety and seek ways to keep me with you." He said the words softly against her lips. "I dwell within you now; we are able to share thoughts with one another. This is my life, Sara; this is what I do. I have no choice but to go. I am a male Carpathian sent by the Prince of my people into the world to protect others from these creatures. I am a hunter. It is the only honor I have left."

There was that aching loneliness in his voice. She had been alone for fifteen years. She couldn't imagine what it would be like to be alone for as long as he had been. Watching endless time go by, the changes in the world, without hope or refuge. Sentenced to destroying his own kind, perhaps even friends. *Honor.* That word had been used often in his diary. She saw the implacable resolve in him, the intensity that swirled dangerously close to the surface of his calm. Nothing she could say would stop him.

Sara sighed softly and nodded. "I think there is much more in you to honor than just your abilities as a hunter, but I understand. There are things I must do that I don't always want to, but I know I couldn't live with myself if I didn't do them." She slipped her arms around his neck and pressed her body close to his. For one moment she was no longer alone in the world. He was solid and safe. "Don't let him harm you. He's managed to destroy everyone I care about."

Falcon held her, his arms cradling her body, every cell needing her. It was madness to hunt when he was so close to turning and the ritual had not been completed, but he had no choice. The wind beat at the window, the branches of trees sweeping against the house in a kind of fury. "I will be back soon, Sara," he assured her softly.

"Let me go with you," she said suddenly. "I've faced him before."

Falcon smiled. His soul smiled. She was beautiful to him, nearly unbelievable. Ready to face the monster right beside him. He bent once more and found her mouth with his. A promise. He made it that. A promise of life and happiness. And then he was gone, wrenching open the door while he still could, while his honor was strong enough to overcome the needs of his body. He simply dissolved into mist, mixing with the rain for camouflage, and streamed through the night air, away from the shelter and temptation of her body and heart.

Sara stepped out onto the porch after him, still blinking, unsure where he had gone, it had happened so quickly. "Falcon!" His name was a cry wrenched from her soul. The wind whipped her hair into a frenzy. The rain doused her clothes until the silk was nearly transparent. She was utterly alone again.

You will never be alone again, Sara. I dwell within you as you are within me. Speak to me; use your mind, and I will hear you.

She held her breath. It was impossible. She felt a flood of relief and sagged against the column of her porch for support. She didn't question how his voice could be in her mind, clear and perfect and sexy. She accepted it because she needed it so desperately. She jammed her fist in her mouth to stop herself from calling him back to her, forgetting for a moment that he must be reading her thoughts.

Falcon laughed softly, his voice a drawling caress. *You are an amazing woman, Sara. Even to be able to translate my letters to you. I wrote them in several languages. Greek, Hebrew. The ancient tongue. How did you accomplish such a feat?* He was traveling swiftly across the night sky, scanning carefully, looking for disturbances that would signal the arrival of the undead. Sometimes blank spaces revealed the vampire's lair. Other times it would be a surge of power or an unexpected exodus of bats from a cave. The smallest detail could provide clues to one who knew where to look.

Sara was silent a moment, turning the question over in her mind. She had been obsessed with translating the strange documents wrapped so carefully in oilskin. Perseverance. She had *needed* to translate those words. Sacred words. She remembered the feeling she had each time she touched those scrolled pages. Her heart had beat faster, her body had come to life, her fingers had smoothed over the fibers more times than she wanted to count. She had known that those words were meant for her. And she had seen his face. His eyes, the shape of his jaw, the long flow of his hair. The aching loneliness in him. She had known that only she would find the right translation.

My parents taught me Greek and Hebrew and most of the ancient languages, but I had never seen some of the letters and symbols before. I went to several museums and all the universities, but I didn't want to show the diary to anyone else. I believed it was meant for me. She had known that the words were intimate, meant only for her eyes. There had been poetry in those words before she had ever translated them. Sara felt tears gathering in her eyes. Falcon. She knew his name now, had looked into his eyes, and she knew he needed her. No one else. Just Sara. *I studied the diary for several months, translated what I could, but I knew it wasn't right, word for word. And then it just came to me. I felt when it was right. I can't explain how, but I knew the moment I hit on the key.*

Falcon felt the curious wrenching in his heart. She could make his soul flood with warmth, overwhelming him with such intense feeling that he was no longer the powerful predator but a man willing to do anything for his lifemate. She humbled him with her generosity and her acceptance of what he was. He had written those words, expressing emotions he could no longer feel.

Writing the diary was a compulsion he couldn't ignore. He had never expected anyone to read it, yet he had never destroyed it, unable to do so.

Dawn was a couple of hours away and the vampire would still be lethal. More than likely he was searching for lairs, escape routes, gathering information. Falcon had hunted and successfully battled the vampire for centuries, yet he was growing distinctly uneasy. He should have picked up a trail, yet there were none of the usual signs to indicate the undead had passed over the city. Few of the creatures could achieve such a feat; only a very powerful ancient enemy would have such skills.

You are my heart and soul, Sara. The words I left for you are truth, and only my lifemate would know how to find the key to unlock the code to translate the ancient language. His tone held admiration and an intensity of love that wrapped her in warmth. *I must concentrate on the hunt. This one is no fledgling vampire, but one of power and strength. It requires my full attention. Should you have need of me, reach with your mind and I will hear you.*

Sara crossed her arms across her breasts, moving back onto her porch, watching the sheets of rain falling in silvery threads. She felt Falcon's uneasiness more than heard it in his tone. *If you need me, I will come to you.* She meant it. Meant it with every cell in her body. It felt wrong to have Falcon going alone to fight her battles.

Falcon's heart lightened. She would rush to his aid if he called her. Their tie was already strong, and growing with each passing moment. Sara represented the miracle granted to his species. *Lifemate.*

He was cautious as he moved across the sky, using the storm as his cover. He was adept, able to shield his presence easily. He began surveying the areas most likely to harbor the undead. Within the city, it would be the deserted older buildings with basements. Outside of the city, it would be any cave, any hole in the ground the ancient vampire could protect.

Falcon found no traces of the enemy, but the uneasiness in him began to grow. The vampire would have already attacked Sara if he had known for certain where she was. Obviously, he had vented his rage because he *hadn't* found her, and he had hoped to frighten her into betraying her presence. That left one other avenue open to Falcon. He would have to find the vampire's kill and trace him from there. It would be a painstakingly slow process and he would have to leave Sara alone for some time. He reached for her. *If you feel uneasy, call for me at once. Anything at all, Sara, call for me.*

He felt her smile. *I have been aware of this enemy for half my life. I know when he is close, and I have managed to escape him time after time. You take care of yourself, Falcon, and don't worry about me.* Sara had been alone a long time and was an independent, self-sufficient woman. She was far more worried about Falcon than she was about herself.

The rain was still pouring down, the wind blowing the droplets into dismal heavy sheets. Falcon felt no cold in the form he had taken. Had he been in his natural body, he would have regulated his body temperature with ease.

The storm was a deterrent to seeking his enemy by using scent, but he knew the ways of the vampire. He found the kill unerringly.

The body was in an alleyway, not far from where Sara's sewer children had rushed Falcon. His uneasiness grew. The vampire obviously had become adept at finding Sara. There was a pattern to her behavior, and the undead capitalized on it. Once he found the country and the city she had settled in, the vampire would go to the places where Sara would eventually go. The refuges of the lost, the homeless, the unwanted children and battered women. Sara would work in those areas to accomplish what she could before she moved on. Money meant little to her; it was only a means to keep moving and to do what she could to help. She lived frugally and spent little on herself. Just as Falcon had studied vampires to learn their ways, this vampire had studied Sara. Yet she had continued to elude him. Most vampires were not known for their patience, yet this one had followed Sara relentlessly for fifteen years.

It was a miracle that she had managed to avoid capture, a tribute to her courageous and resourceful nature. Falcon's frame shimmered and solidified in the dreary rain beside the dead man. The vampire's victim had died hard. Falcon studied the corpse, careful not to touch anything. He wanted the scent of the undead, the feel of him. The victim was young, a street punk. There was a knife on the ground with blood on the blade. Falcon could see the blade was already corroding. The man had been tortured, most likely for information about Sara.

The vampire would want to know if she had been seen in the area. The echoes of violence were all around Falcon.

He couldn't allow the evidence to remain for the police. He sighed softly and began to summon the energy in the sky above him. Bolts of lightning danced brightly, throwing the alley into sharp relief. The whips sizzled and crackled, white-hot. He directed the energy to the body and the knife. It incinerated the victim to fine ashes and cleansed the blade before melting it.

The flare of power was all around him as the lightning burned like an orange flame from the ground back up to the dark, ominous clouds, where it veined out in radiant points of blue-white heat. Falcon suddenly raised his head and looked around him, realizing that the power vibrating in the air was not his alone. He leaped back, away from the ashes as the blackened ruins came to life. An apparition of horror rose up with a misshapen head and pitiless holes for eyes.

Falcon whirled, a fraction of a second too late, to meet the real attack. A claw missed his eye and raked his temple. Razor-sharp tips dug four long furrows into his chest. The pain was excruciating. Hot, fetid breath exploded in his face and he smelled rotting flesh, but the creature was a blur, disappearing as Falcon struck instinctively toward the heart.

His fist brushed thick fur and then empty air. At once, the beast within Falcon rose up, hot and powerful. The strength of it shook him. There was a red haze in front of his eyes, chaos reigning in his mind. Falcon spun around as he took to the sky, barely avoiding slamming bolts of energy that blackened the alley and took out the sides of the already crumbling building. The sound was deafening. The beast welcomed the violence, embraced it. Falcon was fighting himself as well as the vampire, battling the hunger that could never be assuaged.

Falcon? Her voice was a breath of fresh air, pushing aside the call of the kill. *Tell me where you are. I feel danger to you.* It was the naked concern in her voice that allowed him to control the raging demon, to push it aside despite the desire for violence.

Falcon struck fast and hard, a calculated risk, flying toward the bizarre figure made of ash, his fist outstretched before him. The ashes scattered in a whirlwind, rising high like a tower of grotesque charcoal. For an instant a form shimmered in the air as the vampire attempted to throw a barrier between them. Falcon drove through the flimsy structure, again feeling the brush, this time of flesh, but the creature had managed to dissolve again. The vampire was gone, vanishing as swiftly as it had appeared.

There was no trace of the monster, not even the inevitable blankness. Falcon searched the area carefully, thoroughly, looking for the smallest clue. The longer he searched, the more he was certain that Sara was hunted by a true ancient, a master vampire who had managed to elude all hunters throughout the centuries.

Falcon moved through the sky warily. The vampire would not strike at him again now. Falcon had been tested, and the ancient had lost the advantage of surprise. The enemy now knew he was up against an experienced hunter well versed in battle. He would go to ground, avoid contact in the hopes that Falcon would pass him by.

A clap of thunder echoed across the sky. A warning. A dark promise. The vampire was staking his claim, despite the fact that he knew a hunter was in the area. He would not give Sara up. She was his prey.

Sara was waiting for Falcon on the small porch, reaching for him with eager arms. Her gaze moved over him fearfully, assessing him for damage. Falcon wanted to gather her into his arms and hold her against his heart. No one had ever welcomed him, worried about him, had that look on her face. Anxious. Loving. She was even more beautiful than he remembered. Her clothes were soaked with rainwater, her short hair spiky and disheveled, her eyes enormous. He could drown in her eyes. He could melt in the heat of her welcome.

"Come into the house," Sara said, touching his temple with gentle fingers, running her hands over him, needing to feel him. She drew him into her home, out of the night air, out of the rain. "Tell me," she urged.

Falcon looked around him at the neat little room. It was soothing and homey. Comforting. The stark contrast between his ugly, barren existence and this moment was so extreme, it was almost shocking. Sara's smile, her touch, the worry in her eyes—he wouldn't trade those things for any treasure he had ever come across in his centuries on earth.

"What happened to you, Falcon? And I don't mean your wounds." The fear for him she felt deep within her soul had been overwhelming in those moments before their communication.

Falcon shoved a hand through his long hair. He had to tell her the truth. The demon in him was stronger than ever. He had waited too long, been in too many battles, made too many kills. "Sara," he said softly. "We have a few choices, but we must make them swiftly. We do not have the time to wait until you fully understand what is happening. I want you to remain quiet and listen to what I have to say, and then we will have to make our decisions."

Sara nodded gravely, her eyes on his face. He was struggling, she could see that clearly. She knew he feared for her safety. She wanted to smooth the lines etched so deeply into his face. There was blood smeared on his temple, a thin trail that only accented the deep weariness around his mouth. His shirt was tattered and bloody, with four distinct rips. Every cell in her body cried out to hold him, to comfort him, yet she sat very still, waiting for what was to come.

"I have tied us together in life or death. If something were to happen to me, you would find it very difficult to continue without me. We must get to the Carpathian Mountains and my people. This enemy is an ancient and very powerful. He is determined that you are his, and nothing will deter him from hunting you. I believe you are in danger during both the hours of sunlight and darkness."

Sara nodded. She wasn't about to argue with him. The vampire had been relentless in his pursuit of her. She had been lucky in her escapes, willing to run at the smallest sign that he was near. Had the vampire stalked her silently, he would have had her, she was certain, but he didn't seem to credit her ability to ignore his summons. "He's used creatures during the day before." She looked down at her hands. "I burned one of them." She admitted it in a low voice, ashamed of herself.

Falcon, feeling her guilt like a blow, took her hands, turned them over, and placed a kiss in the center of each palm. "The vampire's ghouls are already dead. They are soulless creatures, living on flesh and the tainted blood of the vampire. You were lucky to escape them. Killing them is a mercy. Believe me, Sara, they cannot be saved."

"Tell me our choices, Falcon. It is nearly morning and I'm feeling very anxious for you. Your wounds are serious. You need to be looked after." She could hardly bear the sight of him. He was smeared with blood and so weary he was drooping. Her fingers smoothed back stray strands of his long black hair.

"My wounds truly are not serious." He shrugged them off with a casual ripple of his shoulders. "When I go to ground, the soil will aid in healing me. While I am locked within the earth, you will be alone and vulnerable. During certain hours of the day I am at my weakest and cannot come to your aid. At least not physically. I would prefer that you remain by my side at all times to know you are safe."

Her eyes widened. "You want me to go beneath the earth with you? How would that be possible?" There were things left undone, things she needed to do in the daylight hours. Business hours. The world didn't accommodate Falcon's people so readily.

"You would have to become fully like me." He said it softly, starkly. "You would have all the gifts of my people, and also the weaknesses. You would be vulnerable during daylight hours, and you would require blood to sustain your life."

She was silent for a moment, turning his words over in her mind. "I presume that if I were like you, that would not be so abhorrent to me. I would crave blood?"

He shrugged. "It is a fact of our lives. We do not kill; we keep our prey calm and unknowing. I would provide for you, and it would not be in such a way that you would find it uncomfortable."

Sara nodded her acceptance of that even as her mind turned over his use of the word *prey.* She had lived in the shadows of the Carpathian world for fifteen years. His words weren't a shock to her. She drew Falcon toward the small bathroom where she had a first aid kit. He went with her because he could feel her need to take care of him. And he liked the feel of her hands on him.

"I can't possibly make a decision like this in one night, Falcon," she said as she ran hot water onto a clean cloth. "I have things I have to finish and I'll need to think about this." She didn't need to think too long or too hard. She wanted him with every fiber of her being. She had already learned in the short time while he was off chasing her enemy what it would be like to be without him.

Sara leaned into him and kissed his throat. "What else?" Her full breasts brushed against his arm, warm, inviting. Very gently she dabbed at the lacerations on his temple, wiping away the blood. The wounds on his chest were deeper. It looked as if an animal had raked claws over his chest, ripping his shirt and scoring four long furrows in the skin.

"I came very close to losing my control this night. I need to complete the ritual so we are one and you are my anchor, Sara. You felt it; you sensed the danger to me and called me back to you. Once the ritual is complete, that danger would no longer exist." He made the confession in a low voice, his overwhelming need evident in his husky tone. He couldn't think straight when she was so close to him, the roar in his head drowning out everything but the needs of his body.

Sara caught his face in her hands. "That's it? That's the big confession?" Her smile was slow and beautiful, lighting her eyes to a deep violet. "I want you more than anything on this earth." She bent her head and took possession of his mouth, pressing her body close to his, her rain-wet silken tank top nearly nonexistent, her breasts thrusting against him, aching with need. A temptation. An enticement. There was hunger in her kiss, acceptance, excitement. Her mouth was hot with her own desire, meeting the demands of his. Raw. Earthy. Real.

She lifted her head, her gaze burning into his. "I have been yours for the last fifteen years. If you want me, Falcon, I'm not afraid. I've never really been afraid of you." Her hands pushed aside his torn shirt, exposing his chest and the four long wounds.

"You have to understand what kind of commitment you are making, Sara," he cautioned. He needed her.

Wanted her. *Hungered* for her. But he would not lose his honor with the most important person in his life. "Once the ritual is complete, if you are not with me below the ground while I sleep, you will fight a terrible battle for your sanity. I do not wish this for you."

CHAPTER FIVE

Sara blinked, drawing attention to her long lashes. Her gaze was steady. "Neither do I, Falcon"—her voice was a seductive invitation—"but I'd much rather fight my battles briefly than lose you. I'm strong. Believe in me." She bent her head, pressed a kiss into his shoulder, his throat. "You aren't taking anything I'm not willing to give."

How could she tell him, explain to him that he had been her only salvation all those long, endless nights when she'd hated herself, hated that she was alive and her family dead? How could she tell him he had saved her sanity, not once, but over and over? All those long years of holding his words close to her, locked in her heart, her soul. She knew she belonged with Falcon. She knew it in spite of what he was. She didn't care that he was different, that his way of surviving was different. She only cared that he was real, alive, standing in front of her with his soul in his eyes. Sara smiled at him, a sweet, provocative invitation, and simply drew her tank top over her head so that he could see her body, the full, lush curves, the darker peaks. Sara dropped the sodden tank top in a little heap on top of his shirt. She tilted her chin, trying to be brave, but he could see the slight trembling of her body. She had never done such an outrageous thing in her life.

Falcon found the nape of her neck, his fingers curling possessively as he dragged her close to him. His wounds were forgotten, his weariness. In that moment everything was forgotten but that Sara was offering herself to him. Pledging to give her life and her body into his keeping. Generously. Unconditionally.

Falcon thought she was the sexiest thing he had ever seen in all his years of existence. She was looking at him with enormous eyes so vulnerable his insides turned to mush. His breath slammed right out of his lungs. His body was so hot, so hard, so tight, he was afraid he might shatter if he moved. Yet he couldn't stop himself. His hand of its own volition drifted down her throat to cup her breast. Her skin was incredibly soft, softer even than it looked. It was shocking the way he felt about her, the sheer intensity of it. Where he had never wanted or needed, where no one had mattered, now there was Sara to fill every emptiness in him. His fingertips brushed over the curve of her breast, an artist's touch, explored the line of her ribs, the tuck of her waist, returned to cup her lush offering.

His black gaze burned over her possessively, scorching her skin, sending flames licking along the tips of her breasts, her throat, her hips, between her legs. And then he bent his head and drew her breast into the hot, moist cavern of his mouth.

Sara cried out, clutched his head, her fingers tangling in the thick silk of his hair, her body shuddering with pleasure. She felt the strong, erotic pull of his mouth in the very core of her body. Her body clenched tightly, aching, coiled with edgy need.

Falcon skimmed his hand down the sleek line of her back. *Are you certain, Sara? Are you certain you want the complete intimacy of our binding ritual?* He sent her the picture in his head: his mouth on her neck, over her pulse, the intensity of his physical need of her. He was already pulling her closer, devouring her skin, the lush curves so different from the hard planes and angles of his own body.

If Sara had wanted to pull back, it was already far too late. She was lost in the arcing electricity, the dazzling lightning dancing in her bloodstream. The images and the sheer pleasure in his mind, darkly erotic, only added to the firestorm building in her body. She had never experienced anything so elemental, so completely right, so completely primitive. She needed to be closer to him, skin to skin. The need was all-consuming, as hot as the sun itself, a firestorm raging, crowning, until there was nothing else, only Falcon. Only feeling. Only his fierce possession. She cradled his head to her breast, arcing deeper into his mouth while her body went liquid hot.

She wrapped one leg around his hips, pushing her heated center against the hard column of his thigh, a hard friction, moving restlessly, seeking relief. Her hands were tugging at his clothes, trying to get them off him while his mouth left flames on her neck, her breasts, even her ribs. His hands skimmed the curve of her hips, taking the silken pajamas down her thighs so the material pooled on the floor in a heap. He caught her leg and once more wrapped it around his hips so that she was open to him, pressed, hot and wet, tight against him.

Falcon's mouth found hers in a series of long kisses, each inflaming her more than the last. His hands were possessive on her breasts, her belly, sliding to her bottom, the inside of her thigh.

She was hot and wet with her need of him, her scent calling to him. Falcon's body was going up in flames. Sara had no inhibitions about letting him know she wanted him, and it was a powerful aphrodisiac. Her body moved against his, rubbing tightly, open to his exploration. She was pushing at his clothes, trying to get closer, her mouth on his chest, her tongue swirling to taste his skin. He removed the barrier of his clothing in the easy manner of his people, using his mind so that her hands could find him, thick and hard and full and throbbing with need. The moment her fingers stroked him, little firebombs seemed to explode in his bloodstream.

She knew him intimately, his thoughts, his dreams. She knew his mind, what he liked, what he needed and wanted. And he knew her. Every way to please her. They came together in heat and fire, yet for all his enormous strength, his desperate need, his touch was tender, exploring her body with a reverence that nearly brought tears to her eyes. His mouth was everywhere, hot and wild, teasing, enticing, promising things she couldn't conceive of.

Sara clung to him, wrapped her arms around his head, tears glistening like diamonds in her eyes, on her lashes. "I've been so alone, Falcon. Never go away. I don't know if you're real or not. How could anything as beautiful as you be real?"

He lifted his head, his black eyes drifting over her face. "You are my soul, Sara, my existence. I know what being alone is. I have lived centuries without home or family. Without being complete, the best part of me gone. I never wish to be apart from you." He caught her face between his hands. "Look at me, Sara. You are my world. I would not choose to be in this world without you. Believe in me." He bent his head to fasten his mouth to hers, rocking the earth for both of them.

Sara had no idea how they ended up in the bedroom. She was vaguely aware of being pressed against the wall, a wild tango of drugging kisses, of hot skin and exploring hands, of moving through space until the comforter was pressed against her bare body, her skin so sensitive she was gasping with the urgency of her own needs.

His mouth left hers to trace a path over her body, the swell of her breasts, her belly, his tongue trailing fire in its wake. His hands parted her thighs, held her tight as her body exploded, fragmented at the first stroking caress of his tongue.

Sara cried out, her hands fisting in his wealth of thick, long hair. She writhed under him, her body rippling with aftershocks. "Falcon." His name came out a breathy whispered plea.

"I want you ready for me, Sara," he said, his breath warming her, his tongue tasting her again and again, stroking, caressing, teasing until she was crying out again and again, her hips arcing helplessly into him.

His body blanketed hers, skin to skin, his heavier muscles pressed tightly against her softer body so that they fit perfectly. Falcon was careful with her despite the wildness rising within him. He watched her face as he began to push inside her body. She was hot, velvet soft, a tight sheath welcoming him home. The sensation was nothing like he had ever imagined, pure pleasure taking over every cell, every nerve. In the state of heightened awareness that he was in, his body was sensitive to every ripple of hers, every clench of her muscles, every touch of her fingers. Her breath—just her breath gave him pleasure.

He thrust deeper until her breath came in gasps. Until her body coiled tightly around his. Until her nails dug into his back. She was so soft and welcoming. He began to move, surging forward, watching her face, watching the loss of control, feeling the wildness growing in him, reveling in his ability to please her. He thrust harder, deeper, over and over, watching her rise to meet him, stroke for stroke. Her breasts took on a faint sheen, tempting, enticing, a lush invitation.

Falcon bent his head to her, his dark hair sliding over her skin so that she shuddered with pleasure, so that she cried out with unexpected shock at another orgasm, fast and furious.

Sara knew the moment his mouth touched her skin. Scorched her skin. She knew what he would do, and her body tightened in anticipation. She wanted him wild and out of control. His tongue found her nipple, lapped gently. His mouth was hot and greedy, and she heard herself gasp out his name. She held him to her, arcing her body to offer him her breast, her hips moving in perfect rhythm with his.

His mouth moved to the swell of her breast, just over her heart, his teeth scraping gently, nipping, his tongue swirling. Sara thought she might explode into a million fragments. Her body was so hot and tight and aching. "Falcon . . ." She breathed his name, a plea, needing to fulfill his every desire.

His hands tightened on her hips, and he buried himself deep inside her body and inside her mind, his teeth sinking into her skin so that white-hot lightning lashed through her, through him, until she was consumed by fire. Devoured by it. She cradled his head, but her body was rippling with pleasure, again and again until she thought she might die from it. Endless. On and on, again and again.

His tongue swirled lightly over the small telltale pinpricks. He was trembling, his mind a haze of passion and need. He whispered softly to her, a command as he lifted her head to the temptation of his chest. Falcon felt Sara's mouth move against his skin. His body tightened, a pain-edged pleasure nearly beyond endurance. With Sara firmly caught in his enthrallment, he indulged himself, coaxing her to take enough blood for a true exchange. His body was hard and hot and aching with the need for relief, the need for the ecstasy of total fulfillment. He closed the wound in his chest and took possession of her mouth as he awakened her from the compulsion.

And then he was surging into her, wild and out of control, taking them closer and closer to the edge of a great precipice. Sara clung to him, her softer body rising to meet his with a wild welcome. Falcon lifted his head to look at her, wanting to see the love in her eyes, the welcome, the intense need for him. Only him. No other. It was there, just as when she had first recognized him. It was deep within her soul, shining through her eyes for him to see. Sara belonged to him. And he belonged to her.

Fire rushed through him, through her. A fine sheen of sweat coated their skin. His hands found hers and they moved together, fast and hard and incredibly tender. She felt him swell within her, saw his eyes glaze, and her own body tightened, muscles clenching and rippling with life. His name caught in her throat, his breath left his lungs as they rushed over the edge together.

They lay for a long while, holding one another, their bodies tangled together, skin to skin, his thigh over hers, in between hers, his mouth and hands still exploring. Sara cradled him to her, tears in her eyes, unbelieving that he was in her arms, in her body, one being. She would never be alone. He filled her heart and her mind the way he filled her body.

"We fit," he murmured softly. "A perfect fit."

"Did you know it would be like this? So wonderful?"

He moved then, rising from the bed and bringing her up with him, taking her to the shower. As the water streamed off them, he licked the water from her throat, followed the path of several beads along her ribs. Sara retaliated by tasting his skin, sipping the water beads as they ran low along his flat, hard belly. Her mouth was hot and tight, so that he had to have her again. And again. He took her there in the shower. They made it as far as the small dresser, where he found the sight of her bottom too perfect to ignore. She was receptive, as hot and as needy as Falcon, never wanting the night to end.

The early morning light filtered through the closed curtains. They lay together on the bed, talking together, holding each other, hands and mouths stroking caresses in between words. Sara couldn't remember laughing so much; Falcon hadn't thought he knew how to laugh. Finally, reluctantly, he leaned over to kiss her.

"You must go if you are going to do this, Sara. I want you high in the Carpathian Mountains before nightfall. I will rise and come straight to you."

Sara slid from the bed to stand beside the bust she had made so many years earlier. She didn't want to leave him. She wanted to remain curled up beside him for the rest of her life.

Falcon didn't need to read her mind to know her thoughts; they were plain on her transparent face. For some reason, her misgivings made it easier for him to allow her to carry out her plans. He stood up, his body crowding close to hers. He needed sleep; he needed to go to ground and fully heal. Mostly he needed to be with Sara.

"I'm afraid that if I leave, I might never get the children. The officials are disturbed because I'm asking for all seven of them and there are no records." Sara's fingers twisted together in agitation.

"Mikhail will be able to get rid of the red tape for us. He has many businesses in this area and is well known." Falcon brought her fingers to the warmth of his mouth to calm her. "I have not been to my homeland in many years, but I am well aware of everything that is happening. He will be able to assist us."

"How do you know so much if you've been away?" Sara wasn't ready to trust a complete stranger with something so important as the children.

He smiled and tangled his fingers in her hair. "The Carpathian people speak on a common mental pathway. I hear when hunters have gone through the land or some trauma has taken place. I heard when our Prince nearly lost his lifemate. Not once, but on two occasions. I heard when he lost his brother and then his brother returned to him. Mikhail will assist you. When you reach the area, he will find you in the evening and you will be under his protection. I will rise as soon as possible and come straight to you. He will assist us in finding a good location for our home. It will be near him and within the protection of all Carpathians. I have marked the trails for you in the mountains." Falcon bent his head to the temptation of her breast, his tongue lapping at the tight, rosy peak. His hair skimmed over her skin like so much silk. "You must be very careful, Sara. You cannot think you are safe because it is daylight. The undead are locked within the earth, but they are able to control their minions. This vampire is an ancient and very powerful."

Her body caught fire, just like that, liquid flames

rushing through her bloodstream. "I will be more than careful, Falcon. I've seen what he does. I'm not going to doing anything silly. You don't have to worry. After I contact my friends and get a call through to my lawyer, I'll be going straight to the mountains. I'll find your people," she assured. Her heart was beating a little too fast at that thought, and she knew he heard it. Her own hearing was far more acute than it had been, and the thought of food made her feel slightly sick. Already she was changing, and the idea of being separated from Falcon was frightening. Sara lifted her chin determinedly and flashed him a reassuring smile. "Once I set everything up, I'll get on the road." Her fingers were continually sliding over the bust of Falcon's head, lovingly following the grooves marking the waves in his hair.

Watching her, knowing that statue had been her solace in years past, Falcon felt his heart turn over. He gathered her close to him, his touch possessive, tender, as loving as he could make it. "You will not be alone, Sara. I will heed your call, even in my most vulnerable hour. Should your mind start to play tricks on you, telling you I am dead to you, call me and I will answer."

Sara molded her body against his, clinging to him, holding him close so that he felt real and strong and very solid. "Sometimes I think maybe I dreamed of you for so long I'm hallucinating, that I made you up and any minute you'll disappear," she confessed softly.

His arms tightened until he was nearly crushing her against him, yet there was great tenderness in the way he held her. "I never dared to dream, even to hope. I had accepted my barren existence. It was the only way to survive and do my duty with honor. I am not ever going to leave you, Sara." He didn't tell her he was terrified at the thought of going to ground while she faced danger on the surface. She was a strong woman, and she had survived a long, deadly duel with the vampire completely on her own. He couldn't find it in him to insist she do things his way simply for his comfort.

Sara was touching his mind, could read his thoughts, the intensity of his fear for her safety. A wave of love swept through her. She turned her face up to his, hungrily seeking his mouth, wanting to prolong her time with him. His mouth was hot and dominant, as hungry as hers. As demanding. A fierce claim on her. He kissed her chin, her throat, found her mouth again, devouring her as if he could never get enough. There was an edginess to his kiss now, an ache. A need.

Sara's leg slid up his leg to wrap around his waist. She pressed against the hard column of his thigh, grinding against him, so that he felt her invitation, her own demand, hot and wet and pulsing with urgency.

Falcon simply lifted her in his arms, and she wrapped both legs around his waist. With her hands on his shoulders, her head thrown back, she lowered her body to the thick hardness of his. He pressed against her moist entrance, making her gasp, cry out as he slowly, inch by inch, filled her completely. Sara threw back her head, closed her eyes as she began to ride him, losing herself completely in Falcon's dark passion. They took their time, a long, slow tango of fiery heat that went on and on as long as they dared. They were in perfect unison, reading each other's minds, moving, adjusting, giving themselves completely, one to the other. When they were spent, they leaned against the wall and held one another, their hearts beating the same rhythm, tears in their eyes. Sara's head was on his shoulder and Falcon's head rested on hers.

"You cannot allow anything to happen to yourself, Sara," he cautioned. "I have to go now. I cannot wait much longer. You know I cannot be without you. You will remember everything I have said to you?"

"Everything." Sara tightened her hold on him. "I know it's crazy, Falcon, but I love you. I really do. You've always been with me when I needed you. I love you."

He kissed her, long and tender. Incredibly tender. "You are my love, my life." He whispered it softly and then he was gone. Sara remained leaning against the wall, her fingers pressed against her mouth for a few moments. Then she sprang into action.

She worked quickly, packing a few clothes and tossing them in her backpack, making several calls to ask friends to keep an eye on the children until she could return. She had every intention of coming back for them as soon as she sorted out the extensive paperwork and set up a home for them. She was on the road heading toward the Carpathian Mountains within an hour.

She needed the darkness of sunglasses, although the day was a dreary gray with ominous clouds overhead. Her skin prickled with unease as rays of sunlight pushed through the thick cloud covering to touch her arm as she drove. She tried not to think about Falcon locked deep within the ground. Her body was wonderfully sore. She could feel his touch on her, his possession, and just the thought of him made her hot with renewed desire. She couldn't prevent her mind from continually seeking his. Each time she touched on the void, her heart would contract painfully, and it would take tremendous effort to control her wild grief. Every cell in her body demanded that she go back, find him, make certain he was safe.

Sara tilted her chin and kept driving, hour after hour, leaving the cities for smaller villages until she was finally in a sparsely populated area. She stopped twice to rest and stretch her cramped legs, but continued steadily, always driving up toward the region Falcon had so carefully marked for her. She was concentrating so hard on finding the trail leading into wild territory that she was nearly hit by another vehicle as it overtook her and roared by. It shot past her at breakneck speed, a larger, much heavier truck with a camper. She was forced to veer off the narrow track to keep from being shoved off the trail. The vehicle went by her so quickly she nearly missed seeing the little faces peering out at her from the window of the camper shell. She nearly missed the sounds of screams fading into the forest.

Sara froze, her mind numb with shock, her body nearly paralyzed. The children. Her little ones, the children she had promised safety and a home. They were in the hands of a puppet, a ghoul. The walking dead. The vampire had taken a human, enslaved him, and programmed the creature to take her children as bait. She should have known, should have guessed he would discover them. She gave chase, hurtling along the narrow, rutted trail, clinging to the steering wheel as her truck threatened to break apart.

Two hours later, she was completely and hopelessly lost. The ghoul was obviously aware that she was following and it simply drove where no vehicle should have been able to go, racing dangerously through hairpin turns and smashing his way through vegetation. Sara attempted to follow, driving at breakneck speed through the series of turns, wheels bouncing over the rough pits in the roads. Once a tree was down directly across her path and she had to take her truck deeper into the forest to get around it. She was certain the ghoul had shoved the tree there to block her pursuit, to delay her. The trees were so close together, they scraped the paint from the sides of her truck. She couldn't believe she could possibly have lost the other vehicle; there weren't that many roads to turn onto. She tried twice to look at the map on the seat beside her, but with the terrible jouncing, it was impossible to focus. Branches scraped the windshield; twigs snapped off with an ominous sound.

With her arms aching and her heart pounding, Sara managed to maneuver her truck back onto a faint trail that might pass for a road. It was very narrow and ran along a deep, rocky ravine that looked like a great crack in the earth. In places, the boulders were black and scarred as if a war had taken place. The branches slapped at her truck as it rushed through the trees along the winding road. She would have to pull over and consult the map Falcon had given her.

His name immediately brought a welling of grief, of fear that he was lost to her, but Sara attempted to push the false emotion aside, grateful that he had prepared her for such a possibility. A sob welled up, choking her; tears blurred her vision but she wiped them away, wrenching at the wheel determinedly when her truck nearly bounced off the road from a particularly deep rut.

This couldn't be happening. The children, *her* children in the hands of the vampire's evil puppet. A flesh-eating ghoul. Sara wanted to continue driving as fast as she could, terrified that if she stopped she would never be able to catch them. She was well aware that it was late afternoon and once the ghoul delivered the children to the vampire, she had little hope of saving them.

Sara sighed softly and slowed the truck with great reluctance, pulling to the side of the trail. A steep cliff rose up sharply on her left. It took tremendous discipline to force herself to stop her vehicle and spread the map out in front of her. She needed to look for places where she could have gotten off the track, where the ghoul could have gotten away from her. She found she was nearly choking with grief. She shoved the door open and, leaving the vehicle running, jumped out where she could breathe the cool, crisp, fresh air.

Falcon. She breathed his name. Wanted him. Dashing the tears away, Sara grabbed the map from the seat and stared down at the clearly marked trail. Where had the ghoul turned off? How had she missed it? She had been driving as fast as she dared, yet she had still lost sight of the children.

A terrible sense of failure assailed her. She spread the

map out on the hood of the truck and glared at the markings, waiting for inspiration, for some tiny clue. Her fingernails beat out a little tattoo of frustration on the metal hood. All around her was the sound of the wind whipping through the trees and out over the cliffs into empty space. But some sixth sense warned her she was not alone.

Sara turned her head. The creature was lumbering toward her, his blank expression a hideous reminder that he was no longer human. There would be no reasoning with him, no pleading with him. He had been programmed by a master of cunning and evil. She let out her breath slowly, carefully, centering herself for the attack. Sara crouched lower on the balls of her feet, her mind clear and calm as the thing neared her. Its eyes were fixed on her, its fingers clenching and unclenching as it shuffled forward. She didn't dare allow it to get its hands on her. Her world narrowed to the thing approaching her, her mind clear, as she knew it would have to be.

She waited until the creature was nearly on top of her before she moved. She used her speed, whirling in a spin, generating power as her leg lashed out, the edge of her foot catching the ghoul's kneecap in an explosion of violence. She sprang away, out of reach of those clawed hands. The creature howled loudly, spittle spraying into the air, a thick drool oozing from the side of its mouth. The eyes remained dead and fixed on her as its leg buckled with an audible crack. Unbelievably, it lurched toward her, dragging its useless leg but coming at her steadily.

Sara knew its kneecap was broken, yet it continued toward her relentlessly. Sara had faced such a thing before, and she knew it would keep coming even if it had to drag itself on the ground. She angled sideways, circling to the ghoul's left in an attempt to slide past it. It bothered her that she couldn't hear the children, that none of them were crying or yelling for help. With her hearing so acute, Sara was certain she would have been able to hear whimpers coming from the ghoul's truck, but there was an ominous silence.

She stood her ground, shaking her arms to keep them loose. The ghoul swiped at her with its long arm, its huge, hamlike fist missing her face as she ducked and slammed her foot into its groin, then straight up beneath its chin. It howled, the sound loud and hideous, its body jerking under the assault, but it only rocked backward, jolted for a moment. Sara had no choice but to slip out of its reach.

It was a lesson in sheer frustration. No matter how many times she managed to score a kick or hit, the creature refused to go down. It howled, spittle exploding from its mouth, but its eyes were always the same, flat and empty and fixed on her. It was like a relentless machine that never stopped. As a last resort, Sara tried luring it near to the edge of the ravine in the hope that she could push it over, but it stood for a moment, breathing heavily, and then turned unexpectedly and lumbered away from her into heavier brush and trees.

Sara hastily scrambled to her truck, her heart pounding heavily. A thunderous crash made her swing her head around. To her horror, the ghoul's heavier vehicle was mowing down brush and even small trees, roaring out of the forest like a charging elephant, aimed straight at the side of her truck. More out of reflex than rational thought, her foot slammed down hard on the accelerator.

Her truck slewed sideways, fishtailed, the tires spinning in the dirt. Sara's heart nearly stopped as the larger vehicle continued straight at her. She could see the driver's face as it loomed closer. It was masklike, the eyes dead and flat. The ghoul appeared to be drooling. She could hear the screams of the children, frightened and alone in the madness of a world they couldn't hope to understand. At least they were alive. She had been afraid that their former silence meant the ghoul had murdered them.

The truck hit the side of hers, buckling the door in on her and shoving her vehicle closer to the edge of the steep ravine. Sara knew she was going to go over the crumbling cliff. Her small truck slid, metal grinding, children screaming, the noise an assault on her sensitive ears. A strange calmness invaded her, a sense of the inevitable. Her fingers wouldn't let go of the steering wheel, yet she couldn't steer, couldn't prevent the truck from sliding inch by inch, foot by foot toward the edge of the cliff.

Two wheels went over the edge, the truck tilted crazily, and then she was falling, tumbling through the air, slamming into the ravine, sliding and rolling. The seatbelt tightened, a hard jolt, biting into her flesh, adding to the mind-numbing pain. *Falcon.* His name was a soft sigh of regret in her mind. A plea for forgiveness.

Falcon was wrenched from his slumber, his heart pounding, his chest nearly crushed in suffocation. He was far from Sara, unable yet to aid her. He would build a monstrous storm to help protect his eyes so he could rise early, but he still would not reach her in time. *Sara*. His life. His heart and soul. Terror filled him. Took him like a crushing weight. *Sara*. His Sara, with her courage and her capacity for love.

She was already in the Carpathian Mountains, caught in the trap the vampire had laid for her. He had no choice. Everyone of Carpathian blood would hear, and that included the undead. It was a risk, a gamble. Falcon was an ancient presumed dead. He had never declared his allegiance to the new Prince and he might not be believed, but it was Sara's only chance.

Falcon summoned his strength and sent out his call. *Hear me, brethren. My lifemate is under attack in the mountains near you. You must go to her aid swiftly as I am far from her. She is hunted by an ancient enemy and he has sent his puppets to acquire her. Rise and go to her. I warn all within my hearing, I am Falcon, a Carpathian of ancient blood, and I will be watching to protect her.*

CHAPTER SIX

There was a swirling fear in Sara's mind, in his. Falcon burst through the soil and into the sky. Light assailed his sensitive eyes and burned his skin, but it didn't matter. Nothing mattered except that Sara was in danger. One moment he was merged mind to mind with Sara; in the next microsecond of time, there was a blank void. He had an eternity to feel the helpless terror roiling in his gut, the fist clamping his heart like a vise, the emptiness that had been his world, now unbearable, unthinkable, a blasphemy after knowing Sara. Falcon forced his mind to work, reaching relentlessly into that blank void for his very soul. For his life. For love.

Sara. Sara, answer me. Wake now. You must wake. I am on my way to you, but you must awaken. Open your eyes for me. He kept his voice calm, but the compulsion was strong, the need in him raw. *Sara, you must wake.*

The voice was far away, coming from within her

throbbing head. Sara heard her own groan, a foreign sound. She was raw and hurting everywhere. She didn't want to obey the soft command, but there was a note she couldn't resist. The voice brought with it awareness, and with awareness came pain. Her heart began to pound in terror.

She had no idea how long she had been unconscious in the wreckage of the truck, but she could feel the metal pressing on her legs and glass cutting her body. She was trapped in the twisted metal, shattered glass all around her, blood running down her face. She didn't want to move, not when she heard movement close to her. She squeezed her eyes shut and willed herself to slip back into oblivion.

Relief washed over Falcon, through him, shook him. For a moment he went perfectly still, nearly falling from the sky, nearly unable to hold the image he needed to stay aloft. His mind was fully merged with Sara's, buried within hers, worshiping, examining, nearly numb with happiness. She was alive. She was still alive! Falcon worked at controlling his body's reaction to the sheer terror of losing her, the unbelievable relief of knowing she was alive. It took discipline to lower his heart rate, to steady his terrible trembling. She was alive, but she was trapped and hurt.

Sara, piccola, *do as I ask, open your eyes.* Keeping his voice gentle, Falcon gave her no choice, burying a compulsion within the purity of his tone. He felt pain sweeping through her body, a sense of claustrophobia. She was disoriented; her head was pounding. Now his fear was back again in full force, although he kept it hidden from her. Instead, it was trapped in his heart, in his deepest soul, a terror such as he had never known before. He was moving fast, streaking across the sky as quickly as possible, uncaring of the disturbance of power, uncaring that all ancients in the area would know he was racing toward the mountains. She was alone, hurt, trapped, and hunted.

Sara's eyes obeyed his soft command. She looked around her at the crushed glass, the twisted wreckage, and the sheered-off top of her truck. Sara wasn't certain she was still actually inside the vehicle. She couldn't recognize it as a truck any longer. It looked as if she were trapped in a smashed accordion. The sun was falling in the mountains, a shadow spreading across the rocky terrain.

She heard a noise, the scrape of something against what was left of her truck, and then she was looking into the face of a woman. Sara's vision was blurry, and it took a few moments of blinking rapidly to bring the woman into focus. Sara remembered how she had gotten in her predicament, and it frightened her to think of how much time might have passed, how close the ghoul might be. She tried to move, to look past the woman. When she moved, her body screamed in protest and a shower of safety glass fell around her. Her dark glasses were missing, and her eyes burned so that they wept continually.

"Lie quietly," the woman said, her voice soothing and gentle. "I am a doctor and I must assess the severity of your injuries." The stranger frowned as she lightly took Sara's wrist.

Sara felt very disoriented, and she could taste blood in her mouth. It was far too much of an effort to lift her head. "You can't stay here. Something was chasing me. Really, leave me here; I'll be fine. I've got a few bruises, nothing else, but you aren't safe." Her tongue felt thick and heavy and her tone shocked her, thin and weak, as if her voice came from far away. "You aren't safe," she repeated, determined to be heard.

The woman was watching her carefully, almost as if she knew what Sara was thinking. She smiled reassuringly. "My name is Shea, Shea Dubrinsky. Whatever is chasing you can be dealt with. My husband is close by and will aid us if necessary. I'm going to run my hands over you and check you for injuries. If you could see your truck, you would know what a miracle it is that you survived."

Sara was feeling desperate. Shea Dubrinsky was a beautiful woman, with pale skin and wine-red hair. She looked very Irish. She was serene despite the circumstances. It was only then that the name registered. "Dubrinsky? Is your husband Mikhail? I've come looking for Mikhail Dubrinsky."

Something flickered in Shea Dubrinsky's eyes behind her smoky sunglasses. There was compassion, but something else, too, something that made Sara shiver. The doctor's hands moved over her impersonally, but thoroughly and gently. Sara knew that this woman, this doctor, was one of *them. The others.* Right now Shea Dubrinsky was communicating with someone else in the same manner Sara did with Falcon. It frightened

Sara nearly as much as the encounter with the ghoul. She couldn't tell the difference between friend and foe.

Falcon. She reached for him. Needed him. Wanted him with her. The accident had shaken her so that it was difficult to think clearly. Her head ached appallingly and her body was shaky, trembling beyond her ability to control it. It was humiliating for someone of Sara's strong nature. *She is one of them.*

I am here. Do not fear. No one can harm you. Look directly at her, and I will observe what you see. There was complete confidence in Falcon's voice and he swamped her with waves of reassurance, the feel of strong arms stealing around her, gathering her close, holding her to him. The feeling was very real and gave her confidence.

She speaks to another. She says her name is Dubrinsky and her husband is close. I know she speaks to him. She has called him to us. Sara said it with complete conviction. The woman looked calm and professional, but Sara felt what was happening, knew that Shea Dubrinsky was communicating with some other even though Sara could not see anyone else.

Sara gasped as the woman's hands touched sore places. She tried to smile at the other woman. "I'm really okay, the seat belt saved me, although I hurt like crazy. You have to get away from here." She was feeling a bit desperate searching for signs of the ghoul. Sara tried to move and groaned as every muscle in her body protested. Her head pounded so that even her teeth hurt.

"Stay very quiet for just a moment," Shea said softly, persuasively, and Sara recognized a slight "push" toward obedience. Falcon was there with her, sharing her mind, so she wasn't as afraid as she might have been. She believed in him. She knew he would come, that nothing would stop him from reaching her side. "Mikhail Dubrinsky is my husband's brother. Why are you seeking him?" Shea spoke casually, as if the answer didn't matter, but once again, there was that "push" toward truth.

Sara made an attempt to raise her hand, wanting to remove the broken glass from her hair. Her head was aching so much it made her feel sick. "For some reason, compulsion doesn't work very well on me. If you are going to use it, you have to use it with much more strength." She was struggling to keep her eyes open.

Sara! Focus on her. Stay focused! Falcon's command was sharp. *I sent a call ahead to my people to alert them to find you. Mikhail did have brothers, but you must remain alert. I must see through your eyes. You must stay awake.*

Shea was grinning at her a little ruefully. "You are familiar with us." She said it softly. "If that is the case, I want you to hold very still while I aid you. The sun is falling fast. If you are hunted by a puppet of the undead, the vampire will be close by and waiting for the sun to sink. Please remain very quiet while I do this." Shea was watching Sara's face for a reaction.

There was a movement behind Shea and she turned her head with a loving smile. "Jacques, we have found the one we were seeking. She has a lifemate. He is watching us through her eyes. She is one of us, yet not." Out of courtesy she spoke aloud. There was a wealth of love in her voice, an intimacy that whispered of total commitment. She turned back to Sara. "I will attempt to make you more comfortable, and Jacques will get you out of the truck so we may leave this place and get to safety." There was complete confidence in her gentle tones.

Sara wanted the terrible pounding in her head to go away. She couldn't shift her legs; the wreckage was entombing her as surely as a casket. Falcon's presence in her mind was the only thing that kept her from sliding back into the welcoming black void. She struggled to stay alert, watching Shea's every move. The unknown Jacques had not come into her line of vision, but she felt no immediate threat.

Shea Dubrinsky was graceful and sure. There were no rough edges to her, and she seemed completely professional despite the bizarre way she was healing Sara. Sara actually felt the other woman inside her, a warmth, an energy flowing through her body to soothe the terrible aches, to repair from the inside out. She was amazed that the terrible pounding in her head actually lessened. The nausea disappeared.

Shea leaned over to unfasten the seat belt that was biting into Sara's chest. "Your body has suffered a trauma," she said. "There will be extensive bruising, but you're very lucky. Once we are safe, I can make you much more comfortable." She moved out of the way to allow her lifemate access to the wreckage.

Sara found herself staring up at a man with a singularly beautiful face. His eyes, as he took off his sunglasses, were as old as time, as if he had seen far too much. Suffered far too much. He pushed the glasses onto Sara's face, bringing a measure of relief to her burning eyes. Shea brushed Jacques's hand with hers, the lightest of gestures, but it was more intimate than anything Sara had ever witnessed. She could feel the stillness in Falcon, could feel him gathering his strength should there be need.

"Hold very still," Jacques cautioned softly. His voice held the familiar purity that seemed to be a part of the Carpathian species.

"He has the children. Go after him. If you're like Falcon, you have to go after him and get the children back. He's taking them to the vampire." *Falcon, I'm all right. You must find the children and keep them from the vampire.* She was beginning to panic, thinking much more clearly now that the pain was receding.

Jacques grasped the steering column and gave a wrench, exerting strength so that it bent away from her, giving her more room to breathe. "The ghoul will not reach the vampire. Mikhail has risen and he will stop the puppet from reaching his master." There was complete confidence in Jacques's soft voice. "Your lifemate must be on his way, perhaps already close to us. All heard his warning, although he is not known to us." It was a statement, but Sara heard the question in his words.

She watched his hands push the crumbling wreckage from around her legs so that she could move. The relief was so tremendous she could feel tears gathering in her eyes. Sara turned her head away from the probing gaze of the stranger. At once warmth flooded her mind.

I am with you, Sara. I feel your injuries and your fear for the children, but this man would not lie to you. He is the brother of the Prince. I have heard of him, a man who has endured much pain and hardship, who was buried alive by fanatics. Mikhail will not fail to rescue the children.

You go; don't worry about me. You make certain the children are safe!

She didn't know the Prince. She knew Falcon and she trusted him. If the children could be snatched away from the vampire, he would be the one to do it. And he was closer now, she was certain of it. His presence was much stronger and it took little effort to communicate with him.

"I am going to help you out of there," Jacques warned.

Sara had desperately wanted to be free of the wreckage of her truck, but now, faced with the prospect of actually moving, it didn't seem the best of ideas. "I think I'll just sit here for the rest of my life, if you don't mind," she said.

To her shock, Jacques smiled at her, a flash of white teeth that lit his ravaged eyes. It was the last thing she'd expected of him, and she found herself smiling back. "You do not frighten very easily, do you?" he asked softly. He gave no sign that the light of day hurt his eyes, but she could see they were red and streaming. He endured it stoically.

Sara lifted a trembling hand to eye level and watched it shake. They both laughed softly together. "I'm Sara Marten. Thanks for coming to my rescue."

"We could do no other, with your lifemate filling the skies with his declaration." The white teeth flashed again, this time reminding her of a wolf. "I am Jacques Dubrinsky; Shea is my lifemate."

Sara knew he was watching her closely to see what effect his words had on her. She knew Falcon was watching Jacques through her eyes, catching every nuance, sizing up the other man. And Jacques Dubrinsky was well aware of it, too.

"I am going to lift you out of there, Sara," he said gently. "Let me do the work. I have never dropped Shea, so you do not need to worry," he teased.

Sara turned her head to look at the other woman. She lifted an eyebrow. "I don't think that's much of a reassurance. She's much smaller than I am."

Shea grinned at her, a quick, engaging smile that lit her entire face. "Oh, I think he's up to the task, Sara."

Jacques didn't give her any more time to think about it. He lifted her out of the wreckage and carried her easily to a flat spot in the high grass, where his lifemate bent over her solicitously. The movement took Sara's breath away, sent pain slicing through her body. Shea carefully brushed glass from Sara's hair and clothing. "You have to expect to be a bit shaky. Tell your lifemate we are going to take you to Mikhail's house. You will be safe there, and Raven and I can look after you while Jacques joins the men in the hunt for these lost children."

I want the male to stay near you while I am away.

Sara heard the underlying irony in Falcon's voice and she laughed softly. The thought of any male near Sara was disconcerting to him, but he needed to know she was safe.

Sara's relief that Falcon was close and was searching

for the children was enormous. She could breathe again, yet, inexplicably, she wanted to cry.

Shea knelt beside her, took her hand, and looked into her eyes. "It's a natural reaction, Sara," she said softly. "It's all right now, everything is going to be all right." Unashamedly she used her voice as a tool to soothe the other woman. "You are not alone; we really can help."

"Falcon says the vampire is ancient and very powerful," Sara said in warning. She was struggling to appear calm and to control the trembling of her body. It was humiliating to be so weak in front of strangers.

Jacques swung his head around alertly, his eyes black and glittering, his entire demeanor changed. All at once he looked menacing. "Is she able to travel, Shea?"

Shea was straightening slowly, a wary look on her beautiful face. A flutter of nerves in Sara's stomach blossomed into full-scale fear. "He's here, isn't he? The ghoul?" She bit her lip and made a supreme effort to get to her feet. "If he's close to us, then so are the children. He can't have handed them off to the vampire." To her horror, she only managed to get a knee under her before blackness began swirling alarmingly close.

"The ghoul is making his way quickly to his master," Jacques corrected. "The vampire probably has summoned the ghoul to him. The undead is sending his warning, a challenge to any who dare to interfere with his plans."

Shea slipped her arm around Sara to keep her from falling. "Do not try to move yet, Sara. You are not ready to stand." The woman turned to her lifemate. "We can move her, Jacques. I think it best to hurry."

They know something I don't. Sara rubbed her pounding head, frustrated that she was unable to see or hear the things heralding danger. *Something is wrong.*

At once she could feel Falcon's reassurance, his strong arms, warmth flooding her, though he was many miles away. *The vampire is locked within his lair, but he is sending his minions across the land searching for you. The male wishes to take you to safety.*

Do you really want me to go with him? I feel so helpless, Falcon. I don't think I could fight my way out of a paper bag.

Yes, Sara, it is best. I will be with you every moment.

The sky was becoming dark, not because the sun was setting but because the winds had picked up, whirling faster and faster, gathering dust, dirt, and debris together, drawing it into a towering mass. Swarms of insects assembled, masses of them, the noise of their wings rivaling the wind. *The children will be so afraid.* Sara reached out for assurance.

Falcon wanted to gather her close, hold her to him, shelter her from the battles that would surely take place. He sent her warmth, love. *I will find them, Sara. You must stay alert so I can guard you while we are apart.*

For some reason, Falcon's words humbled her. She wanted to be at his side. She needed to be at his side.

Jacques Dubrinsky leaned down to Sara. "I understand how you feel. I dislike to be away from Shea. She is a researcher, very important to our people." He looked at his lifemate as he gathered Sara easily into his arms. His expression was tender, mixed with pride and respect. "She is very single-minded, focused on what she is doing. I find it somewhat uncomfortable." He grinned ruefully, sharing his confession candidly.

"Wait!" Sara knew she sounded panic-stricken. "There's a backpack in the truck, I can't leave it. I can't." Falcon's diary was in the wooden box. She carried it everywhere with her. She was not about to leave it.

Shea hesitated as if she might argue, but obligingly rummaged around in the wreckage until she triumphantly came up with the backpack. Sara had her arms outstretched and Shea handed it to her.

Jacques lifted an eyebrow. "Are you ready now? Close your eyes if traveling swiftly bothers you."

Before she could protest, he was whisking her through space, moving so fast that everything around her blurred into streaks. Sara was happy to be away from the wreckage of her truck, from the fierce wind and the swarms of insects blackening the sky. She should have been afraid, but there was something reassuring about Jacques and Shea Dubrinsky. Solid. Reliable.

She had the impression of a large, rambling house with columns and wraparound balconies. She had no time to get more than a quick look before Jacques was striding inside. The interior was rich with burnished wood and wide open spaces. It all blended together— art, vases, exquisite tapestries, and beautiful furniture. Sara found herself in a large sitting room, pressed into one of the plush couches. The heavy drapes were pulled, blotting out all light so only soft candles lit the room, a relief to eyes sensitive to the sun.

Sara removed Jacques's sunglasses with a shaky

hand. "Thank you. It was thoughtful of you to lend them to me."

He grinned at her, his teeth gleaming white, his dark eyes warm. "I am a very thoughtful kind of man."

Shea groaned and rolled her eyes. "He thinks he's charming, too."

Another woman, short with long black hair, glided into the room, her slender arm circling Jacques's waist with an easy, affectionate manner. "You must be Sara. Shea and Jacques alerted me ahead of time that they were bringing you to my home. Welcome. I've made you some tea. It's herbal. Shea thinks your stomach will tolerate it." She indicated the beautiful teacup sitting in a saucer on the end table. "I'm Raven, Mikhail's lifemate. Shea said you were searching for Mikhail."

Sara glanced at the tea, leaned back into the cushions, and closed her eyes. Her head was throbbing painfully and she felt sick again. She wanted to curl up and go to sleep. Tea and conversation sounded overwhelming.

Sara! Falcon's voice was stronger than ever. *You must stay focused until I am at your side to protect you. I do not know these strangers. I believe they do not intend you harm, but I cannot protect you if there be need, unless you stay alert.*

Sara made an effort to concentrate. "I have had a vampire hunting me for fifteen years. He killed my entire family and he's stolen children he knows matter a great deal to me. All of you are in great danger."

Jacques's eyebrows shot up. "You eluded a vampire for fifteen years?" There was a wealth of skepticism in his voice.

Sara turned her head to look at Shea. "He isn't nearly as charming when you've been around him a while, is he?"

Shea and Raven dissolved into laughter. "He grows on you, Sara," Shea assured.

"What?" Jacques managed to look innocent. "It is quite a feat for anyone to escape a vampire for fifteen years, let alone a human. It is perfectly reasonable to think there has been a mistake. And I am charming."

Raven shook her head at him. "Don't count too heavily on it, Jacques. I have it on good authority that the inclination to kick you comes often. And humans are quite capable of extraordinary things." She picked several pieces of glass from Sara's clothes. "It must have been terrifying for you."

"At first," Sara agreed tiredly, "but then it was a way of life. Running, always staying ahead of him. I didn't know why he was so fixated on me."

Shea and Raven were lighting aromatic candles, releasing a soothing scent that seeped into Sara's skin, made its way into her lungs, her body, and lessened the aches. "Sara," Shea said softly, "you have a concussion and a couple of broken ribs. I aligned the ribs earlier, but I need to do some work to ensure that you heal rapidly."

Sara sighed softly. She just wanted to sleep. "The vampire will come if he finds out I'm here, and you'll all be in danger. It's much safer if I keep moving."

"Mikhail will find the vampire," Jacques said with complete confidence.

Allow the woman to heal you, Sara. I have heard rumors of her. She was a human doctor before Jacques claimed her.

Sara frowned as she looked at Shea. "Falcon has heard of you. He says you were a doctor."

"I still am a doctor," Shea reassured gently. "Thank you for your warning and your concern for us. It does you credit, but I can assure you, the vampire will not be allowed to harm us here. Allow me to take care of you until your lifemate arrives." Her hands were very gentle as they moved over Sara, leaving behind a tingling warmth. "Healing you as a Carpathian rather than a human doctor is not really all that different. It is faster, because I heal from the inside out. It won't hurt, but it feels warm."

Raven continued to remove glass from Sara's clothing. "How did you meet Falcon? He is unknown to us." She was using a soft, friendly voice, wanting to calm Sara, to reassure her that she would be safe in their home. She also wanted any information available to be transferred to her own lifemate.

Sara leaned into the cushions, her fingers tight around the strap of her backpack. She could hear the wind, the relentless, hideous wind as it howled and moaned, screamed and whispered. There was a voice in the wind. She couldn't make out the words, but she knew the sound. Rain lashed at the windows and the roof, pounded at the walls as if demanding entrance. Dark shadows moved outside the window—dark enough, evil enough to disturb the heavy draperies. The material could not prevent the shadows from reaching into the room. Sparks arced and crackled, striking something they couldn't see. The howls and moans increased, an assault on their ears.

"Jacques." Shea said the name like a talisman. She slipped her hand into her lifemate's larger one, looking up at him with stark love shining in her eyes.

The man pulled his lifemate closer, gently kissed her palm. "The safeguards will hold." He shifted his stance, gliding to place his body between the window and the plush chair where Sara was sitting. The movement was subtle, but Sara was very aware of it.

The sound of the rain changed, became a hail of something heavier hitting the windows and pelting the structure. Raven swung around to face the large rock fireplace. Hundreds of shiny black bodies rained down from the chimney, landing with ugly plops on the hearth, where bright flames leaped to life, burning the insects as they touched the stones. A noxious odor rose with the black smoke. One particularly large insect rushed straight toward Sara, its round eyes fixed malevolently on her.

CHAPTER SEVEN

Falcon, in the form of an owl, peered at the ground far below him. He could see the ghoul's truck through the thick vegetation. It was tilted at an angle, one tire dangling precariously over a precipice. A second owl slipped silently out of the clouds, unconcerned with the wicked wind or lashing rain. Falcon felt a stillness in his mind, then a burst of pleasure, of triumph, a glowing pride in his people. He knew that lazy, confident glide, remembered it well. Mikhail, Vladimir Dubrinsky's son, had his father's flair.

Falcon climbed higher to circle toward the other owl. It had been long since he had spoken to another Carpathian. The joy he felt, even with a battle looming, was indescribable. He shared it with Sara, his lifemate, his other half. She deserved to know what she had done for him; it was she who had enabled him to feel emotion. Falcon went to earth, landing as he shifted into his own form.

Mikhail looked much as his father had before him. The same power clung to him. Falcon bowed low, elegantly. He reached out, clasping Mikhail's forearms in the manner of the old warriors. "I give you my allegiance, Prince. I would have known you anywhere. You are much like your father."

Mikhail's piercing black eyes warmed. "You are familiar to me. I was young then. You were lost to us suddenly, as were so many of our greatest warriors. You are Falcon, and your line was thought to have been lost when you disappeared. How is it you are alive and yet we had no knowledge of you?" His grip was strong as he returned the age-old greeting between warriors of their species. His voice was warm, mellow even, yet the subtle reprimand was not lost on Falcon.

"Your father foresaw much in those days, a dark shadowing of the future of our people." Falcon turned toward the truck teetering so precariously. He began to stride toward the vehicle, with Mikhail in perfect synchronization. They moved together almost like dancers, fluid and graceful, full of power and coordination. "He called us together one night, many of us, and asked for volunteers to go to foreign lands. Vlad did not order us to go, but he was very much respected, and those of us who chose to do as he asked never thought of refusing. He knew you were to be Prince. He knew that you would face the extinction of our species. It was necessary for you to believe in your own abilities, and for *all* our people to believe in you and not rely on those of us who were older. We could not afford a divided people." Falcon's voice was gentle, matter-of-fact.

Mikhail's black eyes moved over Falcon's granite-honed face, the broad shoulders, the easy way he carried himself. "Perhaps advice would have been welcomed."

A faint smile touched Falcon's sculpted mouth, hinted at warmth in the depths of his eyes. "Perhaps our people needed a fresh, new perspective without the clutter of what once was."

"Perhaps," Mikhail murmured softly.

The ghoul had climbed from the truck and moved around the vehicle as if examining it. It didn't look up at the two Carpathian males, or acknowledge their presence in any way. Suddenly it placed its back against the truck, dug its feet into the rocky soil, and began to strain.

The sky erupted with black insects, so many the air seemed to groan with the numbers, raining from the sky with a fury equal to a tempest. From inside the truck, the children began to scream as the metal shrieked. The vehicle was being inched slowly but inevitably over the edge of the cliff.

Falcon put on a burst of preternatural speed, catching the ghoul by the shoulder and whirling it away from the truck. He trusted Mikhail to stop the children from going over. The insects were striking at him, stinging, biting, hitting his body, thousands of them, going for his eyes and nose and ears. Falcon was forced to dissolve into vapor, throwing up a quick barricade around himself as he reappeared behind the ghoul.

The creature swung around awkwardly, dragging one leg as it attempted to turn to face Falcon. Its eyes glowed

a demonic red. It was making strange noises, somewhere between growling and snarling. It swiped at Falcon with razor-sharp nails, missed by inches. Falcon
stayed just out of reach, watching closely. The ghoul
was a mindless puppet to be used by its master. The
vampire must have known that Falcon was an ancient,
easily able to destroy such a creation, so it made little
sense that the creature would attempt to fight him, yet
that was exactly what the ghoul did. The macabre puppet grasped Falcon, fumbling to get its hands locked
around Falcon's neck.

Falcon easily broke the grip, shattering the thick
bones and wrenching the ghoul's head. The crack was
audible despite the intensity of the wind and the loud
clacking of the insects as they hit the ground. The ghoul
seemed to glow for a moment, the eyes lighting an eerie
orange in the darkness, the skin sloughing off as if the
creature were a snake rather than a man.

"Get those children out of here," Falcon called out
gravely, backing away from the creature. The light coming from inside the ghoul was becoming brighter, giving
off a peculiar luminescence. "It is a trap."

Mikhail was tossing the children to safer ground.
Three little girls and four boys. He leaped out of the way
as the truck teetered precariously and then tumbled over
the edge. He had shielded the children's minds, knowing they had been terror-stricken for most of the day.
The oldest child, a boy, couldn't have been more than
eight. Mikhail sensed that each of them was special in
some way, each had psychic ability.

Insects were raining from the sky, dropping around

them to form thick, grotesque piles of squirming bodies. Although Mikhail had erected a barrier over them and had shielded their minds, the children were staring in wide-eyed horror at the bugs. Mikhail heard Falcon's soft warning, glanced at the ghoul, and immediately shifted his shape, becoming a long, winged creature, the fabled dragon. Using his mind to control the children, he forced them to climb onto his back. They clung to him, their bodies trembling, but they accepted what was happening without real comprehension. Mikhail took to the air, laying down a long red-orange flame, incinerating all of the hideous beetles and locusts within his range.

I will transport the children to safety.

Go now! Falcon was alarmed for the Prince, alarmed for the children. The ghoul was spinning, creating a peculiar whirlwind motion reminiscent of a minitornado. The winds were furious, blowing the insects in all directions, even sucking them up into the sky. The glow was bright enough to hurt Falcon's sensitive eyes. *In all my long centuries of battles with the undead and their minions, this is a new phenomenon.*

New to me also. Mikhail was winging quickly through the waning light in the sky, battling the ferocity of the wind and the thick masses of insects attacking from all directions. *The undead is indeed powerful to create this havoc while he still lies within his lair. He is without doubt an ancient.*

I sent word to your brother to wait to fight him, as I am certain this one is as old and as experienced as I am. I hope he listens to Sara.

Mikhail, in the body of the dragon, sighed. He hoped so, too. Immediately he touched Jacques's mind, relayed what had transpired and their conclusions.

Falcon moved carefully away from the ghoul, attempting to put distance between them. *The undead baited a trap, drew us away from Sara using the children and the ghoul. He will go after her.* Each direction Falcon chose, the grotesque creature turned with him in perfect rhythm, matching his flowing motions as if they were dance partners. *Get out of here now, Mikhail. Do not wait for me. This thing has attached itself to me like a shadow. A lethal and difficult spell to break. He is a bomb. Get to Sara.*

I will not be happy if such a despicable creature harms you. There was an edge of humor to Mikhail's soft voice. An edge of worry.

I am an ancient. This one will not defeat me. I am concerned only with the safety of you and the children. And with the delay in reaching Sara. It was the truth. Falcon might not have seen such a thing before, but he had supreme confidence in his own abilities. Already he was working at removing the binding attachment from his cells. It was a deep shadowing, as though the ghoul had managed to embed its molecules into Falcon's. Falcon tried various methods but could not find where the binding was impressed into his body. The ghoul was white-hot, blossoming like a mushroom and emitting a strange low hum. Time was running out.

Falcon ran his hands down his arms, across his chest. At once he felt the strange warmth emanating from his chest. Of course. The four long furrows the vampire had carved into his chest! The undead had left the spell in Falcon's chest, spoor for the ghoul to recognize, to adhere itself to. Falcon transmitted the information immediately to the Prince as he hastily began to detach himself from the monstrous time bomb.

The humming was louder, pitched much higher as the insects clacked with more intensity. The bugs were in a kind of frenzy, flying in all directions, swarming, attempting to scratch their way through the barrier Falcon had erected around himself. He had no time to think about poisonous insects; he had to turn his full attention to removing the hidden shadowing on his body. The vampire's fingerprints were etched deep beneath Falcon's skin.

Falcon glided quickly toward the ravine, drawing the ghoul away from the forest. As he twisted this way and that, taking the vampire's puppet with him at every step, he was examining his body from the inside out. He had missed those tiny prints marring his skin, pressed deeply into the lacerations he had already healed. So small, so lethal. He concentrated on scraping the nearly invisible marks from under his skin. It took tremendous discipline to work as he moved, using only his mind, leading the macabre ghoul right over the edge of the cliff. He was floating over empty space, enticing the unholy creature to take the last step that would send it plummeting to the rocks below. The explosion, when it came, could be contained deep within the ravine. Falcon worked rapidly, knowing that if the ghoul was attached to him, even by such tiny and invisible threads, the explosion would kill him.

The ghoul was in the air with him now, and Falcon began the descent slowly, taking the hideous thing where it could do no harm, even as he continued to find each print in the furrows on his chest. The whirling hot light suddenly shuddered, slipped, as if hanging by only a few precarious threads. The humming was now at fever-pitch, a merciless, unrelenting screaming in his head that made it difficult to think.

Falcon shut out the noise, increasing his speed, knowing he was close to throwing off the ghoul, knowing it was close to the end of its run. The vampire was waiting for sunset, holding Falcon away from Sara as surely as if he had imprisoned him. The ghoul pulsed with red-orange light through the white-hot glow just as Falcon sloughed off the last of the vampire's marks. The puppet began to fall, dropping away as Falcon rose swiftly toward the roiling clouds.

Falcon dissolved into mist as he rushed away from the screeching bomb. The explosion was monumental, a force that blew insect parts in all directions, carved a crater into the side of the ravine, and set the brush on fire. Falcon immediately doused the flames with rain, directing the heavy clouds over the steep ravine as he turned toward Mikhail's home, picking the directions out of the Prince's mind.

When Falcon made contact with Mikhail, he found him engaged in conversation with a human male, cautioning the man to protect the children. He knew he need not worry about the children; Mikhail would never place them in a dangerous situation. *Sara, I am some distance away but I will reach you soon.*

* * *

Falcon! Sara pushed herself upright despite her dizziness, staring in horror at the hideous beetle scurrying across the floor toward her. It was staring directly at her, watching her, marking her. And she knew what it was. Just as Falcon could use her eyes to see what was happening around her, the vampire was using the beetle's. The hard shell was on fire, the smell atrocious, but it was moving unerringly toward her, the eyes fixed on her. *He knows where I am. He'll kill all these people.* She was terrified, but Sara couldn't live with more guilt. If this monster wanted her so badly, perhaps the solution was simply to walk out the door and find him.

No! Falcon's voice was strong, commanding. *You will do as I say. Warn the male that this enemy is an ancient, most likely one of the warriors sent out by Mikhail's father who turned vampire. The sun has not yet set, we have a few minutes. The male must use delaying tactics until we arrive to aid him.*

Jacques simply stepped on the large insect, flames and all, crushing the thing beneath his foot, smothering the flames. Sara cleared her throat and looked at Jacques with sorrow in her eyes. "I'm so sorry. I didn't mean to bring this enemy to you. He's an ancient, Falcon says, most likely one of the warriors Mikhail's father sent out."

Raven smoothed back Sara's hair with gentle fingers. Jacques hunkered down so he was level with Sara. His expression was as calm as ever. "Tell me what you know, Sara. It will aid me in battle."

Sara shook her head, had to suppress a groan as her

head throbbed and pulsed with pain. "Falcon says to delay the battle, to wait for him, and for Mikhail."

"Heal her, Shea," Jacques ordered gently. "The sun has not set and the vampire is locked deep within the earth. He knows where she is and will come to us, but the safeguards will slow him. We have time. Mikhail will make his way here, and her lifemate will come also. This ancient enemy is a powerful one."

The children, Falcon. What of the children? Sara was finding it difficult to think, with the grotesque remains of the insect on the immaculate shining wood floor.

The children are safe, Sara. Do not worry about them. Mikhail has taken them to a safe house. A man, a human, known to him and our people, is there to watch over them. They will be safe while we are hunting your enemy.

Sara inhaled sharply. Hadn't the others seen what she had? The vampire had penetrated the safeguards and had found her, had watched her through the eyes of its servant. Now the children she wanted to adopt were being taken to a perfect stranger. *Who is this man? How do you know of him, Falcon? Maybe you should go there yourself. They must be so afraid.*

Mikhail trusts this man. His name is Gary Jansen, a friend to our people. He will look after the children until we have destroyed the vampire. We cannot afford to draw the undead to them a second time. Mikhail will not leave them frightened. He is capable of helping them to accept this human and their new situation.

Sara lifted her chin, trying to ignore the terrible pounding in her head. "Do you know someone called

Gary? Mikhail is taking the children to him." She knew she sounded anxious but she couldn't help it.

Shea laughed softly. "Gary is a genius, a man very much involved with his work. He flew out here from the States to help me with an important project I'm working on." As she spoke she silently signaled her lifemate to lift Sara and transport her to one of the underground chambers below the house. "I wish I'd been there to see the expression on his face when Mikhail showed up at the inn with several frightened children. Gary is a good man and very dedicated to helping us discover why our children are not surviving, why there are so few female children born, but I can't imagine him attempting to take care of little ones all by himself."

"You are enjoying the thought way too much." Jacques's laughter was low, a pleasant sound in contrast with the loud, frightening noises outside the home. "I cannot wait to tell the human you are pleased with his new role."

"But he *will* take care of them." Sara sought reassurance even as Jacques lifted her high into his arms.

Raven nodded emphatically. "Oh, yes, there's no need to worry. Gary would never abandon the children, and all Carpathians are bound to protect him should he have need. Your children will be very safe, Sara." As they moved through the house, she indicated a framed picture on the wall. "That is my daughter, Savannah. Gary saved her life."

Sara peered at the picture as they went by. The young woman was beautiful, but she looked the same age as

Raven. And she looked vaguely familiar. "She's your daughter? She looks your age."

"Savannah has a lifemate." Raven touched the frame in a loving gesture. "When they are small, our children look very young, but their bodies grow at about the same rate as a human child for the first few years. It is only when our people reach sexual maturity that our growth rate slows. That is one reason we have trouble reproducing. It is rare for our women to be able to ovulate for a good hundred years after having a baby. It has happened, but it is rare. Shea believes it is a form of population control, just as most other species have built-in controls. Because Carpathians live so long, nature, or God, if you prefer, built in a safeguard. Savannah will be returning home quite soon. They would have returned immediately upon their union, but Gregori, her lifemate, has received word of his lost family and wishes to meet with them first." Raven's voice held an edge of excitement. "Gregori is needed here. He is Mikhail's second in command, a very powerful man. And, of course, I've missed Savannah."

Sara was suddenly aware that they were going swiftly through a passageway. Raven's chatter had distracted her from her headache and from the danger, but mostly from the fact that they were moving steadily downward, beneath the earth. She felt the leap of her heart and instantly reached out for Falcon. Mind to mind. Heart to heart. *We can only have a child once every hundred years.* She said the first thing she thought of, then was embarrassed that she had whispered a secret dream, now a regret. She longed for a house filled with children.

With love and laughter. With all the things she had lost. All the things she had long ago accepted she would never have.

We have seven children, Sara, seven abandoned, half-starved, very frightened children. They will need us to sort out their problems, love them, and aid them with their unexpected gifts. The three girls may or may not be lifemates for Carpathians in sore need, but all will need guidance. We will have many children to love in the coming years. Whatever your dream, it is mine. We will have a home and we will fill it with children and laughter and love.

He was closer, he was on his way to her. Sara wrapped herself in his warmth, in his words. *This is my gift to you.* A dark dream she would embrace. Reach for.

"Where are you taking me?" Sara's anxiety was embarrassing, but she couldn't seem to hold it in check. Falcon had to be able to find her.

She heard the reassurance of his soft laughter. *There is no place they could take you where I could not find you. I am in you as you are in me, Sara.*

"What you are feeling is normal, Sara," Raven said softly. "Lifemates cannot be apart from one another comfortably."

"And you have a concussion," Shea reminded. "We're taking you where you will be safe," she assured again, calmly, patiently.

The passageway wound deep within the earth. Jacques took Sara through what seemed like a door in the solid rock to a large, beautiful chamber. To Sara's grateful surprise, it looked like a bedroom. The bed was large and inviting. She curled up on it the moment

Jacques put her down, closing her eyes and wanting just to go to sleep. She felt that even a few minutes' rest would make her feel better. The comforter was thick and soothing, the designs unusual. Sara found herself tracing the symbols over and over.

The candles leaped to life, flickering and dancing, casting shadows on the walls and filling the room with a wonderful aroma. Sara was barely aware of Shea's healing touch with all the precision of a surgeon. Sara could only think of Falcon. Could only wait for him deep beneath the earth, hoping they would all be safe until he arrived.

CHAPTER EIGHT

The attack came immediately after sunset. The sky rained fire, streaks of red and orange dropping straight down toward the house and grounds. Long furrows in the ground appeared, moving quickly, darting toward the estate, tentacles erupting near the massive gates and columns surrounding the property. Bulbs burst through the earth, spewing acid at the wrought-iron fence. Insects fell from the clouds, oozed from the trees. Rats rushed the fence, an army of them, round beady eyes gleaming. There were so many bodies the ground was black with them.

Beneath the earth Jacques lifted his head alertly. His lifemate was performing her healing art. His eyes met Raven's over Sara's head. "The ancient one has sent his army ahead of his arrival. The house is under attack."

"Will the safeguards hold?" Raven asked with her usual calm. She was already reaching out to Mikhail.

They were still separated by many miles, yet his warmth flooded her immediately.

"Against his servants, the safeguards will certainly hold. The ancient one is attempting to weaken the safeguards so that he can more easily penetrate our defenses. He knows that Mikhail and Sara's lifemate are on their way. He thinks to have a quick and easy victory before their arrival." Jacques was calm, his black eyes flat and cold. He was banishing all emotion in preparation for battle. His arms were around Shea's waist, his body pressed close, protectively toward her. He bent his head to kiss her neck, a light, brief caress before moving away.

Raven caught his arm, preventing him from leaving the chamber. "Mikhail and Falcon say this one is dangerous, a true ancient, Jacques. Wait for them, please."

He looked down at her hand. "They are all dangerous, little sister. I will do what is necessary to protect the three of you." Very gently he removed her hand from his wrist, gave her an awkward, reassuring pat, a gesture at odds with his elegance.

Raven smiled at him. "I love you, Jacques. So does Mikhail. We don't tell you nearly enough."

"It is not necessary to say the words, Raven. Shea has taught me much over the years. The bond between us is very strong. I have much to live for, much to look forward to. I have finally convinced my lifemate that a child is worth the risks."

Raven's face lit up, her eyes shiny with tears. "Shea didn't say a word to me. I know she's always wanted to have a baby. I'm happy for you both, I really am."

Shea returned to her body, swaying from the intense effort of healing Sara. She staggered toward Jacques. He caught her to him, drew her gently into his arms, buried his face in the mass of wine-red hair. "Is Sara going to be all right?" he asked softly. There was a wealth of pride in his voice, a deep respect for his lifemate.

Shea leaned into him, turned up her face to be kissed. "Sara will be fine. She just needs her lifemate." She stared into Jacques's eyes. "As I do."

"Neither you nor Raven seems to have much faith in my abilities. I'm shocked!" Jacques's chagrined look had both women laughing despite the seriousness of the situation. "I have my brother attempting to pull his Prince routine on me, giving me orders not to engage the enemy until His Majesty returns. My own lifemate, brilliant as she is, does not seem to realize I am a warrior without equal. And my lovely sister-kin is deliberately delaying me. What do you think about that, Sara?" He arced one eyebrow at her.

Sara sat up slowly, pushed her hand through her tousled, spiky hair. Her head was no longer pounding and her ribs felt just fine. Even the aches from the bruises were gone. "I don't know about your status as a warrior without equal, but your lifemate is a miracle worker." She had the feeling that Raven and Shea spent a great deal of time laughing when they were together. Neither seemed in the least intimidated by Jacques, despite the gravity of his appearance.

"I cannot argue with you there," Jacques agreed.

Shea grinned at Sara, her face pale. "He has to say that. It is always best to compliment one's lifemate."

"And that is why you and Raven are casting aspersions upon my battle capabilities." Once more Jacques kissed his lifemate. With his acute hearing, he could hear the assault upon the estate.

Sara could hear it, too. She twisted her fingers together anxiously. "He's coming. I know he is."

"Do not fear him, Sara," Shea hastened to assure her. "My lifemate has battled many of the undead and will do so long after this one is gone." She turned her gaze on her husband. "Raven will provide for me while you delay this monster. You will return to me unharmed."

"I hear you, little red hair, and I can do no other than obey." His voice was soft, an intimate caress. He simply dissolved into vapor and streamed from the chamber.

Sara made an effort to close her mouth and not gape in total shock. Raven, one arm wrapped around Shea's waist, laughed softly. "Carpathians take a little getting used to. I ought to know."

"I must feed," Shea said, her gaze steady on Sara's. "Will it alarm you?"

"I don't know," Sara said honestly. For no reason at all, the spot along the swell of her breast began to throb. She found herself blushing. "I suppose I should get used to it. Falcon and I were waiting until I had settled the red tape with the children before we"—she sought the right word—"finalized things." She lifted her chin. "I'm very committed to him." It seemed a pale way of explaining the intensity of her emotions.

"I am amazed he allowed you the time. He must be extraordinarily certain of his abilities to protect you," Raven said. "Feed, Shea. I offer freely that you may be at full strength once again." She casually extended her wrist to Shea. "Carpathian males usually have a difficult time at the first return of their emotions. They have to contend with jealousy and fear, the overwhelming need to protect their lifemate and the terror of losing her. They become domineering and possessive and generally are a pain in the neck." Raven laughed softly, obviously sharing the conversation with her lifemate.

Sara could feel her heart racing as she watched in horrified fascination while Shea accepted nourishment from Raven. Although it was bizarre, she could see no blood. She was almost comforted by the completely un-selfish act between the two women. Sara was humbled by Shea's gift of healing. She was humbled by the way she was accepted so completely into their circle, a close family willing immediately to aid her, to place their lives directly in the path of danger for her.

"Are you really planning to have a child?" Raven asked as Shea closed the tiny pinpricks in her wrist with a sweep of her tongue. "Jacques said he has finally con-vinced you." There was a slight hesitation in Raven's voice.

Sara watched shadows chase across Shea's delicate features. Sara had always wanted children, and she sensed that Shea's answer would be important to her dreams, also.

Shea took a deep breath, let it out slowly. "Jacques wants a child desperately, Raven. I have tried to think like a doctor, because the risks are so high, but it is diffi-cult when everything in me wants a child and when my lifemate feels the same. It was a miracle Savannah survived; you know that, you know how difficult it was. It took both Gregori and me that first year of fighting for her life, along with Mikhail and you. I have improved the formula for infants, since we cannot feed them what was once the perfect nourishment. I do not know why nature has turned on our species, but we are fighting to save every child born to us. Still, knowing all this does not stop me from wanting children. I know now that if something happened to me, Jacques would fulfill my wish and raise our child until he or she has a family. I will choose a time soon and hope we are successful with the pregnancy and keeping the child alive afterward."

Sara stood up carefully, a little gingerly, a frown on her face. She could hear the sizzle of fire meeting water, of insects and other frightening things she had no knowledge of. She could hear clearly, even envision the battle outside, the army of evil seeking to break through the safeguards protecting those within the walls of the house. Yet she felt safe. Deep below the earth, she felt a kinship with the two women. And she knew Falcon was on his way. He would come to her. For her. Nothing would stop him.

It seemed crazy, yet perfectly natural, to be in this chamber talking intimately with Raven and Shea while, just above them, the ancient vampire was seeking entrance. "Will I have problems having a child once I become fully like Falcon?" Sara asked. It had not occurred to her that she would not be able to have a child once she was a Carpathian.

Shea and Raven both held out their hands to her. A

gesture of camaraderie, of compassion, of solidarity. "We are working very hard to find the answers. Savannah survived and two male children, but no other females. We have much more research to do, and I have developed several theories. Gary has flown out from the United States to aid me, and Oregon will follow in a few weeks. I believe we can find a way to keep the babies alive. I even believe I'm close to finding the reason why we give birth to so few females, but I am not certain that, even once I know the cause, I can remedy the situation. I do believe that every female who was human at one time has a good chance of having a female child. And that is a priceless gift to our dying race."

Sara paced the length of the room, suddenly needing Falcon. The longer she was away from him, the worse it seemed to be. Need. It crawled through her, twisted her stomach into knots, took her breath away. She accepted it, had known the need long before she had known the reality of Falcon. She had carried his journal everywhere with her, his words imprinted on her mind and in her heart. She had needed him then; now it was as if a part of her were dead without him.

"Touch his mind with yours," Raven advised softly. "He is always there for you. Don't worry, Sara, we will be here for you, too. Our life is wonderful, filled with love and amazing abilities. A lifemate is worth giving up what you had."

Sara pushed a hand through her hair, tousling it further. "I didn't have much of a life. Falcon has allowed me to dare to dream again. Of a family. Of a home. Of belonging with someone. I'm not afraid." She suddenly laughed. "Well . . . maybe I'm nervous. A little nervous."

"Falcon must be an incredible man," Shea said.

Not that incredible. Jacques never quite relinquished his touch on Shea. Over the years he had managed to relearn many things that had once been wiped from his mind, but he needed his lifemate anchoring him at all times. Before, he would have been jealous and edgy; now there was a teasing quality to his voice.

Shea laughed at him. Softly. Intimately. Sent him her touch, erotic pictures of twining her body around his. It was enough. She was his lifemate. His world.

Sara watched the expressions chase across Shea's delicate features, knowing exactly what was transpiring between Shea and her lifemate. It made Sara feel as if she really were a part of something, part of a family again. And Raven was right, the moment she reached for Falcon, he was there, in her mind, enfolding her in love and warmth, in reassurance. She wrapped her arms around herself to hold him close to her, felt him in her mind, heard him, the soft whispers, the promises, his supreme confidence in his abilities. It was all there in an instant.

"Sara." Raven brought Sara's attention back to the women, determined to keep it centered on them rather than on the coming battle. "Whose children are these that the vampire went to so much trouble to acquire?"

Sara suddenly smiled, her face lighting up. "I guess they are mine now. I found them living in the sewers. They had banded together because of their difference from most. All of them have psychic abilities. Three little girls and four boys. Not all of their talents are the same, but they still knew, as young as they are, that they needed one another. I had great empathy with them because I grew up feeling different, too. I wanted to give them a home where they could feel normal."

"Three little girls?" Shea and Raven exchanged a long, gleeful grin. Shea shook her head in astonishment. "You are truly a treasure. You've brought us an ancient warrior. We may learn much from him. You have seven little ones with psychic talent, and you are a lifemate. Tell me how it is that you accept our world so readily."

Sara shrugged. "Because of the vampire. I saw him killing in the tunnels of a dig my parents were on. Two days later he killed my whole family." She lifted her chin a little as if in preparation for condemnation, but both women only looked sad, their gazes compassionate. "He chased me for years. I always kept moving to stay ahead of him. Vampires have been part of my life for a long time. I just didn't understand the difference between vampires and Carpathians."

"And Falcon?" Raven prompted.

Sara heard a sudden hush outside the house, as if the wind were holding its breath. The night creatures stilled. She shivered, her body trembling. The sun had set. The vampire had risen and was hurtling through space to reach the estate before Falcon and Mikhail had a chance to return.

Sara was positive that both women were aware of the vampire's rising, but they remained calm, although they linked hands. She took a deep breath, wanting to follow their examples of tranquillity. "Falcon has been my salvation for fifteen years. I just didn't know he was real. I found something that belonged to him." *This is my gift to you. Sara, lifemate to Falcon.* She held his words tightly to her. "I saw him clearly, his face, his hair, his every expression. I felt as if I could see into his heart. I knew I belonged with him, yet he was from long ago and I was born too late."

Falcon, winging his way strongly through the falling night felt her sorrow. He reached out to her, flooding her mind with the sheer intensity of his love for her. *You were not born too late, my love. Accept what is and what has been given to us. A great gift, a priceless treasure. I am with you now and for all time.*

I love you with all my heart, with every breath.

Then believe that I will not allow this monster to tear us apart. I have endured centuries of loneliness, a barren existence without your presence. He will not take you from me. I am of ancient lineage and much skilled. Our enemy is indeed powerful, but he will be defeated.

Sara's heart began to ease its frantic racing, slowing to match the steady beat of Falcon's heart. Deliberately he breathed for her, for them, a shadow in her head as much for his own peace of mind as for hers. He was well aware of the vampire moving swiftly toward the house to find Sara. The foul stench was riding on the night wind. The creatures of the evening whispered to him, scurried for cover to avoid the danger. Falcon had no way of communicating with Mikhail and Jacques without the vampire hearing. He could use the standard path of telepathy used by their people, but the vampire would certainly hear. Mikhail and Jacques shared a blood tie and had their own private path of communication the undead could not share. It would make the planning of a battle against an ancient vampire much easier.

Falcon felt heat sizzling through the air as the first real attack was launched by the vampire. The vibrations of violence sent shock waves through the sky, bouncing off the mountain peaks so that wicked veins of lightning rocked the black, roiling clouds. The avian form he was using could not withstand such force. He tumbled through the sky, falling toward earth. Falcon abandoned that form and shifted into vapor. The wind changed abruptly, because a gale force, blowing the droplets of water in the opposite direction from where he wished to go. Falcon took the only avenue safely open to him; he dropped to earth, landing in the form of a wolf, running flat out on four legs toward his lifemate and the Prince's estate.

Despite the miles separating them, Mikhail ran into the same problem. It was no longer safe or expedient to travel through the air. He took to the ground, a large, shaggy wolf running at top speed, easily clearing logs in his path.

Jacques surveyed the sky thick with locusts and beetles, the arrows of flame and the spinning black clouds veined with forks of lightning. Tentacles erupted along the inside of the gates, a small inconvenience announcing the first break in the safeguards. He was calm as he withered the tentacles and protected the structure from the fire and insects. He began to throw barriers up, small, flimsy ones that took little time to build yet would cost the vampire time to destroy. Minutes counted now. Every moment that he managed to delay the ancient vampire gave Mikhail and Falcon a chance to reach them.

I have been in many battles, yet this is the first time I have encountered a vampire so determined to break through obvious safeguards. Jacques sent the information to his brother. *He knows this is the home of the Prince, that the women are protected by more than one male, yet he is persistent. I think we should send the women deep within the earth and you should stay away until this enemy is defeated.*

What of the human woman? The advice didn't slow Mikhail down. The wolf was running flat out, not breathing hard, nature's perfect machine.

I will protect her until her lifemate arrives. We will defeat this vampire together. Mikhail, you have a duty to your people. If Gregori were here—

Gregori is not here, Mikhail interrupted wryly. *He is off with my daughter neglecting his duty to protect the Prince.* There was a hint of laughter in his voice.

Jacques was exasperated. *The undead is unlike anything we have faced. He has not flinched at anything I have thrown at him. His attack has never faltered.*

It seems that this ancient enemy is very sure of his abilities. Mikhail's voice was a soft menace, a weapon of destruction if he cared to use it. There was a note of finality that Jacques recognized immediately. Mikhail was racing through the forest, so quickly his paws barely brushed the ground. He felt the presence of a second wolf close by. Smelled the wild pungent odor of the wolf male. A large animal burst through the heavy brush, rushing at him on a diagonal to cut him off.

Mikhail was forced to check his speed to avoid a collision. The heavier wolf contorted, wavered, took the shape of a man. Mikhail did so also.

Falcon watched the Prince through thoughtful, wary eyes. "I believe it would be prudent on our part to exchange blood. The ability to communicate privately may come in handy in the coming battle."

Mikhail nodded his agreement, took the wrist that Falcon offered as a gesture of commitment to the Prince. Mikhail would always know where Falcon was, what he was doing if he so desired. He took enough for an exchange and calmly offered his own arm in return.

Falcon had not touched the blood of an ancient in many centuries, and it rushed through his system like a fireball, a rush of power and strength. Courteously he closed the pinpricks and surveyed Vladimir's son. "You know you should not place yourself in harm's way. It has occurred to me that you could be the primary target. If you were to be killed by such a creature, our people would be left in chaos. The vampire would have a chance of gaining a stranglehold on the world. It is best if you go to ground as our last line of defense. Your brother and I will destroy the undead."

Mikhail sighed. "I have had this conversation with Jacques and do not care to repeat it. I have fought countless battles and my lifemate is at risk, as well as the villagers, who are my friends and under my protection." His shape was already wavering.

"Then you leave me no choice but to offer my protection since your second is not present." There was an edge to Falcon's voice. His body contorted, erupted with hair, bent as feet and hands clawed.

"Gregori is in the United States collecting his lifemate." It was enough, a reprimand and a warning.

Falcon wasn't intimidated. He was an ancient, his lineage old and sacred, his loyalties and sense of duty ingrained in him. His duty was to his Prince; honor demanded that he protect the man from all harm no matter what the cost.

They were running again, fast and fluid, leaping over obstacles, rushing through the underbrush, silent and deadly while the skies rained insects and the mist thickened into a fogbank that lay low and ugly along the ground. The wolves relied on their acute sense of smell when it became nearly impossible to see.

They burst into the clearing on the edge of the forest. The ground erupted with masses of tentacles. The writhing appendages reached for them, squirming along the ground seeking prey. The two wolves leaped nearly straight into the air to avoid the grasping tentacles, danced around walls of thorns, and skidded to a halt near the tall, double, wrought-iron gates.

Falcon angled in close to Mikhail, inserting his body between the Prince and a tall, elegant man who appeared before them, his head contorting into a wedge shape with red eyes and scales. The mouth yawned wide, revealing rows of dagger-sharp teeth. The creature roared, expelling a fiery flame that cut through the thick fog straight at them.

Jacques exploded from the house, leaping the distance to the gate, then jumping over to land on the spot where the undead had been. The vampire used its preternatural speed, spinning out of reach. He hissed into the night air, a foul, poisonous blend of sound and venom. Vapor whirled around his solid form, green and then black. A noxious odor was carried on the blast. The vapor simply dissolved into thousands of droplets of water, spreading on the wind, an airborne cloud of depravity.

The hunters pressed forward into the thick muck. Falcon murmured softly, his hands following an intricate pattern. At once the air was filled with a strange phosphorescent milky whiteness. The trail left by the undead was easily seen as dark splotches staining the glowing white. Falcon took to the clouds, a difficult task with the air so thick and noxious. The splotches scattered across the heavens, tiny stains that seemed to spread and grow in all directions, streaking like dark comets across the night sky.

The vampire could only go in one direction, yet the stains were scattering far and wide, east and south, north and west, toward the village, high over the forest, along the mountain ridge, straight up, blowing like a foul tower and falling to earth as dark acid rain.

On the ground the rats and insects retreated, the walls of thorn wavered and fell, the tentacles retreated beneath the earth. Near the corner of the gate, a large rat stared malevolently at the house for several moments. Teeth bared, the rodent spat on the gate before it whirled around and scurried away. The wrought iron sizzled and smoked, the saliva corroding the metal and leaving behind a small blackened hole.

Mikhail sent out a call to all Carpathians in the area to watch over the villagers. They would attempt to cut off the vampire's source of sustenance. With the entire region on alert, he hoped to find the vampire's lair quickly. He signaled the other two hunters to return to the house. Chasing the vampire when there was no clear trail was a fool's errand. They would regroup and form a plan of attack.

"This one is indeed an ancient," Jacques said as they took back their true forms at the veranda of the Prince's home. "He is more powerful than any other I have come across."

"Your father sent out many warriors. Some are still alive, some have chosen the dawn, and a few have turned vampire," Falcon agreed. "And there is no doubt that this one has learned much over the years. But he had fifteen years to find Sara, yet she escaped. A human, a child. He can and will be defeated." He glanced toward the gate. "He left behind his poisonous mark. I spotted it as we came in. And, Jacques, thank you for finding Sara so quickly and getting her to safety. I am in your debt."

"We have much to learn of one another," Mikhail said, "and the unpleasant duty of destroying the evil one, but Sara must be able to go to ground. She is beneath the earth in one of the chambers. For her protection, it is best that you convert her immediately."

Falcon's dark eyes met his Prince's. "And you know this can be safely done? In my time such a thing was never tried by any but the undead. The results were frightening."

Mikhail nodded. "If she is your true lifemate, she must have psychic abilities. She can be converted without danger, but it is not without pain. You will know instinctively what to do for her. You will need to supply her with blood. You must use mine, as you have no time to go out hunting prey."

"And mine," Jacques volunteered generously. "We will have need of the connection in the coming battle."

CHAPTER NINE

Sara was waiting for Falcon in the large, beautiful chamber. Candles were everywhere, flames flickering so that the glowing lights cast shadows on the wall. She was alone, sitting on the edge of the bed. The other women had been summoned by their lifemates. Sara jumped up when Falcon walked in. She wore only a man's silken shirt, the tails reaching nearly to her knees. A single button held the edges together over her generous breasts. She was the most beautiful thing he had ever seen in all his centuries of existence. He closed the door quietly and leaned against it, just drinking her in. She was alive. And she was real.

Sara stared up at him, her heart in her eyes. "It seems like forever."

Her voice was soft but it washed over him with the strength of a hurricane, making his pulse pound and his senses reel. She was there waiting for him with that

CHRISTINE FEEHAN

same welcome on her face. Real. It was real, and it was just for him.

Falcon held out his hand to her, needing to touch her, to see that she was alive and well, that the healer had worked her miracle. "I never want to experience such terror again. Locked within the earth, I felt helpless to aid you."

Sara crossed to his side without hesitation. She touched his face with trembling fingertips, traced every beloved line—the curve of his mouth, his dark eyebrows—and rubbed a caress along his shadowed jaw. "But you did come to my aid. You sent the others to me, and you were always with me. I wasn't alone. More than that, I knew you would save the children." There was a wealth of love in her voice that stole his heart.

He bent his head to take possession of her tempting mouth. She was soft satin and a dark dream of the future. He took his time, kissing her again and again, savoring the way she melted into him, the way she was so much a part of him. *Are you ready to be as I am? To be Carpathian and walk beside me for all time?* He couldn't say it aloud but whispered it intimately in her mind while his heart stood still and his breath caught in his lungs. Waiting. Just waiting for her answer.

You are my world. I don't think I could bear to be without you. She answered him in the way of his people, wanting to reassure him.

"Is this what you want, Sara? Am I what you want? Be certain of this—it is no easy thing. Conversion is painful." Falcon tightened his hold on her possessively, but he had to tell her the truth.

"Being without you is more painful." Her arms crept around his neck. She leaned her body against his, her soft breasts pushing against his chest, her body molding to his. "I want this, Falcon. I have no reservations. I may be nervous, but I am unafraid. I want a life with you." Her mouth found his, tiny kisses teasing the corners of his smile, her teeth nibbling at his lower lip. Her body was hot and restless and aching for his. Her kiss was fire and passion, hot and filled with promises. She gave herself into his keeping without reservation.

He melted inside. It was an instant and complete meltdown, his insides going soft and his body growing hard. She tore him up inside as nothing had ever done. No one had ever penetrated the armor surrounding his heart. It had been cold. Dead. Now it was wildly alive. His heart pounded madly at the love in her eyes, the touch of her fingertips, the generous welcome of her body, the total trust she gave him when her life had been one of such mistrust.

His kiss was possessive, demanding. Hot and urgent, the way his body felt. His hands went to her waist in a soft caress, slid upward to cup the weight of her breasts in his hands. But his mouth was pure fire, wild and hot even when his hands were so tender. He slipped the single button open, his breath catching in his throat, and he stepped back to view the lush temptation of her breasts. "You are so beautiful, Sara. Everything about you. I love you more than anything. I hope you know that. I hope you are reading my mind and you know that you are my life." His finger trailed slowly down the valley between her breasts to her navel. His body reacted, that painful ache of urgent demand. And he let it happen.

Sara watched his eyes change, watched the way his body changed, and she smiled, unafraid of the wildness she glimpsed in him. Wanting it. Wanting him crazy for her. She unbuttoned his shirt, slipped it from his shoulders. Leaning forward, she pressed a row of kisses along his muscles, her tongue sliding around his nipple. She smiled up at him as she rubbed her hand over the bulging material of his trousers, her fingers deftly freeing him from the tight confines. Her hand wrapped around the thick length of him, simply held him for a moment, enjoying the freedom of being able to explore. Then she hooked her thumbs into the waistband of the trousers to remove them. "I think you're beautiful, Falcon," she admitted. "And I know that I love you."

He wrapped his arm around her waist, dragged her to him, his mouth fusing with hers, all at once aggressive, demanding, a little primitive. Sara met him kiss for kiss. His hands were everywhere; so were hers. He slid his palm over her stomach, wanting to feel a child, his child, growing there, wanting everything at once—her, a child, a family, everything he had never had. Everything he'd believed he never could have. His fingers dipped lower into the thatch of tight curls, cupped her welcoming heat even as his mouth devoured hers. "I know I should slow down," he managed to get out.

"There's no need," she answered, feeling the exact same sense of wild urgency. She needed him. Wanted him. Every inch of him buried deep within her merging their two halves into one whole.

Shadows danced on the wall from the flickering candle-light, threw a soft glow over Sara's face. He lifted his head as he slowly, carefully, pushed two fingers deep inside her. He wanted to watch the pleasure in her eyes. She held nothing back from him, not her thoughts, her desires, or her passion. She gasped, her body tightening, clamping around his fingers, hot and needy. She moved against his hand, a slow, sexy ride, her head thrown back to expose her throat, her breasts a gleaming enticement in the candlelight.

He pushed deeper into her, felt the instant answering wash of hot moisture. Very slowly he bent his head to her throat. His tongue swirled lazily. His teeth nipped. He hid nothing from her, his mind thrusting into hers, sharing the perfect ecstasy of the moment with her, his body's reaction and the frenzy of heated passion. His fingers penetrated deep into her feminine channel as he buried his teeth in her throat. The lightning lanced both of them, hot and white, a pain that gave way to an erotic fire. She was hot and sweet and just as wild as he was. Falcon was careful to keep his appetite under control, taking only enough blood for an exchange. His mouth left her throat with a soothing swirl of his tongue; he lifted her with only one arm wrapped around her waist and took her to the bed. All the time, his fingers were sliding in and out of her, his mouth was fused to hers, the pleasure blossoming and spreading like wild-fire through both of them.

She expected to find the taking of her blood disgusting, but it was erotic and dreamy, almost as if he had drawn a veil over her mind, ensnaring her in his dark passion. Yet she shared his mind and knew he had not. She also shared the intensity of his pleasure in the act, and it gave her courage.

"It isn't enough, Falcon. I want more, I want you in my body, I want us together." Her voice was breathless against his lips, her hands sliding over him eagerly, tracing each defined muscle, urging his hips toward hers.

He kissed her throat, her breasts, swirling his tongue over her nipples, along her ribs, around her belly button. Then she was gasping, rising up off the bed, her hands clutching fistfuls of his hair as he tasted her. She was shattering with the sheer intensity of her pleasure. Falcon could transport her to other worlds, places of beauty, emotion, and physical rapture.

He rose above her, a dark, handsome man with long, wild hair and black, mesmerizing eyes. There was a heartbeat while he was poised there, and then he surged forward, locking them together as they were meant to be, penetrating deeply, sweeping her away with him. He began to move, each stroke taking him deeper, filling her with a rush of heat and fire. She rose to meet him, craving the contact, wanting him deep inside, all the time her body winding tighter and tighter, rushing toward that elusive perfection.

Sara gasped as he thrust deeper still, the fiery friction clenching every muscle in her body, flooding every cell with a wild ecstasy. Then he was merging their minds, thrusting deep as his body took hers. She felt his pleasure, he felt hers, body and mind and heart, a timeless dance of joy and love. They soared together, exploding, fragmenting, waves of release rocking the earth so that they clung together with hearts pounding and shared smiles.

Falcon held her tightly, buried his face in her neck, whispered soft words of love, of encouragement before reluctantly untangling their bodies.

They lay on the bed together . . . waiting. Her heart was pounding, her breath coming too fast, but she tried valiantly to pretend that everything was perfectly normal. That her entire world was not about to be changed for all eternity.

Falcon held her in his strong arms, wanting to reassure her, needing the closeness as much as she did. "Do you know why I wrote the journal?" He kissed her temple, breathed in her scent. "A thousand years ago, the words welled up inside me when I could feel nothing, see nothing but gray images. The emotions and words were burned into my soul. I felt I needed to write them down so I would always remember the intensity of my feelings for my lifemate. For you, Sara, because even then, a thousand years before you were born, more even, I felt your presence in my soul. A tiny flicker and I needed to light the way." He kissed her gently, tenderly. "I guess that doesn't make much sense. But I felt you inside of me and I had to tell you how much you mattered."

"Those words saved my life, Falcon. I wouldn't have survived without your journal." She leaned into him. She would survive this, as well. She was strong and she would see it through.

"I shudder to think what trouble the children are giving this poor stranger who has been called into service," Falcon teased, wanting to see her smile.

Sara nibbled at his throat. "How long will it take us to get the children in a real home? Our home?"

"I think that can be arranged very fast," Falcon assured, his fingers sliding through her thick, silken hair, loving the feel of the sable strands. "The one wonderful thing about our people is that they are very willing to share what they have. I have jewels and gold stashed away. I was going to turn it over to Mikhail to aid our people in any way possible, but we can ask for a house."

"A large house. Seven children require a large house."

"And a large staff. We will have to find someone we trust to watch over the children during the day," Falcon pointed out. "I am certain Raven and Shea will know the best person to contact. The children have very special needs. We will have to aid them . . ."

She turned her head, frowning at him. "You mean manipulate them."

He shrugged his powerful shoulders, unperturbed by her irritation. "It is our way of life in this world. We must shield those who provide sustenance for us, or they would live in terror. Officials who do not want to hand us these children are easily persuaded otherwise. To keep the children from being afraid and allow them to become more used to their environment and more accepting of a new lifestyle, it will be necessary. It is a useful gift, Sara, and one we depend on to keep our species from discovery."

"The children want to live with me. We have discussed it on many occasions. I would have taken them to my home immediately but I knew that eventually the vampire would come. I was attempting to set up a safe house for them, a refuge where I could see them without endangering them. But the officials continually put roadblocks in my way, mostly to charge more money. But the children knew I was trying. They believed in me, and they won't be afraid of a new life."

"You will not be with them during the day, Sara. We must ensure that they trust the humans we will have to rely on to guard them during those hours."

Just then a ripple of fire moved through Sara's body. She put her hand over her stomach and turned her head, meeting his shadowed gaze. He put his hand over hers.

He bent to kiss her, a kiss of sorrow, of apology. "I would spare you this pain if I could." He whispered it against her skin. His body trembled against hers.

She caught his hand, twining their fingers together. Her insides were burning alarmingly. "It's all right, Falcon. We knew it was going to be like this." She wanted to reassure him even though every muscle was cramping and her body was shuddering with pain. "I can do this. I want to do this." She allowed nothing else to enter her mind. Not fear. Not growing terror. It had no place, only her complete belief in him, in them. In her decision. A convulsion lifted her body, slammed it back down. Sara tried to crawl away from him, wanting to spare him.

Falcon caught at her, his mind firmly entrenched in hers. *Together,* piccola. *We are in this together.* He could feel the pain ripping through her body and he breathed deeply, evenly, determined to breathe for both of them, protecting her as best he could. He wanted, *needed,* to

CHRISTINE FEEHAN

take the pain from her, but even with his great strength and all of his powers, he could not alleviate the terrible burning as her organs were reshaped. He could only shoulder part of the terrible pain and share her suffering. He held her as her body rid itself of toxins. Never once did he detect a single moment when she blamed him or wavered in her choice to join him.

For Falcon, time inched by slowly, an eternity, but he forced serenity into his mind, determined to be as accepting as Sara. Determined to be everything she needed, even if all he could do was believe that everything would turn out perfectly. In the centuries of his existence, he had mingled with humans and had seen extraordinary moments of bravery, but her steadfast courage astounded him. He shared his admiration of her, his belief in her ability to ride above the waves of pain and the convulsions possessing her body. She took each moment separately, seeking to reassure him when each wave ebbed, leaving her spent and exhausted.

Once, she smiled and whispered to him. He couldn't hear her, even with his phenomenal hearing. *Having a baby is going to be a piece of cake after this.* There was a wry humor in her soft voice brushing at the walls of his mind. Falcon turned his head away to keep her from seeing the tears in his eyes at the evidence of her deep commitment to him.

The moment he knew it was safe to send her to sleep, Falcon commanded it, opening the earth to allow the healing properties to aid her. Carpathian soil, more than any other, rejuvenated and healed its people, yet they could use whatever was available, as he had been doing for centuries. He had forgotten the soothing richness of his homeland. Falcon carefully cleaned the bedchamber, removing every trace of illness and evidence of Sara's conversion. He took his time, relying on the other two Carpathian males to hold a watchful vigil against further assaults by the ancient vampire. It had been far too long since he had been home, since he had known the comfort of being with his own people, the luxury of being able to depend on others.

Falcon took the sustenance offered to him by Jacques, again grateful for the powerful blood supplied by an ancient of great lineage. He rested for an hour, deep within the earth, his arms wrapped tightly around Sara.

When Falcon was certain that Sara was completely healed, he brought her to the surface, laying her carefully on the bed, her naked body stretched out, clean and fresh, the lit candles releasing a soothing, healing fragrance. His heart was pounding, his mouth dry. *Sara. My life. My heart and soul. Awake and come to me.* He bent his head to capture her first breath as a Carpathian. His other half.

Sara woke to a different world. The vivid details, the smells and sounds, were almost too much to take in. She clung to Falcon, fitting her body trustingly into his. They both could hear her heart pounding loudly, frantically.

He kissed the top of her head, rubbed his chin over the silken strands of her hair. "Ssh, my love, it is done now. Breathe with me. Let your heart follow the rhythm of mine."

Sara could hear everything. *Everything.* Insects. The murmur of voices in the night. The soft, hushed flight of an owl. The rustle of rodents in nearby brush. Yet she was far beneath the earth in a chamber constructed of thick walls and rock. If she could hear everything, so could all people of this species.

Falcon smiled, his teeth immaculately white. "It is true, Sara," he agreed, easily monitoring her thoughts. "We learn discretion at a very young age. We learn to tune out what is not our business. It becomes second nature. You and I have been alone far too long; we are now a part of something again. The adjustment will take some time, but life is an exciting journey now, with you by my side."

Against his shoulder she laughed softly. "Even before I ever underwent conversion, I could read you like a book. Stop being afraid for me. I am strong, Falcon. I made the decision fifteen years ago that you were my life. My everything. You were with me in my dreams, my dark lover, my friend and confidant. You were with me in my darkest hours when everything was bleak and hopeless and I had no one. All my days, all my nights, you were in my heart and mind. I know you. I lived only because of your words. I would never have survived without your journal. Really, Falcon. You know my mind, you know I am telling the truth. I am not afraid of my life with you. I want it. I want to be with you."

He felt humbled by her tremendous generosity, her gift to him. He answered her the only way he could, his kiss tender and loving, expressing with his body the deep emotion that could not be described by words. "I still cannot believe I found you," he whispered softly.

Her arms circled his neck, her soft breasts pressed

tightly against his chest. She shifted her legs in invitation, wanting his body buried deep in hers. Wanting the safe anchor of his strength. "I still can't believe you're real and not my fantasy, the dream lover I made up from a vision."

Falcon knew what she needed. He needed the same reassurance. Sara. His Sara. Never afraid of appearing vulnerable to him. Never afraid of showing her desires. His mouth found hers, shifting the heavens for both of them. Her body was warm and welcoming, his haven, a refuge, a place of intimacy and ecstasy. The world fell away from them. There was only the flickering candle-light and the silk sheets. Only their bodies and long, leisurely explorations. There was gasping pleasure as they indulged their every fantasy.

Much, much later, Falcon lay across the bed, his head in her lap, enjoying the feel of the cool air on his body, the way her fingers played through his hair. "I cannot move."

She laughed softly. "You don't have to move. I like where you are." Her breath tightened, caught in her throat as he blew warm air gently, teasingly, across her thighs. Her entire body clenched in reaction, so sensitized by their continual lovemaking that Sara didn't think she would ever recover.

"Ahh, but I do, my love. I have our enemy to hunt. No doubt he is close and very anxious to finish his work and leave these mountains. He cannot afford to bide his time here." Falcon sighed. "There are too many hunters in this area. He will want to leave as soon as possible. As long as he is alive, the children and you will never be safe." He turned his head slightly to swirl a small caress along her inner thigh with his tongue. His hair slid over her skin so that she throbbed and burned in reaction.

"Stop trying to distract me," she said. His arm was around her, his palm cupping her buttocks, massaging gently, insistently. It was very distracting, rendering her nearly incapable of rational thought.

"And all this time I thought you were distracting me." His voice was melodic with amusement. Deliberately he slid his finger along her moist core. "You are incredibly hot, Sara. Did you stay in my mind while we made love? Did you feel how tightly you wrapped around me? The way your body feels to me when I'm surrounded by your heat? Your fire?" He pushed two fingers into her, a long, slow stroke. "The way your muscles clamp around me?" He let out his breath slowly. "Yes. Just like this. There is nothing else like it in this world. I love everything about your body. The way you look." He withdrew his fingers, brought them to his mouth. "The way you taste."

Her body rippled to life as she watched him insert his fingers into his mouth as if he were devouring her all over again. He smiled, knowing exactly what he was doing to her. Sara laughed softly, happily, the sound carefree. "If we make love again, I'm certain I'll shatter into a million pieces. And you, crazy man, will not be in any shape to go chasing after vampires if you touch me one more time. So if you're determined to do this, behave yourself."

He kissed the inside of her thigh. "I thought I was behaving just fine."

She caught a fistful of his hair. "What I think is that you need me to bag the vampire. To bring him right to you."

He sat up, his black gaze wary all at once. "You just stay right here where I know you are perfectly safe."

"I'm not the safe type, Falcon, I thought you knew that by now. I expect a partnership and I'm not willing to settle for less," she said firmly.

He studied her face for a long moment, reached out to trace the shape of her breast, sending a shiver through her body at his feather-light touch. "I would not want less than a partnership, Sara," he answered honestly. "But you do not fully comprehend what would happen if something should harm you."

She laughed at him, her eyes suddenly sparkling like jewels. "I don't think you fully comprehend what would happen if something should harm *you*."

"I am a hunter, Sara. Please trust my judgment in this."

"More than anything I do trust your judgment, but it is very biased at the moment, isn't it? It makes no sense not to use the one person he would come out into the open to find. You know that if he chased me for fifteen years, he isn't going to stop. Falcon"—she placed a hand on his chest, leaned forward to kiss his chin—"he will show himself if he thinks he has a serious chance of getting to me. If you don't use me as bait, everyone will continue to be in danger. Our children are frightened and in the care of a total stranger. These people have been good to us; we don't want to bring them and the surrounding villagers trouble." She pushed a hand through her short sable hair. "I know I can bring him out into the open. I have to try. I can't be responsible for any more deaths. Every time he follows me to a city and I read about a serial killer in the papers, I feel as if I had brought him there. Let me do this, Falcon. Don't look so stubborn and intimidating. I know you understand why I have to do this."

Falcon's hard features slowly softened. His perfectly sculpted mouth curved into a smile. He framed her face between his hands and bent his head to kiss her. "Sara, you are a genius." He kissed her again. Slowly. Thoroughly. "That is exactly what we will do. We will use you as bait and trap ourselves a master vampire."

She raised an eyebrow, not trusting the sudden grin on his face.

CHAPTER TEN

Sara sat on a boulder, dipped her hand into the small pool of water, and looked up at the night sky. The clouds were heavy and dark, blotting out the stars, but the moon was still valiantly attempting to shine. White wisps of fog curled here and there along the forest floor, lending an eerie appearance to the night. An owl sat in the high branches of the tree to her left, completely still and very aware of every movement in the forest. Several bats wheeled this way and that overhead, darting to catch the plethora of insects flying through the air. A rodent scurried through the leaves, foraging for food, drawing the attention of the owl.

Sara had been out for some time, simply inhaling the night. Her favorite perfume mingled with her natural scent and drifted through the forest so that the wildlife were very aware of her presence. Sara stood up slowly and wandered back toward the house. Rare night blossoms caught her attention and she stopped to examine one. Her fresh scent mingled with the fragrant flower and was carried on the breeze, wafting through the forest and high into the trees. A fox sniffed the air and shivered, crouching in the heavy underbrush near the boulder where the human had been.

There was a soft sound in the vegetation near her feet. Sara froze in place, watching the large rat as it foraged in the bushes quite close to her. Too close to her. Between her and the house. She backed away from the rodent, back toward the interior of the forest. She glanced toward the boulder, judging its height. Vampires were one thing, rats quite another. She was a bit squeamish when it came to rats.

When Sara turned back, a man stood watching her. Tall. Gaunt. With gray skin and long white hair. The vampire stared at her through red-rimmed eyes. Eyes filled with hatred and rage. There was no false pretense of friendship. His bitter enmity showed in every deep line of his ravaged face. "After all those wasted years. At last I have you. You have cost me more than you will ever know. Stupid, pitiful woman. How ridiculous that a nothing such as you should be a thorn in my side. It disgusts me."

Sara retreated from him, backing the way she had come until her legs bumped against rock. With great dignity she simply seated herself on the boulder and watched him in silence; her fingers twisting together were the only sign of fear. This was the monster who had murdered her family, taken everyone she had loved, virtually taken her life from her. This tall, gaunt man with hollow cheeks and venomous eyes.

"I have nearly limitless power, yet I need a little worm like you to complete my studies. Now Falcon's stench is all over you. How that sickens me." The vampire laughed softly, tauntingly, spittle flying into the air, fouling the wind. "You did not think I knew who he was, but I knew him well in the old time. A stooge to do the Prince's bidding. Vladimir lived long with Sarantha, yet he sent us out to live alone. His sons stayed behind, protected by him, yet we were sent to die alone. I did not choose death but embraced life, and I have studied much. There are others like me, but I will be the one to rule. Now that I have you, I will be a god and nothing will touch me. The Prince will bow to me. All hunters will tremble before me."

Sara lifted her head. "I see now. Although you think yourself all-powerful, a god, you still have need of me. You have followed me for fifteen years, a puny human woman, a child when you found me, yet you could not catch up to me."

He hissed, an ugly, frightening sound, a promise of brutal retaliation.

Sara frowned at him, sudden knowledge in her eyes. "You need me to find something for you. Something you can't do yourself. You killed everybody I loved, yet you think I will help you. I don't think so. Instead I intend to destroy you."

"You do not have any idea of the pain I can inflict on you. The things I can make you do. I will derive great pleasure in bending you to my will. You have no idea how powerful I am." The vampire's parody of a smile exposed stained, jagged teeth. "I will enjoy seeing you suffer as you have been a plague to me for so long. Do not worry, my dear, I will keep you alive a very long time. You will find the tomb of the master wizard and the book of knowledge that will give me untold power. I have acquired several of his belongings, and you will know where the book is when you hold these items. Humans never know the true treasures for what they are. They lock them up in museums few people ever visit, and none see what is truly valuable. They believe that wizards and magic are mere fairy tales, and they live in ignorance. Humans deserve to be ruled with an iron fist. They are cattle, nothing more. Prey only, food for the gods."

"Perhaps that is your impression of humans, but it is a false one. Otherwise how could I have evaded you for fifteen years?" Sara asked mildly. "I am not quite so insignificant as you would like me to believe."

"How dare you mock me!" The vampire hissed, his features contorting with hatred as he suddenly looked around warily. "How is it you are alone? Are your keepers so inept they would allow you to walk around unprotected?"

"Why would you think they are not guarding me? They are all around me." She sounded truthful, sincere.

His eyes narrowed and he pointed one daggerlike fingernail at her. Had she denied it, he would have been far more wary, but she was too quick to give the hunters away. "Do not try my patience. No Carpathian hunter would use his lifemate to bait a trap. He would hide you deep in the earth, coward that he is, knowing I am too powerful to stop." He laughed softly, the sound a hideous screech. "It is your own arrogance that has caused your downfall. You ignored his orders and came out into the night without his knowledge or consent. That is a weakness of women. They do not think logically, always whining and wanting their way." His dagger-sharp finger beckoned her. "Come to me now." He used his mind, a sharp, hard compulsion designed to hurt, to put tremendous pressure on the brain even as it demanded obedience.

Sara continued to sit serenely, a slight frown on her soft mouth. She sighed and shook her head. "That has never worked on me before. Why should it now?"

Cursing, the vampire raised his arm, then changed his mind. The vibration of power would have given him away immediately to the Carpathian hunters. He stalked toward her, covering the short distance between them, his strides purposeful, his face a mask of rage at her impertinence.

Sara sat perfectly still and watched him come to her. The vampire bent his tall frame, extending his dagger-tipped bony fingers toward her. Sara exploded into action, only it was Falcon's fist slamming hard into the chest cavity of the undead, as he returned to his true form. As Falcon did so, the vampire, with a look of sheer disbelief, stumbled back so that the fist barely penetrated his chest plate. Overhead, Jacques, in the shape of the owl, launched himself from the branches and flew straight at the undead, talons outstretched. The small fox grew in stature, shape-shifting into the tall, elegant frame of a male hunter, and Mikhail's hands were already weaving a binding spell to prevent the vampire from shifting or vanishing.

Pressed from the air, caught between the hunters and unable to flee, the vampire launched his own attack, risking everything in the hopes of defeating the one Carpathian whose death might force the other two to pause. Calling on every ounce of power and knowledge he possessed, he slammed his fist into Falcon's elbow, shattering bone. Then he whirled away, his body replicating itself over and over until there were a hundred clones of the undead. Half the clones initiated attacks using stakes or sharp-pointed spears; the others fled in various directions.

Jacques, in the owl form, drove talons straight through the head of a clone, going through empty air so that he was forced to pull up swiftly before hitting the ground. The air vibrated with power, with violence and hatred.

Each of the clones on the attack was weaving a different spell, and sprays of blood washed the surrounding air a toxic crimson. Falcon's mind shut off the pain of his shattered elbow as he assessed the situation in that one heartbeat of time. It was all he had. All he would ever have. In that blink of an eye the centuries of his life passed, bleak and barren, stretching endlessly until Sara. *This is my gift to you.* She was his life. His soul. His future. But there was honor. There was what and who he was, what he stood for. He was guardian of his people.

She was there with him. His Sara. She understood that he had no other choice. It was everything he was.

Without regret, Falcon flung his body between his Prince and the vampire moving in for the kill. A multitude of razor-sharp spears pierced Falcon's body, taking his breath, spilling his life force onto the ground in dark rivers. As he toppled to earth, he reached out, slamming both open hands into the scarlet fountain on the vampire's chest, leaving his prints like a neon sign for the other hunters to target.

Sara, sharing Falcon's mind, reacted calmly, already knowing what to do. She had made good use of Falcon's knowledge and she shut down his heart and lungs instantly, so that he lay as still as death on the battlefield. She concentrated, holding him to her, a flickering, dim light that wanted to retreat from pain. She had no time for sorrow. No time for emotion. She held him to her with the same fierce determination of the Carpathian people's finest warrior as the battle raged on around him.

Mikhail saw the ancient warrior fall, his body riddled with holes. The Prince was already in motion, snapping the spears like matchsticks as he drove forward, directing Jacques with his mind. The clones tried to regroup to throw the hunters off the scent, but it was too late. The vampire had revealed himself in his attack, and Mikhail locked onto Falcon's marks, as certain as fingerprints.

The undead snarled his hatred, shrieked his fury, but the holding spell bound him. He could not shift his shape and it was already too late. The Prince buried his fist deep, following the twisted path the ancient warrior had mapped out. Jacques took the head, slicing cleanly, a delaying tactic to give his brother time to extract the black, pulsating heart. The sky rained insects, great stinging bugs, and pellets of ice and rain.

Mikhail calmly built the charge of energy in the roiling clouds. All the while, the black heart jumped and crawled blindly, seeking its master. Blisters rose on the ground and on their arms as the scarlet spray embedded itself in their skin. The fury of the wind whipped them, moaning and hissing a dark promise of retaliation. Mikhail grimly continued, calling upon nature, directing a fiery orange ball from the sky to the pulsing heart. The thing was incinerated with a noxious odor and a cloud of black smoke.

The body of the vampire jerked, the head rolled, the eyes staring at Falcon's still form with a hatred beyond anything the hunters had ever witnessed. A hand moved, the dagger-tipped claws reaching for the fallen warrior as if to take him along on the path to death. The orange ball of energy slammed into the body, incinerating it immediately, then leaping to the head to reduce it to a fine powder of ashes.

Jacques took over the cleansing of the earth, and then their own skin, erasing the evidence of the foul creature which had gone against nature itself.

Raven met her lifemate at the door, touching his arm, sharing his deep sorrow, offering him comfort and warmth. "Shea has gone ahead to the cave of healing, opening the earth and taking the candles we will need. Jacques has brought Falcon there. The soil is rich and will aid her work. I have summoned our people to join with us in the healing chant." She turned to look at Sara.

Sara stood up slowly. She could see compassion,

even sorrow, on Raven's face. Tears streaked Raven's cheeks and she held out both hands. "Sara, they have brought him to the best place possible, a place of power. Shea says . . ." She choked back a sob and pressed a fist to her mouth even as she caught Sara's hand in hers. "You must come with us quickly to the cave of healing."

Mikhail stepped back, avoided her eyes, his features a mask of granite, but Sara knew what he was thinking. She touched his arm briefly to gain his attention. "I was sharing his mind when he made the decision. It was a conscious decision, one he didn't hesitate to make. Don't lessen his sacrifice by feeling guilty. Falcon believes you're a great man, that the loss of your life would be intolerable to him, to your people. He knew exactly what he was doing and what the cost might be. I am proud of him, proud of who he is. He is an honorable man and always has been. I completely supported his decision."

Mikhail nodded. "You are a fitting lifemate for an ancient as honorable as Falcon. Thank you for your kindness in such a bleak hour, Sara. It is a privilege to count you among our people. We must go to him rapidly. You have not had time to become used to our ways, so I ask that you allow me to take your blood. Falcon's blood runs in my veins. I must aid you in shape-shifting to get to this place of healing."

She met his black gaze steadily. "You honor me, sir."

Raven's fingers tightened around Sara's as if holding her close, but Sara could barely feel the contact. Her mind was firmly entrenched in Falcon's, holding him to her, refusing to allow him to slip away despite the gravity of his injuries. She felt the prick of Mikhail's teeth on her wrist, felt the reassuring squeeze of Raven's hand. Nothing mattered to Sara but that flickering light so dim and far away.

Mikhail placed the image of an owl in her mind, and she actually felt the wrenching of her bones, the contorting of her body, and the sudden rush of air as she took flight. But there was only Falcon, and she didn't dare let go of that fading light to look at the world falling away from her as she winged her way to the cave of healing.

Deep beneath the earth, the air was heavy and thick with the aroma of hundreds of scented candles. Sara went to Falcon, shocked at the terrible wounds in his body, at his white, nearly translucent skin. Shea's body was an empty shell. Sara was vividly aware of her in Falcon's body, valiantly repairing the extensive damage. The sound of chanting—ancient, beautiful words in a language she recognized yet didn't know—filled the chamber. The ancient language of the Carpathians. Those not present were there nonetheless, joined mind to mind, sending their powers of healing, their energy, to their fallen warrior.

Sara watched the Prince giving his blood, far more than he could afford, yet he waved the others off and gave until he was weak and pale, until his own brother forced him to replenish what he had given. She watched each of the Carpathians, strangers to her, giving generously to her lifemate, reverently, paying a kind of homage to him. Sara took Falcon's hand in hers and watched as Shea returned to her own body.

Shea, swaying with weariness, signaled to the others to pack Falcon's terrible wounds with saliva and the deep rich earth. She fed briefly from her lifemate and returned to the monumental task of closing and repairing the wounds.

It took hours. Outside the cave the sun was climbing, but not one of the people faltered in their task. Sara held Falcon to her through sheer will, and when Shea emerged, they stared at one another across his body, both weary, both with tears shimmering in their eyes.

"We must put him to ground and hope that the earth works its magic. I have done all I can do," Shea said softly. "It's up to you now, Sara."

Sara nodded. "Thank you. We owe you so much. Your efforts won't be wasted. He'll live. I won't allow anything else." She leaned close to her lifemate. "You will not die, do you hear me, Falcon?" Sara demanded, tears running down her face. "You will hold on and you will live for me. For us. For our children. I am demanding this of you." She said it fiercely, meaning it. She said it with her heart and her mind and her soul. Gently she touched his beloved face, traced his worn features. *Do you hear me?*

She felt the faintest of stirrings in her mind. A warmth. Soft, weary laughter. *Who could not hear you, my love? I can do no other than comply.*

The house was large, a huge, rambling home built of stone and columns. The veranda wrapped around the entire structure on the lower story. A similar balcony wrapped around the upper story. Stained-glass windows greeted the moon, beautiful unique pieces that soothed the soul. Sara loved every single thing about the estate. The overgrown bushes and thick stands of trees. The jumbles of flowers that seemed to spring up everywhere. She would never tire of sitting on the swing on her porch and looking out into the surrounding forest.

It was still difficult to believe, even after all these months, that the vampire was truly out of her life. She had been firmly in Falcon's mind when he assumed her shape. Her thoughts and emotions had guided his disguised body. Falcon buried deep, so that the vampire would fail to detect him. The plan had worked, the vampire was destroyed, but it would take a long while before she would wake without being afraid. She could only hope that the book the vampire had been searching for would remain hidden, lost to mortals and immortals alike. The fact that the undead had gone to such lengths to find the book could only mean that its power was tremendous. In the wrong hands, that book could mean disaster for both mortals and immortals.

Falcon had told Sara he'd known the vampire as a young boy growing up. Vladimir had sent him to Egypt while Falcon had gone to Italy. Somewhere along the way, Falcon had chosen honor, while his boyhood friend had wanted ultimate power. Sara rocked back and forth in the swing, allowing the peace of the evening to push the unpleasant thoughts from her mind.

She could hear the housekeepers in the kitchen talking quietly together, their voices reassuring. She could hear the children, upstairs in their bedrooms, laughing and murmuring as they began to get ready for bed. Falcon's voice was gentle as he teased the children. A pillow fight erupted as if often did, almost on a nightly basis.

You are such a little boy yourself. The words appeared in Falcon's mind, surrounded by a deep love that always took his breath away. Sara loved him to have fun, to enjoy all the simple things he had missed in his long life. And she was well aware Falcon loved her for that and for the way she enjoyed every moment of their existence, as if each hour were shiny and new.

They attacked me, the little rascals. Sara could see the image of him laughing, tossing pillows as fast as they were thrown at him.

Yes, well, when you are finished with your war, your lifemate has other duties for you. Sara leaned back in her swing, tapped her foot impatiently as a small smile tugged at her soft mouth. Deliberately she thought of her latest fantasy. The pool of water she had discovered by the waterfall in the secluded cliffside. Tossing her clothes aside. Standing naked on the boulder stretching her arms up in invitation to the moon. Turning her head to smile at Falcon as he came up to her. Leaning forward to chase a small bead of water across his chest, down his belly, then lower, lower.

The air shimmered for a moment and he was standing in front of her, his hand out, a grin on his face. Sara stared up at him, taking in his long silken hair and his mesmerizing dark eyes. He looked fit and handsome, yet she knew there were still faint scars on his body. They were etched in her mind more deeply than in his skin. Sara went to him, flowed to him, melted into him, lifting her face for his kiss, knowing he could move the earth for her.

"I want to check out this pool you have discovered," he whispered wickedly against her lips. His hands moved over her body gently, possessively.

She laughed softly. "I had every confidence you would."

A DREAM OF
STONE & SHADOW

by

Marjorie M. Liu

PROLOGUE

It began with a knife in the heart. As usual. A fine sharp blade needling deep into the beating muscle, stilling it with a stab and cut. Charlie did not cry out. There was no real use. He was accustomed to death, and the price was not too high, given the exchange. He simply closed his eyes and laid himself down, let darkness creep in until he died.

Only then was it safe to dream.

It was always dark where Mrs. Kreer put her. Damp, too. Emma did not like to imagine what made her backside and legs moist as she curled up against the wall to rest. Andrew said it was piss—that this place was a regular shit-hole, and that they put her here because she was shit, too.

She wrapped her arms around her knees, hugging them tight to her chest. She could feel the cold cement through her blue jeans and rocked in place, hoping to keep her backside from getting numb. She did not want to stand up; it might bring too much attention to her. In the darkness—this heavy, black, and suffocating darkness—things could hide that she would never see coming. Sometimes she thought she heard, over in the corner, scuffling. A tiny scrape and scrabble. Maybe the brush and flutter of wings or cloth. But she could not see enough to be sure of what moved beyond the circle of her tiny space. Not in this darkness. She couldn't even see her hands. Andrew had put a towel at the foot of the basement door, taped up the edges to keep out the light, until all Emma had left was her mind, the visions and colors that were her thoughts. That was all she was in this place.

Emma liked to imagine herself in different places, clinging feverishly to visions taken from glimpses of the outside. Like trees. She loved the trees. Those were real. Sometimes, when Andrew was slow setting up the cameras, Sarah would lean backwards on the bed and peer out the crack in the blinds and see them, tall and green, cast in sunlight.

Everything else—pictures from the magazines, women who Mrs. Kreer wanted Emma to imitate—she thought they might be real, but she could not be sure. She was not sure of anything, not unless she could touch, smell or taste it. Darkness was real, tangible. It had fingers buried in her hair. It traveled into her lungs with every breath she took.

Mrs. Kreer was real, too. So was her son, Andrew.

Emma did not remember much else that was real, except for her mother. But it had been a long time since she had seen her, and Emma thought she might be dead. She did not remember blood, but she remembered hearing screams from a distance. A loud bang. Emma did not like to think about that. It was not real.

The scuffling sounds in the corner of the basement grew louder. Emma pressed her lips together. No crying for her. Andrew liked tears. He liked it when she was afraid.

But she still squeaked when a low voice said, "Emma."

The voice was so soft that she could not tell if it was a man or woman, and she was not sure she cared. Only, that the darkness around her had finally begun to pay attention, and still she could not see, could not fight— could not fight *this*, not when fists and kicks and teeth meant nothing against the two adults upstairs, who had finally taught her to obey.

"Emma," said the voice again, and this time she thought it was male. Which was worse. The voice was a thing, a cloud, disembodied words floating like spirits. A ghost. She was listening to a ghost.

She squeaked again, pushing up hard against the cold wall, unmindful of the damp. She wrapped her arms around her head and shut her eyes tight. She thought she heard a sigh, but her heart hammered so loud in her ears it was impossible to say.

"Please," whispered the ghost, and the pain in his voice scared her almost as much as his presence. "Please, don't be afraid. I'm here to help you."

Emma said nothing. She felt something warm pass

over the top of her head, and it felt like what she remembered of summer, fresh and green and lovely. The air around her mouth suddenly tasted so clear and clean, she thought for one minute she was outside, in the woods, in the grass and sunlight and sharp air. Emma opened her eyes. Nothing. Darkness.

The ghost said, "Emma. Emma, do you know where you are?"

"No," Emma mumbled, finally finding the strength to speak. The ghost, the darkness, had not hurt her yet. That could change, but until then, she would try to be brave. She would try very hard.

"There are trees," she added. "I see them sometimes."

"Good," said the ghost, and this time Emma did not have to try so hard not to be afraid. His voice was strong and soft—a voice like the heroes had in the cartoons she watched so long ago. She loved those heroes.

"Who are you?" she asked him.

"A friend," he replied, and again Emma felt warmth upon her head, moving slowly down her face. Soothing, like sunlight. She closed her eyes and pretended it was the sun.

The basement door rattled. Emma heard tape rip away. Lines of light appeared above her at the top of the stairs. She turned and looked and saw the outline of a man beside her. She could not see his face, but he was very large. For a moment she was afraid again, but that was nothing to her fear of Andrew and Mrs. Kreer, and she whispered, "Help me."

"I will," the shape said, but Emma did not see his mouth move. She looked closer and thought he had no mouth, no eyes. Faceless. His entire body was nothing but a lighter shade of night. An imprint.

"Andrew's coming," Emma said.

"I won't leave you," he replied.

She begged. "Don't let him touch me."

The ghost said nothing. Emma felt warmth upon her face, and then, quiet: "I'll be right here with you."

"Please," she said, "I want my mommy."

"Emma—"

The door opened. Emma shielded her eyes. Andrew stood silhouetted in the light: narrow and lean, tall and strong. His hair stood up off his head in spikes.

"Time to get you cleaned up," he said, and his voice was not soft, but hard instead; not strong, but thready, with a sharp edge. Emma looked into the darkness beside her, but the ghost was gone. She swallowed hard. Tried not to cry.

And then warmth collected at the back of her neck and she heard, "I'm here," and when Andrew said her name in a bad way, she stood up, still with the sun at her back, and found the strength to hobble up the stairs into the light.

CHAPTER ONE

The hunt was on.

Aggie had a gun chafing her ribs and a very panicked man at her side as she drove ninety miles an hour down a residential backstreet, narrowly missing the jutting bumpers of badly parked vehicles, the slow moving bodies of several elderly men out for a stroll, and one very large garbage can that truly rolled out of nowhere and which required a quick jerk on the wheel, sending Aggie's little red Miata spinning deliriously into an empty intersection. She pulled hard on the emergency brake— the tires squealed; the world spun. The car slammed to a stop. Her partner made a choking sound.

Perfect.

"Oh, God," said Quinn, clutching his chest.

"They're coming," Aggie snapped, rolling down the window. She clicked off the safety on her .22, but kept the gun in its rig. She needed her hands free, and Quinn was the better shot. "Yo, did you hear me? They're almost here, Quinn. Are you ready?"

He made gagging sounds. Aggie wondered if that greasy lunch at Tahoe Joe's was going to make a repeat appearance. The Miata's leather seats were not vomit friendly. But then her vision shifted and she glimpsed Quinn's immediate future, and puke was not involved.

But death was.

Aggie undid Quinn's seatbelt and reached across him to open his door. "Gotta move, gotta move," she murmured, still with the future rolling quick inside her head. They had less than a minute; already she could hear the roar of a powerful engine gunning down a nearby road. So much for a quiet neighborhood. So much for a peaceful life.

"I'm going to kill you," Quinn said, wiping spit from his mouth. "It's the humane thing to do."

"Keep talking, little man," Aggie replied, and shoved him from the car. Quinn was not the most graceful person in the world, but he managed to keep his feet. He gave her a dirty look, which to anyone but Aggie would have felt menacing—those dark eyes, that wild bushy mountain man hair. He was not quite five feet tall—but his extremely short stature meant nothing when he had that expression on his face. Quinn was a law unto himself.

He leaned against the inside of the Miata's open door and reached inside his leather jacket for his gun. He hesitated before drawing the weapon. "Why aren't you getting out of the car?"

"Shut the door," Aggie said, ignoring him. "Get some cover. We don't have any spike strips, so you might need to shoot out some tires, maybe do more if I don't have a clear way into the van."

"Aggie."

"Quinn."

His jaw tightened. "No chicken."

She forced a grin. "I'm but a leaf in the wind. A feather."

"Aggie, no."

The roar of the oncoming car got louder. It was still out of sight, but soon, any second now, it would turn onto this road and . . .

Aggie said, "You have to do this for me, Quinn. Shut the door."

"Bullshit. I won't leave you. I can work from inside the car."

"You can't."

"Agatha," he said, which made her wince. "You take too many risks."

"Risks?" Images passed through Aggie's head, destiny spinning, channels switching, the immediate future spread before her in all its infinite variations, blurring into something more than instinct, something less than conviction, but all of it creating one single *knowing,* one interpretation. Aggie looked at Quinn and saw him in the passenger seat with a bullet in his brain, looked and saw him dead and dying, looked and saw him paralyzed, looked and saw him in a coma, looked and saw and looked and saw and . . .

Aggie's hands tightened around the steering wheel. "The probability of you dying or getting fucked over inside this car within the next thirty seconds is higher than eighty percent. On the street, ten. Make your call, Quinn."

He stared, and she could feel his resistance, his hesitation—she could see it on his face, and *God,* only Quinn would try to argue fate with a pre-cog—but Aggie stared him down with an expression only her mother could have loved, and he finally—reproachful, angry, oh so stubborn—slammed the door shut. He raised his hands over his head so she could see them through the window and flipped her double birdies.

Yeah. It sure was nice to have friends who loved her.

Aggie counted to five. She revved the engine, savoring the roar, ignoring the shaking pit in her stomach and the bone-white of her knuckles around the steering wheel. Quinn moved into position up the street, a small figure huddled behind the bumper of a Cadillac. A good choice; her inner sight clicked and whirred the probabilities, and he came out fine there. No likely injuries.

Maybe. Anything was possible.

"Anything," she murmured, and watched as the target—a green windowless van, sparkling clean—finally turned onto the street. It drove toward her, and Aggie smiled, grim.

She released the Miata's emergency brake and hit the accelerator. No room for mistakes—no room at all to let the men in that Chevy go. Aggie knew what they were about; she and Quinn had been standing in that parking lot at Tahoe Joe's for a reason, as part of their investigation, and there that van had passed them by, and with it blood and screams and all kinds of wrong, all kinds of horror, because those two men in the front seat had something in their possession that made all the probabilities go bad, bad, bad—worse than Aggie had ever realized entering this case. And she and Quinn had to stop them, cut them off, no matter what. Fight the future, and all that jazz.

The world dropped away. Distance died and scenarios played through her mind. If she blocked the road, the driver would put the car in reverse, find a way through one of the tree-lined back alleys connecting the yards of neighborhood homes. Too much risk of a getaway—the odds were in their favor. She had to pin them, disable them, make sure they could not move at all. She had to be a little crazy.

The street was narrow; the possibilities were not endless. She counted on Quinn to do his part and did not let up on the accelerator. The Miata growled. The van ahead of her slowed, but not enough—he thought she was teasing him, that he had enough room in the road and she would squeeze on by.

Aggie gritted her teeth and veered into his lane. Her sight narrowed—the future to a needle point, the eye in a sieve, squeezing—

There was a gunshot. The van's front tire blew out and it swerved. Aggie pulled hard on the steering wheel, moving parallel, ramming the side of her little Miata into the van's broad body. Metal screamed; the passenger door crumpled. Aggie felt her side of the car momentarily lift off the ground as the windshield cracked. She slammed on the brakes, jerking so hard against the seatbelt that all air was pushed from her lungs. She heard a crash—could barely turn her neck—but she managed to move enough to see the van had scraped past her and slammed head-on into a parked car. Lovely, lovely.

Another gunshot; Quinn, with his unnatural aim, making mush of the van's back tire. She heard shouting—struggled to get out of her seatbelt—and glimpsed movement around the back of the van.

It was the driver, swaying on his feet. Tanned, wrinkled, fat nose, with a face screwed up in a snarl that was one part confused, one part afraid, and a whole lot of angry. Aggie recognized him. David Yarns. Notorious for living an unremarkably remarkable life off the radar. A hard man to find, because he never stayed in one place for long. Until now.

Blood trickled down his forehead. Aggie's mind pushed hard for the probabilities, but her gift chose that moment to go dark. No more future. No more live feed to the Book of Coming Things. Bad timing. Real bad. Aggie thought, *I just might be screwed,* and then saw the gun in David's hand, and knew that "might" had just turned into "definitely." Future come, future go.

Quinn, she thought, but there was no way her partner could see Yarns around the back of the van, no way he could stop him as the bastard pointed his gun at her. She ducked just as the windshield shattered above her head; a bullet slammed low into the passenger seat. Terrible aim. Terrible for Quinn, if he had been sitting there.

"Aggie!" Quinn crouched across the street with his gun trained on the van. "Aggie, move!"

Aggie scrambled out of her new car, rolling instantly to the road and pushing her back against the Miata, catching sight of Quinn just as three bullets rocked into the side of her Cadillac, just inches from her face. Quinn narrowed his eyes and squeezed off one round. Aggie heard a scream.

"Aggie!" Quinn shouted. "Where's Yarns?"

She peered over the hood of her car. Yarns was gone, but when she stood up she saw him—hauling ass down the sidewalk. Quinn shouted at her again, but Aggie ignored him, throwing herself into a sprint, racing down the road until she had eaten up enough distance to pull a Starsky and slide over the hood of a parked car onto the grassy shoulder and hard sidewalk. She saw a woman come out of her house with a child in tow; Aggie screamed and waved her gun. The woman fell back inside, eyes wide.

David was quick on his feet. Aggie was a good runner, but he was better. Perverts were always fast.

You can't catch him, Aggie told herself. Not foresight, just common sense. Her gun felt warm and heavy in her hand.

"Stop!" Aggie shouted, but Yarns ignored her. No surprise. She took a deep breath, tried again to see the possibilities, and failed.

Heart in her throat—because she hated doing these things blind—Aggie shot at the sidewalk near his feet. Just a warning. He stumbled, glancing over his shoulder, but did not slow. Aggie could not risk another shot, even to wound. She would just as likely kill the man, and even though he deserved a bullet in the back, she had to play this one on the up and up. Her employer had a good reputation with local law enforcement, but that only took a girl so far. Witnesses were only good if you could talk to them.

Or catch them. Damn.

A gunshot cracked the air. David cried out and fell to the ground, hard. He began to get up—to turn with the gun in his hand—but Aggie heard another shot and the pistol flew from his grip, hitting the sidewalk, spinning away. David went after it, but no luck—another shot, another scream. Gripping his leg, he went down for the second time.

Aggie turned. Quinn stood on the sidewalk behind her, so far away she could barely make out his features. He waved. Job done. Three impossible shots. Aggie imagined there was not a man on earth who could do the same, even with a scope and long-range rifle. Quinn had a very talented brain. Talented enough to let him skim a man with bullets so there was no evidence of real abuse, but with all the force necessary to stun, surprise, make indecent amounts of pain.

David tried to stand, but fell and began crawling down the sidewalk toward his gun. Aggie caught up with him and pressed the muzzle of her .22 against his head.

"I don't think so," she murmured, glancing down at his legs. His jeans had been slit open at the knee; the skin beneath looked red, burned. Some distance away Aggie saw several bits of metal glinting from the base of a tree. Good. Quinn always took care with his bullets.

Aggie kept plastic cuffs in the deep pockets of her denim jacket. It did not take long to secure David's hands behind his back. She did the same for his ankles, binding them to his wrists so that he arched backwards on the ground like a bow. He did not resist or say a word, simply lay with his rough cheek pressed to the concrete, staring. Aggie wished he would fight, give her some excuse. He deserved the worst.

Aggie left him sprawled on the ground and ran back to Quinn and the van. Police sirens curled through the air, closing in. Any minute the cops would roll up and there would be some tough explaining to do. She was not worried. All the evidence she needed was inside that van—everything that would make it easy to explain why she and Quinn had gone ape-shit on two strangers.

Of course, the *how* of that knowledge was another matter entirely, but the agents at Dirk & Steele were good at deflecting those kinds of questions. It came with the territory of keeping secrets, of being different from the rest of the world in profound ways. A life like that cultivated the ability to wheedle around the truth, to protect your own life while still doing good. A necessary evil, one that Aggie supposed lay at the core of her employer's turn-of-the-century foundation. Hiding and helping. Dirk & Steele showed itself off to the public as an internationally respected detective agency, but that was just a mask. A ruse. Underneath ran deeper waters.

The van's second passenger lay on the sidewalk at Quinn's feet. Aggie did not know his name and she was utterly uninterested in learning it. His hands were tied and he bled from a shoulder wound. His gun lay on the driver's seat inside the van.

"Have you checked the interior?" Aggie asked, dreading his answer.

"No," Quinn said. "It took me a hell of a time just to get this guy out."

Not surprising. Most big men did not take kindly to Quinn ordering them around, even with a gun in his hand. It was a height thing. Aggie thought that was funny. Being wicked short had its own superpower: it turned grown adults into dumbasses.

The back door was locked. The keys were still in the ignition. Aggie heard a shuffling sound when she reached into the van to grab them; the front seats were separated from the rest of the vehicle by a steel grill. On the other side hung a black curtain. Aggie's stomach tightened.

She accidentally kicked the gunman in the balls and head on her way to the back of the van. Stomped once on the bullet wound in his shoulder. Smiled when he screamed. Quinn's lips twitched. He was much better at hiding his mean streak than Aggie was.

The police arrived just as she opened the back door. She heard them begin the usual shouting, the typical demands of "hands up, stay still," but she ignored that, staring inside the van at the equipment, the crude bed and props. A makeshift moving film studio.

And there on the carpeted floor, bound and gagged and squirming, was the very young star of the show.

* * *

His name was Rujul, and he was not from America. He spoke very little English, had no papers, and could only tell them—falteringly, mixed with Hindi—that he had been with these men for quite some time.

Rujul did not say the men had hurt him, but he did not need to. Everyone there saw the bruises, the hollowness of his face, the emptiness in his gaze. They saw the stacked and dated tapes inside the van. The boy was not much older than twelve.

"International child smuggling for the sex industry," Quinn said. "Put a fork in my eyes right now."

Aggie said nothing. That she felt sickened was not a strong enough word; neither was rage. Only, a deep abiding calm spread through her aching heart as she watched Rujul disappear into the ambulance, a certainty that someone was going to hurt for this, maybe die, maybe burn in Hell, and she would be there when it happened. Her gift was still dark, the future quiet, but Aggie did not need her inner sight to know the probable outcomes of this particular day.

Her cell phone rang. She glanced at the screen. "It's Roland."

"Perfect timing," Quinn said, his voice quiet, distant. "I need to ask him how he does that."

Aggie was too tired to smile. "He's the boss. His powers are unnatural."

She answered the phone. There was a distinct pause on the other end as Roland Dirk got his bearings—a hitch, a sucking in of breath as his clairvoyant vision kicked in—and then he said, in the succinct way only he was capable, "Fuck."

"Yes," Aggie said. "That's about right."

"I need to buy you a new car," Roland said. "Maybe you can outfit it with a battering ram. Jesus Christ, Aggie."

She did not feel particularly apologetic. "It had to be done. Didn't matter how. We had to get Yarns off the street."

"Yeah. The police called. They said you caught the fucker and his accomplice red-handed. Roughed them up a little."

"I don't think anyone is going to complain. There was a boy with them, Roland. I didn't realize they had a captive until I saw the van with my own two eyes. They were going to get rid of him tonight, with a seventy percent probability of death."

"Any reason why?"

Aggie shook her head. "David and his friend were on their way to a double meeting with a client and smuggler. Future was fuzzy, so I can't give you any names or locations, but it looked to me like they were going to try and sell the kid. Exchange him. And if that didn't work, dump his body in a river. Rujul is twelve, and that's close to puberty. Odds are, they wanted someone younger to take his place."

"I'm going to puke," Quinn muttered.

"I'm with him," Roland said, overhearing. "Holy shit. I hate this."

Understatement of the century. Aggie said, "Today

was just one piece of it. We know David has a boss. We still need to find him."

"And then what?" Quinn asked. He could only hear Aggie's side of the conversation, but it was clear from the look on his face that was enough. "We began investigating these child porn rings because of an increased flux in local kidnappings, but so what? Even if Dirk & Steele devotes all its resources to stopping this industry, it'll be a losing battle. Too much ground to cover, too much money, too many opportunists."

"Too many potential victims," Aggie said. "There's no rest for the wicked when they've got Third World countries and rich perverts playing buffet."

"I don't want to hear this," Roland said. "We do what we can. Maybe it's not enough, maybe today won't even make a dent, but a life is a life. You guys really want to quit after saving that kid and taking David Yarns and his porn mobile off the street? For Christ's sake, give me a break."

His voice was loud enough that Quinn could hear him. He winced. So did Aggie.

"I gotta go," Roland said. "You two take a break. Go somewhere. Stay at home. Read a book. Find people to have sex with. Have sex with each other. I don't care what, but do anything but think of this."

"After everything we've just seen, Roland, that's about as offensive an idea as any I can come up with."

"What?" Quinn asked.

"He wants us to take a vacation," Aggie told him. "And have sex with each other."

"I'm not offended by that," Quinn said. "Really."

"There's more work that needs to be done," Aggie replied.

"And you'll do it," Roland said. "But I need you fresh. The two of you do this much longer and you'll burn out. It's happening already."

"No, it's not."

"Sweetheart, you and the gunslinger are depressed because you saved a kid from a fate worse than death. You tell me how that sounds."

Aggie looked at the phone and gave it the finger.

"Nice try," Roland said. "But that ain't no insult. Now, go. Chew on your ankles somewhere else. I'll deflect the police and the feds if they come looking for you. I'll also try to send Max or one of the other telepaths down to the station to see if they can get close enough to your perverts for a reading on who they might have been contacting. Yarns might have some names floating around his head right about now."

"Good," Aggie said. "But I still hate you."

"I know." Roland snorted. "But that doesn't mean you're fired. I haven't used you up yet. When you're a shriveled husk, then you can collect unemployment."

"And here I thought you liked us all for more than our minds."

"No," Roland said. "I'm a bastard through and through."

He hung up on her. Aggie considered destroying her phone, but the emphasis would be lost, Roland couldn't see her anymore. His clairvoyance was dependent on particular connections.

Quinn shuffled his feet. "We're off the case?"

"Temporarily," Aggie said. "Until we become shiny happy people again."

"Well," Quinn said. "I'm toast."

"Yeah." Aggie sighed. She recalled Rujul's terrified eyes staring at her face as she opened the van door. One boy—one kid rescued—and odds were high that somewhere in the world at least a hundred more had just been recruited to replace him. It was enough to make a person roll up in a ball and cry.

But at least David Yarns and his friend were off the street. Hello, jail. Aggie hoped they got it good. Child molesters did not last long within the prison system; incarceration of any kind was an eventual death sentence. The other prisoners saw to that.

She watched the police walk the scene, taking photographs of the van interior and crash site. She worried about Rujul; the FBI would probably send in its own social worker to evaluate him, and after that—with no papers and no family—he might be deported. Aggie could not imagine what would happen to him then.

"So, now what?" Quinn asked.

"Home," Aggie replied, and for a moment felt something warm against her neck, a deep inexplicable flush that did not seem at all internal. She touched herself; her hand warmed, too. Like a caress, a breath of something heavier than air. Aggie shivered, but not because she was cold.

"What is it?" Quinn asked. "You see something?"

"No," Aggie said, frowning. She rubbed her hands

against her jeans. The warmth around her neck fled, but it left another in its wake, a heat that spread through her body, low into her gut. She did not dare call it erotic, because that would just be weird, but for a moment the sensation opened an ache in her heart, a deep abiding loneliness.

You have never been in love, she thought, and could not understand why now of all times she would think such a startling thing, and why it instilled within her such a deep sense of loss for something she had never had, something she should not miss.

"Aggie," Quinn said, staring.

"Nothing," she told him, forcing herself to focus. "Really, Quinn. I'm going through a blackout at the moment."

"Ah." He said nothing else, but she could tell he did not completely believe her. Which was fine. They were good enough friends to respect the space each of them needed. Working out the devils in the mind—and heart—were sometimes best done in a solitary fashion.

"Will your car drive?" he asked her. She gave him a look and he shrugged.

"Come on," he said, taking her hand. The top of his head only came up to her waist, but his grip was sure and strong. "Let's hit the big street and find a cab."

"I can call one."

"I need the walk," he said, and after a moment, Aggie agreed. A little air, a little sunlight. It was a beautiful day. Best to remind herself of that.

She glanced over her shoulder as they left the crime scene. Looked at her car, the van, the lingering police. She did not see anyone watching them.

But her neck tingled, and she remembered the warmth, the pressure on her skin, and wondered.

CHAPTER TWO

Charlie's brothers were made of stone, so the conversation was rather limited within the confines of his prison. Still, he tried, because he remembered the life of before, the life of midnight runs and wild scents, the life of a bright moon floating halo-like in the sky, full and pregnant in the heavens. A good life, even if much of it had been hidden.

Good, however, was not the word Charlie would use to describe his current circumstances, though in all honesty he thought it possible to feel a small amount of pride that he had done as well as he had. After all, he was not stone. The curse that had taken his siblings had not reached as far on his body—an accident of fate, as far as he was concerned—and though the witch had a taste for his flesh in all manner and form, he had managed to plead some favors with the hag as a matter of courtesy.

The witch had some manners left to her. Not many, but enough.

For example, she cut out his heart whenever he asked her to. Which, in recent days, was quite often. He did not think she minded; hearts were her favorite organ to consume: roasted with peppers, diced and fried with ginger, stewed with carrots and onions. All manners of preparation. Charlie could smell himself now, filling the air with a rich scent that did nothing for his appetite, but which most certainly had the witch's stomach keening high for a taste, perhaps with a dollop of rice.

There was nothing better than a gargoyle when hungering for flesh. Or that's what the witch liked to tell him. Charlie could not, in principle, agree—though he did acknowledge that as far as an endless food supply went, his kind were good to go. Gargoyles were not so very easy to kill.

And destroying their natures? Even more difficult.

That was the reason Charlie's brothers were still cast in stone. If they ever, in their hearts, agreed to the witch's demands of obedience and degradation, the granite would flake away into flesh, crack and turn to dust upon their bodies. All it took was one word: *Yes*.

But, obviously, all three of them were too stubborn for that, and had been for quite some time. Charlie was glad of it. As lonely as he was for their company, he really could not recommend joining the living again, especially with the witch as a mistress. She had, to use the modern colloquial, issues.

Of course, so did Charlie. And one of those issues was a little girl named Emma.

"She's alone," he said to his brothers, who crouched around him in a semicircle, frozen in varying poses of shock and horror. "And they're hurting her for money and pleasure."

It was a hard thing to hear himself say. Charlie hated it. Hated Kreer and her son with a passion second only to his rage at the witch. Perhaps he had grown accustomed to the hag and her whims, but that did not mean he understood them, or that he felt any compassion for her motives. She had stolen his entire family from their lives—good, modern, integrated lives that had taken years to cultivate—and made his brothers nothing more than stone dolls, ornaments who could still think and feel, forced to mark the passing of time in a kind of stupefying torture, while he . . . he lived. Lived, and tried to make the best of it, because some day he would ferret out a way to break the curse, and then, freedom. Sweet and happy freedom.

You are living in a dream world.

Well, yes. Everyone needed goals.

Like helping children escape their prisons, those human captors who in their own ways gave the witch a run for her money. The witch was sick, but at least she never targeted children. Not to Charlie's knowledge, anyway.

But there were others who did, and Emma—poor little Emma, with her dreams so full of heartfelt distress—was the last and final straw. Charlie, during one of his excursions, had felt her from the other end of the world—a small voice, crying out—and he, dead and dreaming, with his soul separated from his body while his heart and lungs and various other organs grew back from the witch's cuts, had broken a cardinal rule of his kind and stepped from the shadows to help her.

He could not stop himself. Gargoyles aided, they protected, and though times had changed and forced his kind to adopt different lives—more human, less circumspect—he could not turn away from his nature, or the child.

And really, what was the danger? No one believed in magic anymore. No one, that is, except those already capable of it—and Charlie didn't think any of them were going to rat him out, assuming of course that those particular elements even paid attention to the life of one insignificant gargoyle. And if they did, then shame on them for letting the witch go on as she had.

He said as much to his brothers, and he pretended they agreed. He also pretended they approved of him summoning in the witch with her long shining knife.

"I was just about to eat," said the hag. Her blond hair bounced in a high ponytail, the ends of which skimmed her pale delicate shoulders. She wore an off the shoulder number, white and glittery. Charlie noted a flush to her cheeks. She looked very girlish.

"Are you also expecting company?" he asked, tracing the sand beneath him with one long silver finger.

"I am," she admitted. "How do I look?"

"I prefer you as a brunette," Charlie said. "You don't look as dangerous."

"Liar." She smiled and her teeth were sharp and

white. "Besides, I don't need to worry about looking dangerous. My guest tonight knows exactly what I am."

"A cannibal?"

"Silly. An *asset*."

That was disturbing. "I thought you preferred working alone."

"What I prefer is that you not ask so many questions. Don't worry," and here she smiled, once again, "I'll take care of you, no matter what."

"How very thoughtful," he said. "Really."

The witch stepped through the circle drawn in the sand: his prison, a mere line of light. She held up the knife and waited.

"My heart, please," he said.

"It is always the quick deaths with you," she said. "And I suppose you want me to remove everything else, after that?"

"Yes," he said.

"You really are peculiar," said the witch. "I can't imagine why you think death is preferable to the company of your brothers."

The witch was not quite as all-knowing as she imagined herself to be. Charlie imagined punching his thumbs through her bright glittering eyes and then eating them like sugarplums. He said, "It's not the company of my brothers I'm trying to get away from."

"Clever," said the witch, and shoved the knife into his bone-plated chest. She missed his heart on purpose, which required hacking at him for some time before she got it right. Blood spattered her face and dress. Charlie's brothers watched.

Charlie, dying, hoped the witch's guest arrived before she had time to change.

The line between life and death was a thin one for a gargoyle, and Charlie, though he had never found much occasion before his captivity to walk it, found that he had some talent navigating the world beyond his body. He could see things about people—private, unconscious things. As a dream, a disembodied soul, almost nothing was hidden. He could peer into hearts and heads, and while he was not so nosy as to pry deep into places he did not belong, being able to explore the world as a ghost did alleviate the suffering he left behind. If only for a little while.

And the witch was totally clueless, which made the experience all the sweeter—and more—because death was also a good opportunity to explore possible avenues of escape for himself and his brothers. Charlie did not know what kind of spell the witch had put them under, only that someone, somewhere, must be familiar with it, or know what could be done to break it. Haunting the witch for that information was impossible, even dangerous. The shields around her thoughts were simply too tight, and Charlie feared pushing—that somehow she would sense him, recognize him, even, and the game would be up. Then there would be no more death. No more escape into the world.

Emma changed everything. Not, perhaps, Charlie's approach to the witch, but his approach to everything else in his life, which suddenly seemed burdened down with unnecessary secrets, the hands of the past reaching out to hold him down. He was not human, and though he had masqueraded as one for years and years, helping this child, even as a ghost, demanded that he give up some of that hard-earned anonymity, the illusion of separation between himself and others, the world and his personal, singular *I*. Never mind that Charlie was a prisoner, that he had lost the right to solitude. Reaching out was far more intimate, because it was his choice, his connection to make, and the consequences would be greater than any the witch could impart upon him.

And it was worth it when Emma, trapped in darkness, turned to the sound of his voice, and though she was afraid she did not lose herself, and though she had been abused so horribly by men, thought *hero* when she listened to him speak.

Words were not enough to express what that did to him, and it was not pride that made him warm, but something deeper—genetic, maybe, a biological imperative that had been suppressed in his psyche until that moment, that bloom of recognition when he thought, *My kind have given up our souls for safety. We murdered ourselves the moment we forgot what we could do for others. What we* should *do, no matter what. No matter the risk. It is not us or them, but all of us, together.*

And he carried that with him the first time he followed Emma from her basement prison into the well-lit living room of an old farmhouse, and found a startling array of equipment: cameras, televisions, sound machines. Thousands and thousands of dollars worth, and farther beyond, in other rooms, he sensed more: offices, computers, editing equipment; an infrastructure dedicated to the subjugation of innocence.

And subjugate they had, Mrs. Kreer and her son, Andrew. Both their minds were tight, as were their hearts—as difficult to read as the witch—but Charlie did not need to push deep to know what they were about. All he had to do was watch, ghostly arms wrapped tight around Emma as Mrs. Kreer carefully applied glossy red lipstick to her small mouth.

Emma hated Andrew—feared him, too—but she thought, *I am not alone and I am warm,* when Charlie kept his word. And so he did not leave her. Not until the filming was over and he felt the tug, the inexorable rush, and he was forced, unwilling, back into his healed body. The living could not exist without the soul—to resist would be committing to a true death, and Charlie was not ready for that.

But he did ask for the knife again. And again. As many murders as he could squeeze into the witch's schedule. He needed to die, and stay dead, for as long as possible. The pain was momentary, easily endured, nothing at all compared to what Emma suffered. What she would continue suffering, unless he helped her.

Charlie's options, though, were rather limited. As a ghost, he had a form, but no real ability to affect his physical surroundings. The best he could do was scare Mrs. Kreer and her son—which he'd tried, on his second visit. The old woman did not give any indication of noticing him, and her son was much the same, except for one violent shiver which was just as likely due to a bad meal rather than Charlie's presence. It was a piss-poor reaction and Charlie had no explanation for it. Emma most certainly could see him when he chose to materialize—though admittedly, he did so with a very toned down version of his face and body. The girl was traumatized enough without seeing what he really looked like.

So. If he could not help Emma himself, he needed to find someone who could. Tricky. The world was a big place. He had almost six billion candidates to choose from. Kind of, anyway. He liked to keep his options open.

He narrowed his search based on location; Emma was being kept in Washington state, in a little town in the mountains northeast of Seattle called Darrington. It took him far too long to discover her location—a weakness on his part, because every time he died he went straight to the child. A compulsion: he needed to know she was all right, still alive. And then, of course, he would say a word or two, and before long his time would run out and back under the knife he would go again.

But Emma was being held on the west coast of the United States, and that seemed as good a place as any to start his search, beginning first with her mother. He knew where she lived; the address was easy to take from Emma's mind. She came from a house in the Cascade Mountains, only several hours away. Charlie went there. Just one thought and *poof.* Faster than light, a speeding bullet.

Charlie did not tell Emma he was going to her mother, and was glad for it. He did not want to tell her what he found: empty shell casings, the decaying body, the blasted face. He did not want to tell her that it appeared no one had found or disturbed the remains, and therefore, no one had reported her as missing. Emma and her mother had lived a very isolated life. Perfect targets, well chosen. It was the ruthlessness that shocked him, though he supposed that was naïve. He had seen enough horrors during his captivity to know better than to underestimate any capacity for cruelty. Especially when performed by those who could command perfect masks, spinning their lies into lives made of illusion. Like the Kreers, who had a perfect reputation in the community they lived in. People . . . liked them. Which was vomit-inducing, but unchangeable.

It made his burden heavier, and though the candidates he found were good men and women, professionals, even that was suddenly not enough. Mere honesty and integrity were not adequate standards; nor was a desire to do good.

Charlie wanted more out of the person who helped Emma. He wanted someone who would throw his or her life into the effort with as much intensity as a parent for a child, with all the dedication and commitment that such devotion required. He wanted someone who would not give up. He wanted someone who would fight to the bitter end to see Emma safe.

He wanted someone who would love the girl as much as he did.

So he drifted—pressured by time and patience, because every day was a day that Emma got hurt—listening to thoughts and hearts, looking and looking for that one bright song. He was relentless, could not remember a time in his life when he had felt such implacable drive, and he wondered at himself, at the way he had spent his life before now; drifting around the world, moving from city to city, immersing himself in books and learning, walking streets only to pretend to be something he was not, because it was easier and safer than wearing his true inhuman face. Casting illusion through shifting shape.

Gargoyles were not the only kind with such gifts of transformation, but Charlie knew those others only by their eyes. Golden and bright, like twin suns. Animals. Pure shape-shifters, in the truest sense of the word. A long time since Charlie had seen one of them. Almost twenty years, at least. He wondered how many were still left in the world, if they outnumbered the gargoyles and other creatures of the arcane and uncanny. In these modern days, what was considered normal vastly outweighed its opposite, though pockets remained, often hiding in plain sight. Clinging desperately to secrets, because the truth was unthinkable. Charlie could not imagine what the media would make of someone like him, what governments and scientists would do to a person so radically different from human. The heart might be the same—all the emotion and passion—but the body, the flesh . . .

Flesh meant nothing. Flesh was nothing but a vehicle for his soul, but a vehicle that Charlie desperately missed as he searched for help. In his body, he could have stormed the farmhouse, taken Emma away—but he was trapped across the ocean, in a city near the sea, and he had nothing to give the little girl but a promise.

I will help you.

Charlie gave up on Washington state and moved to Oregon. Passed over that state in a day. California was his last hope; after that, he would begin moving farther inland. Three days searching, and time was running out; he needed to find someone fast. All those high expectations, his convictions, just might have to fade to the side in order to get the job done.

And he was ready—he was ready to do it, come what may—when he felt a tug on the edge of his spirit. A call.

He followed. He had no choice; he felt like he was listening to Emma for the first time, only this was a boy, tied up in the back of a van that suddenly lurched, slamming the whimpering child against sharp equipment. A man swore. Charlie heard gunshots.

Gunshots, and something stronger. Another mind.

Charlie focused on that mind, binding himself to the imprint of it, and *went,* dropping his spirit into the middle of a storm, a tumult, spinning wild against thoughts of pain and anger, and there, at the center . . .

A woman. Strong—determined—carrying a resolve so stubborn and powerful, Charlie felt it strike his own heart in a perfect sympathetic echo.

She was very tall, with skin the color of deep bronze; a woman easy to hold on to, with shapely legs and a small waist; broad shoulders and strong arms. Nothing girlish about her; just solid strength, easy confidence. And her mind . . .

Charlie lost himself inside her head, rolling through her thoughts, which were impossible and unending and fast—so fast—quicksilver and mercury and lightning rolling into one flashing vision of cars and bullets and dying men and he heard: *I have to stop this—I can't let him go—and—Quinn, be careful—*

He pressed for her name and found—*Agatha*—and there was another man beside her—*Quinn*—but his thoughts were quiet in the shadow of her mind, and Charlie watched, appalled and fascinated and terrified, as Agatha threw herself against death, fearless, all to stop—

A man who hurt children.

Charlie pressed himself deep inside Agatha, burying his soul against her own, sharing her life as she fought with all her strength to take down the man she hunted. When she breathed it was for him, and he breathed for her, curling around her lungs, beating with her heart until it was his heart, until he could not tell where he ended and she began, and it was wrong—wrong to be so close to someone without permission, but he could not help himself because to be in a mind so strong, so wild and chaotic and perfect, was a drug.

He had his champion. Right here. His huntress. The perfect woman for Emma.

The perfect woman for you, a voice whispered.

A bad thought. He had not come looking for himself. His heart did not matter. He had a mission, a little girl to save. She was the only one he had time for.

And besides, humans and gargoyles did not mix. Not ever, and not unless deception was involved. The physical differences were just too great.

Yet he wondered, as he finally untangled himself from her soul, what it would be like. He wondered, because it came to him in increments, bits of stunning truth, that the woman was even more extraordinary than he had first imagined, and he saw things inside her head—impossible things—that made him question once again the world around him, turn the paradigm upside down.

She'll believe me, Charlie realized. *I won't need to hide myself from her. I won't need to pretend I'm a ghost or an angel or a devil.*

With this woman, all he needed was the truth.

Things happened: the child, the police, the waiting punctuated by a phone call. Charlie listened to it all, still judging, tasting Agatha's reactions and thoughts. He wondered at his luck.

Finally, though, Charlie felt his spirit stretch—his body, coming back to life. He readied himself to leave, still floating close, eavesdropping, tasting Agatha's thoughts and the quiet mind of the man beside her. Friends, partners. Dedicated fighters. Not lovers.

The pull got stronger. Charlie could not help himself; at the last moment, he reached out and touched Agatha. Placed the hand of his spirit against her neck, infusing that spot with warmth, with the focus of his heart. He pretended he could feel her skin. He pretended she could feel him.

And when she reached back to touch her neck—startling, unexpected—her hand passed through his and he felt a quiet caress move along the entirety of his soul, strong and lovely and undeniable.

Thousands of miles away, Charlie's heart began beating again. Agatha disappeared.

He opened his eyes. Above him, stone. Beneath him, sand, cool and soft. His wings ached.

The witch was not there waiting for him. Charlie turned his head and looked at his brothers.

"Yes," he said, to their unspoken question. "I found her."

CHAPTER THREE

The future returned to Aggie later that evening.

She was alone, as usual. Mulder and Scully were on the television, squabbling while she sucked down a greasy hamburger and milkshake from the nearby Hardee's. Comfort food—she needed it bad. She also needed to curl up and suck her thumb, but she was trying to be mature about her emotions.

What she really wanted—what she thought would cure the ache in her heart: was to return to the office. There was always someone there burning the midnight oil: Roland, usually, who practically had an apartment attached to his suite. Even if she got a lecture, at least there would be something to do. A distraction, maybe. Anything to take away the vision of Rujul's haunted eyes staring at her from the floor of that van.

God. Roland did not know jack shit about how Aggie relaxed. The job *was* her vacation. Getting things done, being useful. Time off was for pansies. Even crap like today was no deterrent. It just made her want to work harder. She chased memories by making new ones, by doing something good to replace the bad.

Push, and push hard. That was Aggie's motto. It was how she had managed to survive into her mid-twenties and get past the weirdo ignoramuses who could not see beyond her skin color or wild hair; the only way she had been able to grow up as the only multiracial kid within a hundred miles, in a town populated by cheerful white supremacists, well-meaning I-am-going-to-save-your-soul Baptists, and an odd fringe collection of artistic eccentrics, hippies, and poets (who were neither poor nor starving, because they managed to supplement the growing of their words with the growing of weed).

Idaho. A wonderful state.

At least her family life was normal. Good parents, cheerful household, no money problems worth speaking of. Aggie's dad was a lawyer, and his office had perched on the back end of the house, right below her bedroom. Which meant some really great eavesdropping.

And later, games of fate.

Aggie did not move from the couch. *Relax, relax,* she told herself, chanting it until her muscles began to unwind. This episode of the *X-Files* was a good one—all about words and hearts and passion burning, with poor Scully so confused about lust and love. Aggie could not relate, but it made for good television. That, and she kept hoping Mulder and Scully would kiss each other well and good. Having a relationship vicariously through fantasy and excellent scripting was all Aggie had at the moment—and to be honest, it wasn't all that bad. Her imagination was always better than reality, which was capped by her inability to find the right connection with a man she could trust enough to share her secrets.

I can see the future, she wanted to say, one day. Say it, and have the other person believe her. No judgment, no fear, no greed. Just loving acceptance.

Right. Big dreamer. Stupid romantic.

Aggie continued watching television, sinking deeper into a drowsy funk. She kept herself awake only to see the end of the episode, and right at the climax, right when the bad guy jumped Scully with his hands outstretched for blood, something else began to happen inside Aggie's head. Her mind danced with color, flickering brighter than any television screen, and she caught a glimpse of things to come.

It was odd. Aggie almost never saw her own future: a mystery—one she had learned to live with, albeit with some lingering frustration. There were ways around the disability; all she needed was to look at the people around her and she could extrapolate from their readings the things she needed to take care of for herself.

But sitting on the couch she began to see things, and it took her a moment to realize that what she was viewing was for her alone and no other. It certainly had nothing to do with the television—though she did wonder about the actors on the screen. She could receive readings from seeing pictures, moving or otherwise. But no, after a moment of careful scrutiny she decided David Duchovny and Gillian Anderson were not in her head.

But Aggie was. And there was a little girl in front of her. A photograph of a blond child, no older than eight or nine, with pale cheeks and hollow eyes. She was naked. She sat with her legs spread apart.

Aggie squeezed her eyes shut. She fought the visions, but they continued bright, clear, and—*God,* please . . .

She ran to the kitchen, braced herself against the sink, swallowed hard. She did not vomit. She held on, but when her stomach was settled and her mind quiet, she slid to the checkered linoleum and buried her head beneath her arms. The image of the little girl lingered, a ghost in the shell, frozen and staring. There was nothing provocative about that gaze, despite her posture. When Aggie closed her eyes, all she could see were eyes that begged, eyes that whispered, *Help me,* with all the quiet sweet pleading of someone still innocent deep in the core of her heart.

It was a terrible thing to see, and it did not feel like fate. There were no probabilities dancing. All the images inside her head were the same—exactly, precisely the same. Which was impossible. Variation was the game of the universe, the future built upon chaos, shifting constantly, affected by as little as one wrong turn, or a thought gone bad. It was true what they said, that something like the flap of a butterfly wing could set off a storm in Texas—except, here it was not the weather being meddled with, but lives.

This isn't the future, Aggie told herself. *This is a summons.*

But a summons to what? To help the child? And who in the world would be able to summon her?

Roland could, she thought. And there were several other telepaths employed by Dirk & Steele who might have a similar ability. But she trusted her friends. They were family. And no one at the agency would risk betraying those bonds by something so silly and wasteful.

So. This was from someone else. Maybe. Could be she was finally going crazy—the lock-her-up kind—and that her brain was giving out under the stress of having to keep straight the infinite possibilities engaged by every living creature Aggie encountered. It was a hard task for one mushy piece of gray matter, and today had been very stressful. Sometimes she could turn it off—sometimes her brain did it for her—but always, always, the gift waited, lingered.

No, stop it. Don't think like that.

It was too frightening. Insanity was a distinct possibility; there was precedent amongst some members of the agency's recent past. The human body was capable of handling only so much, and the horror for those born different—wired with a few more bells and whistles than the rest of the world—was that psychological help was nonexistent. If you got sick in the head, you took care of it yourself—or relied on a friend to talk you through. You pulled yourself up by the bootstraps; that was the only way to survive.

And even amongst the agents at Dirk & Steele, some were more different than others. Aggie wondered what it was like for the shape-shifters when they got sick. There was no science to account for men who turned into animals, who could sprout wings and fur. None at all; only magic, true miracles, through and through. And to see it, to know and believe it . . .

Nothing was sacred. Anything was possible. Aggie could no longer take her world for granted. Which was far more disturbing than it should have been, considering all that she could do.

Aggie forced herself to stand. There was a reason she never had visions of her future self—she realized that now. It placed her in a peculiar kind of paradox she had no explanation for—a trap of being bound by a future she had not contemplated, might never have considered, had she not been witness to such a forceful invasion of her mind. She felt like a serpent eating its own tail.

She returned to the living room. There was another *X-Files* episode on—a marathon of them. This time, baseball players. Aliens in love. The weird was different from her reality, but equal in terms of off-the-wall intensity.

And you wouldn't trade it for a thing. Weird is what keeps you going, what lets you help people in ways others can only dream of. Like today. You saved a life. No matter how you feel, you rescued a little boy.

One boy out of thousands, maybe millions. Bad numbers, worse odds.

But if she tried hard enough, if she wished long enough, perhaps she could pretend that it was not the number of rescues that mattered, but only that a child was safe, that in a world where there was so much suffering, one act of goodness could mean everything. That she *was* making a difference.

And now another child needed her help.

I need to find that photograph. A hard copy of it, or a

scan on the Internet. It was not enough to view the girl inside her head. There had to be a physical connection. It was the same for many of the other agents at Dirk & Steele; like Roland, who could only see across great distances if there was a telephone involved. E-mail did not cut it. Strange, yes, but those were the breaks. You simply had to take what was offered, no matter the form or shape, and run with it. Make do.

So Aggie went to her computer, swallowed hard before typing in her search parameters, and did just that.

Aggie found the girl in the wee hours of morning, after an exhaustive search that left her sick and tired, hand aching from clutching a pen as she made notes on the children she did find, and who gave her terrible visions of futures to come. At least three of them would be easy to locate by the authorities, and Aggie sent Roland a note with the information, flagging the e-mail red for priority. She knew him; by morning all of her research would be passed on to a paid-to-be-anonymous tipster—a man who had a good reputation with the police, and who could not be traced back to the agency. It had to be that way. No one wanted questions asked. The public jobs Dirk & Steele did were public only because there was no alternative. Most of the agency's work was much more subtle.

But the little girl in question—a new memory, to replace Rujul—finally appeared on a Web site that advertised itself as a forum dedicated to the "visual exploration of the human form." Innocent enough, but when she dug deeper—as the blogs of certain self-assured "child lovers" suggested—she found something far darker than a simple exploration of the human body.

She found children. Lots of children. Hidden beneath layers of links and code, nestled deep inside the core of a site that on the surface was hideously innocuous.

The girl was located on one of the last pages Aggie looked at. It was the same photograph, the same ghostly gaze. Aggie stared, pouring herself into those eyes, hunting for the truth, the future, some shining light she could follow. She wanted to know why this one life was so important that the probabilities fell away, why for once she was the victim of her own unpredictable mind.

Her vision split, curling around the present and future. She saw darkness, utter and complete, a future of darkness that was not the grave, but worse, a living tomb, damp and cold and filled with something more than rodents and insects and other creepy-crawlies of the imagination. She heard movement, saw a flash of light—

And the outline of a man, or the semblance of a man, because at first Aggie thought he was wrapped in a black stocking that covered him from head to foot, but then she realized that no such thing existed, and that what she gazed upon was a shadow. A man. A force, maybe. A presence that in all probable futures whispered *Emma, don't be afraid,* and, *Emma, I came back with help.* And Aggie could see that the girl crouched inside the darkness was not afraid of the shadow, the man. Aggie was not afraid, either. She sensed no premonition of terrible things, just a warmth that sank into her bones . . .

Aggie blinked hard, pulling out. She remembered the

heat that had fallen upon the back of her neck at the crime scene, and touched herself again. Her skin felt ordinary. No caresses, this time.

She swallowed hard and forced herself to look at the girl's photo again. *Emma,* she thought, and bright lights dragged across her eyes as she stared into the face of a narrow man whose hair gelled into dagger spikes, and whose gaze held a hunger that made Aggie think drugs, but worse, because all the probabilities pointed to another kind of taste. Variations of this man appeared to her—in a room with long blinds, and behind him an old woman rubbing her hands down the back of his neck.

Aggie looked hard across the veil of possibilities, but found no clues as to where the little girl was hidden away. Nothing at all, not a vision of the outside, not a bill on a table, no words. No one talked inside her head except to say, *Look at this, do this, hold yourself just so, you little shit.* And then, quieter, gentler, *Emma.*

Even softer, *Agatha.*

Aggie sucked in her breath, hearing her name reverberate across the future probabilities of the child in the picture. Her name, spoken not by the girl, but by the presence, the faceless shadow-man.

Future set, future promised. Aggie had no idea what it all meant, but it made her nervous. She rubbed her arms and gazed around her bedroom. Nothing bounced back at her as out of the ordinary. She looked at the computer screen and touched the little girl's face.

I'll find you. You're alive and I'll find you.

One child out of so many that needed to be saved. But Aggie, looking at Emma's picture, thought she could live with that. Slow but steady. One was not such a lonely number. One was everything when it came to saving lives. Roland was right. Despite the odds, that was nothing to get depressed about.

Aggie printed out Emma's picture. She laid it down on her desk, tasting the future. There was a ninety percent chance the girl would not be physically abused tonight, and there was no danger at all of her dying. Which did not ease the pressure, but it did mean Aggie could rest for an hour or two before continuing her research.

She stripped off her clothes and slipped into bed. Shut her eyes.

Sleep did not come easy, and when it did, a deeper darkness mirrored her thoughts and dreams, a basement, a cave, a place of damp wet things and fear, so much fear.

Until, again, that warmth, that sunlight in shadow that reached down into her bones and blood, right through her heart into her soul—and with it a comfort that stripped away fear, the horror of loneliness. A presence that was solid in that most profound sense that had nothing to do with physicality, but home—heart home, soul home, all those homes that were not walls, but thoughts, feelings, passion.

I am home, Aggie thought, curled up within that darkness. *Wherever I am, I am home.*

Warmth. She became aware of it slowly. Like a charm in her head, seeping through her body as a slow-moving river; sunlight, blinding. It was delicious.

But not right. Part of her, even unconscious, knew that. Recognized the heat.

Aggie opened her eyes.

Her bedroom was dark; through the window blinds, the streetlight outside cast a serrated glow on her ceiling. Nothing moved. She was alone.

"No," said a strange voice. "You're not."

A gasp escaped her—almost a scream—but Aggie clamped her mouth shut and reached for the gun on her nightstand. No one stopped her, but that was no consolation. Nor did she feel better with a weapon in her hand.

She recognized that strong low voice. Remembered it from the future. The heat lingered, oozing through her, and that, too, was familiar: a ghost from her afternoon, standing on that street with Quinn.

"I know you," she said, searching the shadows of her bedroom, trying to keep her voice steady as she found only walls and furniture and piles of laundry on the floor. "I *know* you."

"No." One word, so close she could almost feel the air tremble in front of her face. Aggie leaned backward, sweeping her hand through the spot. Heat collided with her skin.

"No, my ass," Aggie said, trying not to shake. "You have something to do with a little girl I'm investigating. I heard you inside my head. I saw you with her." Never mind revealing her gift. This was already weird. The thing inside her room could not possibly be shocked by anything she could do.

"You might be surprised," he said, and then, quieter, "I need your help. I need you to help *her.*"

"And I need you to show yourself. Right now."

For a moment she thought he would not do it—had to wonder, even, if the very male presence in her room was even capable of it—but just as she began to give it up as a lost cause, a shadow materialized; a figure darker than the air around her, gathering together to form the shape of a large man. He looked solid enough, but Aggie did not take that for granted. He did not have a face.

She tried to see his future, but her gift stalled. He said, "I don't think I have a future."

Aggie gritted her teeth. "You're a mind reader."

"Sometimes."

"Sometimes," she repeated. "My theory on mind readers is that you are or you aren't. It's like being pregnant."

"Then at the moment, I guess you could say I'm having triplets."

"Funny," she muttered, and really it was, though she was damned if she was going to crack a smile and encourage the source of that fine heady sound of irritation and sarcasm floating through her room.

You're forgetting that thing is a mind reader. Pretense is a waste of time.

The shadow grunted. "You can call me Charlie, *Agatha*. And yes, that really is my name, and no, I'm *not* a thing, which you should be ashamed of thinking."

"Anything else?" she asked, unnerved.

"Just that you're right. It *is* a waste of time to pretend with me. I do, however, completely understand your desire to try. Really."

"Gee, that's nice," Aggie said. "You're freaking the

hell out of me, but still, I appreciate the honesty. Maybe you can answer another question."

"I did not manipulate you," Charlie said, with a speed that Aggie found truly annoying. "Sorry. But that *was* what you were going to ask. I did not put that . . . that initial vision of Emma in your head. I've never seen that photograph."

"But you've been with her."

"I was called to her. She was afraid. Desperately afraid. I would have rescued her myself, but . . ." He held up his shadowy hands. "I'm not good with the physical at the moment."

"You're physical enough," she thought, recalling the heat, the warmth spreading through her body. "Maybe a little too touchy-feely."

Body language was all she had to read Charlie. It could have been difficult, but he made it easy. His shoulders slumped, straightened, twitched—an odd little dance of discomfort. This time Aggie did smile, though she doubted it was a particularly pleasant expression.

"It's not," he affirmed.

"Cry me a river," she said, but her annoyance began to fade. It was strange, having a conversation that required no artifice or bumbling, but it was—if she could admit it—almost as fun as it was unnerving. She had a thought; Charlie answered. It was very efficient. She liked that. Except for the strong possibility he could hear and see all her most personal secrets. Yikes.

Don't think about that. Focus. Focus on the why and how. And remember Emma.

Remember Emma. Yes. She could do that with absolutely no effort at all. The girl was part of her now—lodged like a knife in her brain.

"So you need my help," Aggie said, "You, who are so obviously gifted in your own remarkable way. Forgive me if I call you a big fat stinkin' liar."

Charlie made a sound of disgust. "What you can do and what I can do are two very different things. But does it even matter? You know the girl is in trouble."

No denying *that*, but Aggie was not satisfied with easy answers—or attempts to deflect her from the truth. "Why me?" she asked, still trying to wrap her head around the situation, to decide whether or not this was some dangerous elaborate hallucinogenic hoax. "Of all the people in the world, why the hell show up in my bedroom?"

"Because you're perfect," he said. "In your mind, your heart. I was there today when you went after that child molester. You were unstoppable, willing to do anything. Emma needs that."

Aggie remembered heat on her neck, heat spiraling into her body. "Emma needs the police, Charlie. Emma needs more than me."

"If the police were enough, I wouldn't be here. And if you . . . if you weren't enough, I wouldn't be here, either."

"Picky, aren't you?"

Aggie saw no eyes, but he tilted his head, and she had the distinct impression that he was giving her a Look.

"Emma's mother is dead," he said, and the change in his voice from soft to hard was chilling, dangerous.

"Her kidnappers shot the woman in the face. They're ruthless people. I needed someone who wouldn't care about the danger."

"And you think that's me." Anger curled through her gut—not at Charlie, but at Emma's captors. Aggie did not doubt the truth of what he told her; somewhere deep, she knew how bad those people were. She had looked into their eyes, and she knew.

"Yes," whispered Charlie. "It's as bad as you think."

Aggie thought of Rujul, the film studio, the bed, those men with their hard eyes and hard hands. Twelve years old and already he had lived through a nightmare.

"Emma is only ten," Charlie said. "And her nightmare is just beginning."

Aggie blew out her breath. "And you? What do you get out of this?"

"Nothing," he said. "Just my soul. And no, I don't mean that literally."

"I had to wonder," she said. "Seeing as how I can't take anything for granted, anymore."

"I'm sorry for that." His response was cryptic, but also, in a strange way, kind. He stepped toward her, graceful and weightless; he did not walk, but floated.

"What are you?" asked Aggie.

He stopped moving. "I'm me. Just . . . a man."

Bullshit, she thought.

"I don't want to talk about it," he said.

"But this isn't your real body."

"No. My physical self is . . . some distance away. This is just a projection."

A projection with a touch that made me hot.

Oh, bad wording, bad thought. Aggie's cheeks felt red. Charlie twitched, but instead of commenting, he said, "Will you help me? Will you help Emma?"

Aggie put down her gun. There no longer seemed to be any reason to hold it on him. "You already know the answer to that."

"I was trying to be polite."

Aggie briefly closed her eyes. "This is bizarre. I can't believe I'm not screaming yet."

"Neither can I," he agreed, and Aggie cracked another smile. Her smile disappeared when he said, "But you're already used to strange things, so maybe that helps. All your friends, the people you work with . . ." He stopped, looking at her, and Aggie wondered what her face must look like, what he was feeling from her heart, because he said, very softly, like a fireman trying to talk down a kitten, "I won't tell anyone."

"Maybe not," she said, "but it's not the kind of secret just anyone should know. A lot of lives depend on it."

"I understand," he said, and there was something in his voice that made Aggie believe him. She could not help herself. So much confusion, so much happening too fast—but she did know that a little girl named Emma needed help, and this apparition before her had gone to great lengths to find someone who could do the job. That in itself seemed genuine. No ruse. No trap.

Can you be sure of that? You're no mind reader. You don't know his motives for certain.

"I'm not here to hurt you," Charlie said, and then, in a more distant voice, "One of your own was kidnapped. Several months ago, by a . . . a rival organization. And you wonder if this isn't too convenient. Just another lure. All of you have been warned to be careful."

"You really need to stop that," Aggie said.

"But you agree it is faster. And no, I'm not from any group. Though the world is such a large and varied place, I think it was a mistake for any of you to assume you were alone."

Aggie did not want to argue with that. She threw back her bedcovers and stood up. Charlie made a low noise; strangled, choked. She stared at him for a moment, and then realized the problem: she was naked.

"Don't look at me," she said, reaching for a blanket.

"I don't have a choice. In this form, I see everything. I don't have eyes to close."

"That's convenient."

"Well, *yes*," he said, and his tone was so sheepish, so unabashedly . . . boyish, that for a moment Aggie almost laughed out loud. She choked it down, though. Laughter would not do. Now was all business. Aggie had a little girl to save.

She wrapped the blanket tight around her body. "If the people who have Emma are as bad as you say, I want to have additional backup with me. No offense, but as you've pointed out, your mind is willing, but the body is weak. I want to call my partner. My boss, even."

"If you like," the shadow said, though there was something in his tone that made her think he was not terribly excited about the idea. She did not like that; it made her trust him less, and she had no reason to trust him at all.

Aggie held the blanket against her breasts and picked

up her phone. She speed-dialed Quinn, who answered on the third ring. Aggie heard a woman's voice in the background and winced.

"I'm sorry," Aggie said. "I didn't know you had company."

Quinn sighed. "What is it?"

Aggie opened her mouth to tell him, but something overcame her and she stopped. *Take a break before you burn out,* Roland had said, and Quinn was doing just that. Forgetting the pain, burying it. To drag him into another case where the best possible outcome would be just as horrific . . .

"It's nothing that can't wait," she said. "You . . . you have a nice night, Quinn. Just rest."

"Rest wasn't what I had in mind, Aggie."

She heard a giggle on the other end of the line, followed by a sucking sound.

"Right," she said quickly. "G'night."

She hung up the phone and stared at it. Thought about Roland. He might insist that she hand the case over to someone else. She was supposed to be resting, too.

"No backup?" Charlie asked.

"Try not to sound so happy."

"You don't trust me. I understand that. You don't have a reason to."

"All I have is faith and visions of a probable future in my head. In them, you aren't doing anything wrong."

"But all you see are glimpses."

Aggie looked at him, pouring strength into her desire to *see,* and much to her shock, the barrier between herself and the future wavered, broke. Images flashed, probabilities dancing. She saw Charlie's dark body, and it was wrapped tight around something—some*one*—but that person he held, who he embraced . . .

Oh. My. God.

It was her. Aggie was looking at herself. Her eyes were closed, mouth parted, body writhing like an eel, and—*holy shit*—when she moaned, the sound was electric, pure unadulterated pleasure. Aggie pushed for an alternative future, variations, but almost everything she saw was the same. The probabilities were high.

She closed her eyes, whirling away from Charlie to stare at the wall. Her heart pounded so loud, she barely heard him when he said, "Maybe you should get dressed."

"Right," she said, and then, louder: "I'm not sleeping with you."

"I didn't ask you to."

"Well, I won't."

"Glad to hear it. Now *please,* get some clothes on."

"I just want us to be clear."

"Fine," he spat. "I get it. Besides, it's not like I have any usable appendages anyway." He stopped. "Pretend you didn't hear that."

"My hand to God," Aggie said. "I'll never tell a soul that you're impotent."

A strangled sound choked up through his body. Aggie smiled. "Still glad you picked me?"

"I—" Charlie began, then touched his chest. He had no features, so it was impossible to read his expression, but Aggie knew instantly something was wrong. The way he moved was different. Jerky.

"What is it?" she asked.

"I have to go," he said, and his voice was tight, strained. "Emma's in Washington state, in a town called Darrington. Don't wait for me. I'll find you."

"Charlie," Aggie said, but he never said another word. His body split into fragments, like shattered glass, and she pushed her arms into those remains of his shadow and felt a brief comforting warmth before everything that was left of him snapped upward and disappeared.

Gone. She was alone.

Aggie closed her eyes and took a deep breath. Counted to five.

She walked to the nightstand and picked up her gun. She brought the weapon to her desk and set it down on Emma's picture, covering her naked body with the stock and muzzle.

"Okay," she whispered to the girl. "Hold on."

She was going to get a little bit crazy.

CHAPTER FOUR

Aggie caught an early morning flight to Seattle—so early, none of the airport coffee shops were yet open when she boarded the plane. Bad, evil, the work of the devil. She felt very cranky. Thank goodness for first-class seating, purchased in its entirety with her agency credit card. Roland could yak at her later. Which he most undoubtedly would, especially after he read his e-mail, which contained a very short and inexcusably cryptic note:

I had a vision. I'll try not to get shot.

Yeah, he was going to love that.

Aggie had Emma's photo in her wallet. Just a head shot. She did not want to get arrested for carrying child porn. She also had her guns, but those were disassembled and stored in her checked luggage. As were her knives, handcuffs, and other sundry items necessary to being an effective wayward detective.

Her cell phone rang just as she took her seat on the plane. Shit, shit, shit. She had forgotten to turn it off. She glanced at the screen and Roland's name blinked at her.

"Yo," she answered, dreading the man on the other end.

"Jesus Christ," Roland said. "You're on a plane."

"Your powers of observation are only improving with age."

"I want you off, Aggie. Right now."

"Is it going to crash?"

"You tell me."

Aggie glanced at the flight attendant, who continued to smile like a plastic doll throughout all the variations of her immediate future. "That would be a resounding no. Which also means there's no good reason for me to lose my nice warm seat."

Roland swore. Aggie said, "This is important. Another kid's life is at stake."

"That's what tip-offs and local authorities are for, sweetheart. We only get involved when all other avenues have been exhausted."

"And that's this one," Aggie told him. "I'm not being frivolous, Roland, and I haven't become some righteous martyr. The circumstances of this case are . . . unique."

"And you had to be the one to take it?"

"Yes." *I had no choice,* she wanted to tell him, but that would be a lie. She could have said no to Charlie, turned her back. Only, he had chosen too well. Aggie was not a quitter, not when someone needed her. Push, and push hard, no matter what.

Roland said nothing. She heard cracking sounds and

knew it was pencils snapping in half. He kept boxes of them around, just for that purpose.

"Okay," he finally said. "Tell me where you're going and I'll send Quinn after you."

"No," Aggie said. "Not Quinn."

"Got no choice. Most of the guys are overseas, and the newbie shifters are too green for this shit. Eddie's in the fucking hospital for his appendix. We're stretched thin enough as it is, and the New York office has their hands full."

"No," Aggie said again, insistent. "Quinn needs to rest. You were right, what you said yesterday. It's been too much, and he's felt it even worse than me. Leave him alone, Roland."

"I think you've forgotten just who the boss in this out-fit is, Aggie."

"I haven't forgotten," she replied, quiet. "But you're a friend before a boss, and that just can't be helped. You raised us that way."

"My mistake," he muttered. "I'm a lousy sap."

"Just a teddy bear. A big overstuffed one."

"Whatever." He sighed, long and mighty. "Fine, have it your way. Do your thing. Go Solo like Han. If you don't get killed, I'm firing you."

"Thank you."

"Don't. And wipe that fucking smile off your face."

Aggie heard a phone ring in the background; Roland answered it and said a few muffled words. She heard a loud slam, a crash, and then, "Aw, hell."

"Trouble?"

"Dean. He's tearing a hole through Taiwan. You may have to wait in line while I kill him first."

"Be gentle," Aggie said. "He screams like a girl."

"He *will* be a girl when I'm done with him."

Aggie began to mouth off a pithy reply, but the flight attendant tapped the arm of her seat and said, "Time to turn that off, dear."

"I got that," Roland said, as the woman moved up the aisle. "She's hot. What's her future?"

"She's all smiles," Aggie said, and then hesitated. "There's a thirty percent chance she'll stick her heel in a grid as she disembarks the plane. She'll break it off and hit the ground with a twisted ankle and a hitched up skirt."

"Bad, but sexy."

"Uh-huh. Everyone will see her penis."

"Right," Roland said. "Take care."

He hung up the phone.

Almost an hour into the flight, Aggie felt something warm touch her hand. Someone whispered in her ear, "We need to talk."

No one sat in the seat beside Aggie, but she did not want anyone to see her talking to the air about child molesters. She got up and went into the bathroom. Maybe the drone of the engines would be enough to drown her out her voice if she whispered.

Charlie materialized the moment she locked the lavatory doors. It was a small space; he towered over her and she pressed back against the door and counter, banging her head on the paper towel dispenser. Under normal lights he looked different; his body still solid, but the surface textured, almost as though he was made up of an infinite amount of vibrating particles. She wanted to touch him.

"Go ahead," he said. "It's not like we're going to jump each other if you do."

"You just had to bring that up."

Charlie shrugged, and his body moved just like any other, except for his size and grace. He was the perfect rendition of a human. Aggie could not help but think it was all a lie. It also bothered her that he didn't have a face. It made listening to him a strange experience.

"Think Spider-man," Charlie said. "You don't see his mouth move."

"A telepathic apparition who reads comic books," Aggie replied. "Nice. That must be where you get your hero complex."

"Right back at you, *sweetheart*. Or isn't that Wonder Woman underwear you've got on?"

"Fuck you." Aggie patted her hips, frowning. "I thought you couldn't see through clothing."

"I can't." He sounded smug. "I read your mind."

Aggie narrowed her eyes. "I never did like Spider-man, you know. The mask always pissed me off. That, and his stupid sense of humor."

"So cranky," he said. "That line in your forehead is going to become permanent if you're not careful."

Aggie sucked in her breath; Charlie raised a shadowy hand before she could launch a rant. "Sorry. Really. But I look this way for a reason, and believe me, it's better that I do."

"Really? You must be the vainest person I know."

"I'm a person now? How nice."

"Don't distract me. I want to know what you are. Underneath."

Charlie paused. "Does it really matter?"

No, she thought, but said, "I don't know you yet."

"Then maybe this is better," he replied, and there was no amusement in his voice. "You might not like the way I look for real. It might scare you."

"Tell me," she said. "Show me."

He shook his head. "It would only be a distraction. And besides, we've got bigger problems than my appearance. For starters, this toilet is filthy."

Aggie gave up. "Just why are you here?"

"Because Emma is asleep," he said, with a matter-of-fact honesty that took her off-guard. "I wanted to see how you were doing."

"I'm fine," Aggie said.

"You don't look fine." Charlie's hand traced a line across her forehead. Gently, he said, "You're tired. You didn't sleep at all last night."

"I had no time." Aggie tried to ignore the warmth of his hand, the warmth of his spirit, bathing her like some dark sun. Visions split her mind; she saw herself held tight within shadowy arms, head thrown back. . . .

Aggie leaned away, heart thudding in her throat. She tried to speak, but her voice would not work. Charlie said, "You want to know why you keep seeing that."

"Yes," she breathed.

"I don't have an answer," he whispered.

"Are you sure?" She could not believe those words came from her mouth.

Charlie went very still. Aggie did not wait for his response. The unheard possibilities scared her. She said, "What happened last night? Why did you leave so quickly?"

He did not immediately answer, but when he did, he said, "I left because I had to. I didn't have a choice."

"There's always a choice."

"No. Not when it's biological."

Aggie frowned. "I'm not sure I understand what you mean by that. Are you . . . dreaming somewhere? And then your body woke up?"

Charlie twitched, which under the bathroom light looked more like a ripple surging through his body. "Something like that. It's a bit more complicated."

Aggie waited for him to continue. When he did not, she leaned even harder against the lavatory door and folded her arms over her chest.

"You know all my dirt," Aggie said. "Everything. I've got no secrets from you."

"Agatha—"

She held up her hand. "You've managed to deflect every personal question I've thrown at you, and frankly, I find your lack of trust deeply offensive. You're asking me to risk my life for Emma, and that's fine, something I would do anyway. But I expect some reciprocity on your part. Show me a little respect, Charlie."

"You want a reason to trust me."

"Maybe," Aggie said. "Or maybe I just want to figure you out. I don't know who you are."

"I'm a guy who has too much time on his hands."

"You're a guy who helps kids."

"I'm a guy who never helped anyone before this kid."

"I find that hard to believe."

"Don't. I had secrets to keep. It made me selfish. Isolated."

"Secrets. The kind of secrets that let you float around like a ghost and read minds?"

"It's related. Part of a larger picture."

"And last night? Is that picture all biology?"

"Extreme genetics."

"The kind not found in nature?"

"No. I'm all natural. That's the problem."

"I don't see how there's a problem in being yourself," Aggie said.

"Then why do *you* hide what you can do?"

"Because I want to keep being myself without any scrutiny or interference."

"Good answer."

"My momma didn't raise no fool," she said.

"But you still want to know about . . . this."

"Your dream self, yes. I really do."

"It's not easy. The explanation, I mean."

"Just spit it out, Charlie! Mr. All-American Charlie."

For a moment she thought he would not answer, and the frustration that welled up inside her chest mixed unpleasantly with a strong ache of disappointment. She did not know why; it seemed ridiculous to expect any honesty from the . . . individual in front of her.

But she did. And if she did not receive a straight answer, if all she continued to hear was nothing at all . . .

"You play hardball," Charlie said.

"I'm just a hard person," Aggie replied.

"Now who's lying?" He shook his head. "Fine. Okay, then. Okay. You want the truth? I'm . . . I'm not human."

He sounded as though he was declaring his own death. Aggie chewed the inside of her cheek. "You're not human? Really?"

"Not at all."

"Well . . . what are you, then?"

"You work with shape-shifters. I've seen it in your head. Golden eyes. Animals. Occasionally bad-tempered."

"I didn't know their tempers were a racial classification, but yes, I do. Is that what you are?"

"No. My kind are related, though. Distantly."

Aggie covered her eyes. Someone knocked on the door behind her.

"Miss?" asked the flight attendant in a loud voice. "Are you okay in there?"

"Fine!" Aggie shouted back. "My stomach! It's bad! Bad!"

If there was a response, she did not hear one. No one else knocked on the door.

"Okay," she whispered. "You're not human, and you're not a shape-shifter. What else is there?"

"Um, a lot, actually."

"Charlie."

"The technical term is gargoyle. That's what I am. A gargoyle."

Aggie blinked hard. She was going insane. Forget acting crazy; she was already there. "What the hell does that mean? Aren't gargoyles little stone . . . watchdogs, or something?"

"Arf," Charlie said.

"Hey."

"I guess that explains why my mother always kept me on a leash."

Aggie buried her face in her hands. "I hate you."

"You don't even know me. I thought that was the whole point of this."

"I changed my mind."

Charlie laughed, and the sound curled warm in Aggie's stomach. He had a nice laugh. It was deep, soft. Sexy.

He stopped laughing. Aggie's face burned.

"Agatha," he said quietly. "Look at me."

She did, but it was painful. She stared up into his dark featureless mask and said, "So you're a gargoyle. Tell me what that is."

He touched her face—a hand made of darkness, resting soft against her cheek. He was warm; radiance poured through her skin. It felt good. Aggie began to relax.

"Charlie," she said.

"Originally we were demon hunters," he said. "You don't know about any of that. It's early history, not quite prehuman, but close. Things were different in the world. Different in a bad way. My kind kept the balance."

"But things changed."

"Humans came into power. Demons lost their hold

on the earth. When that happened, gargoyles had to find a new reason for being. It wasn't very difficult. There were still things to fight."

"And then things changed some more."

"Yes," he whispered. "We became monsters, the hunted. To survive, we were forced to subvert out natures. Gargoyles can shift their shapes in temporary ways. We made ourselves look human, and took up roles in human societies. Quiet professions, mostly. Anything to keep us off the radar."

"You did a good job. You're not much in the legend books."

"That's probably because we wrote them. Many of us become writers and scholars."

He still touched her. Aggie did not pull away. It was dangerous to keep this up—she had a future to subvert—but his hand was warm and large, and she said, "You don't feel like a dream."

"Neither do you," he said. The plane shook—turbulence. The seatbelt light dinged above her head and she glanced left at the mirror. She did not see Charlie's reflection, which was remarkable, considering just how much room he took up. She felt surrounded by a thundercloud, a shot of night.

Charlie turned his head to follow her gaze. "Oh. That's interesting. And no, I'm not even remotely related to a vampire."

The plane shook again, more violently this time. Aggie braced herself against the door, the counter. Charlie remained effortlessly still.

"Maybe you should go back to your seat."

"Yeah," Aggie said, but she did not move. Someone banged on the door.

"Hey!" shouted a man. "I gotta piss, lady."

"He has to piss," Charlie said. "Best to let him have at it."

She wanted to tell him that the man could tinkle in his pants for all she cared, but she kept her mouth shut. Charlie laughed, low in his throat, and when she turned to unlock the lavatory door she felt a pressure at her waist; warmth, sinking through her clothing. Her breath caught.

"Remember," he whispered playfully in her ear. "You've been ill."

Aggie glanced over her shoulder. Charlie's body had disappeared, but the warmth did not fade. She felt his hands move up her spine—a trail of warmth—and she swallowed hard. She unlocked the door.

A man stood there, and behind him, the flight attendant, who stared at Aggie with concern. Aggie tried to look sick, and hoped it did not come off as turned-on. Warmth burst around the front of her stomach and sides; Charlie, embracing her from behind. Her entire body felt hot.

"Sorry," she mumbled. "I need to sit down."

She pushed down the aisle, ignoring the curious gazes of the other first-class passengers. Charlie never let up the pressure; she felt like she was wearing her own ghost—and God, it felt good.

You need to stop this right now, she thought at him. A moment later, the pressure eased off. Aggie bit back her disappointment. Really, she needed to grow up. This was not any way to conduct an investigation. She was going to rescue an abused child, for Christ's sake.

She also realized the trip to the lavatory was a complete waste. She could have just thought that entire conversation from her seat.

Aggie threw herself down and buckled in, pulled her blanket up to her chin, knocked her seat back, and twisted so she faced the window. She did not want to look at anyone. Sleep. She was going to close her eyes and get some fucking Charlie-free rest.

"I'm hurt," he murmured in her ear.

Go away.

"We still have to talk about how we're going to take care of Emma."

We need to get the local authorities involved. We have to do this on the up and up.

"We don't have time for that. They'll need probable cause. A warrant. We need to get Emma out first. You corner these two, and they'll use her as a hostage."

And then what? Something needs to be done about the old woman and her son. They'll just hurt some other kid. If the police help—

"I could have found some way of going to the local police, but I didn't. That was a last resort."

Are they corrupt?

"Worse. They think Mrs. Kreer and her son are pillars of society. Churchgoers, fund-raisers, volunteers. Those two do it all. Their reputation is perfect."

But they shoot women point-blank in the face so they can make daughters into child porn stars? That doesn't make sense, Charlie. That's high-level crime. Psycho, too.

"True psychopaths are the best pretenders." He sighed, and warmth crept up Aggie's shoulder. "Please. At least consider getting her out first. *Then* call the cops. There won't be any lack of evidence, Agatha. Their house in one big . . . perversion."

Do you know why they do it? What drives them? Even why they chose Emma?

"No. I can't read their thoughts. Their minds are . . . blocked."

"Blocked?" Aggie said out loud, and then settled deeper beneath her blanket. *What the hell does that mean?*

"It means that some humans have stronger natural shields than others. It's unusual, but not unheard of."

Yeah, but why them? They're, uh, not special, are they?

"You mean, gifted? Nonhuman? It's an interesting thought, but I don't think that's the case in this situation."

It would be easier if it was. Emotionally, that is.

"Because you don't like to think of human nature being so inherently cruel?" Warmth spread around Aggie's body, rolling down her arms, lacing through her fingers.

"Yes," she breathed.

"Oh, Agatha," he whispered. "There is nothing in this world that is born truly evil, and maybe it's easier to pretend otherwise, to cast some blame and make it easy on ourselves, but that would be wrong. Evil is everywhere, just the same as goodness, and every living creature has the potential for both."

And choice is the catalyst?

"You tell me. You live your life by probabilities, which are not definitive outcomes."

The future is a tricky thing, Charlie. You can predict

probable outcomes based on the current nature and lean-
ings of an individual, but if that individual changes in
any substantive, or even minor, way, the future is irrevo-
cably altered and the probabilities shift once again.

"In other words, choice defines us. Every choice, little
or big."

Good or evil.

"Or the slippery slopes in-between." Aggie felt the
warm pressure around her body tighten. Her heart beat
a little faster. Her ear suddenly felt hot and she sighed.
Charlie whispered, "I didn't see many variations of the
two of us."

Probable futures are defined by choice, remember?

"Then I suppose we'll be saying yes to each other
quite often."

Aggie said nothing. Despite the bizarre circumstances, being held like this was not at all frightening. It
felt good. Which was also strange, unreal, because it
had been years since she had felt arms around her, and
she had forgotten how nice it was—even if the person
doing the holding was invisible and not quite human.
Whatever that meant.

"Are you going to push me away again?" he breathed
into her ear.

Maybe later.

"Okay," he said; and Aggie bit back a gasp as his
warmth spread through her stomach, pushing up and
up. She felt his hands—those invisible ghostly hands
that were nothing but heat—ride high on her ribs, tracing her body, skimming the undersides of her breasts.

Apparently clothes meant nothing; he could pass right through them.

"If you want me to, I'll stop."

She almost said yes, her *maybe later* turning into *get away from me now*. Asking Charlie to stop touching her was the logical, smart thing to do. She did not know him, she knew she should *not* want him, and even if she did, *Jesus Christ*, they were on a plane. Instead, Aggie found herself sinking deeper beneath the blanket. She wondered if anyone was watching, what they thought.

Charlie said, "They think you've got the stomach flu." And then the heat covered her breasts, and she bit down on her lip to keep from crying out.

"Yes or no, Agatha?" His voice was so close it was as though she could hear him inside her head. She wondered briefly if that were not the case, if they weren't speaking mind to mind.

I'm sure you know that I haven't done this for awhile, she told him.

"Hell," Charlie said. "I can't even get a date."

Aggie smothered a laugh, and just like that, heat began rippling over her skin, pressure easing and deepening, warmth kneading into her body, and she forgot how to speak because one hand moved lower, passing over her stomach, pressing between her legs, burrowing like a thread of fire.

She tried not to squirm, to cry out, but some sound escaped and her body shifted, and she said, *Charlie,* and she imagined he said her name but the blood roared loud in her ears and the pressure tightened, spinning her up, throwing her wide, and she remembered her future with eyes closed and mouth open, groaning like every nerve was being tugged and stroked and sucked, and she thought, *Yes, I understand now.*

She came hard—the hardest and longest of her life, and her body jerked so violently she thought for sure the people around her must realize, but Charlie said, "No, they don't. Just relax and enjoy." And she did.

Again, and again, and again.

Making love to a beautiful woman while in a non-corporeal form had its benefits. Namely, the exotic and very public locations one could perform such acts; such as airplanes, bathrooms, the edge of baggage carousels, the lines at rental car stations—and in rental cars themselves. While parked, of course. Charlie had never been much of a ladies' man—for obvious reasons—but he found himself having an indecent amount of fun giving Agatha surprise orgasms everywhere she went.

His enjoyment was short-lived, though. Guilt weighed him down. Emma was still locked in darkness.

And yet, to see the woman beside him, hear the glow of her thoughts, the warmth she reciprocated inside her heart . . . it was a beautiful thing. And yes, fun.

"You're killing me," Aggie said, gasping as she sat in the driver's seat of her rented Taurus. "I barely made it out of that airport alive. I thought the security guards were going to arrest me. Or call an ambulance. I almost needed a wheelchair to make it this far."

"You did very well hiding your reactions," Charlie said. "After the fifth or sixth, you just looked . . . constipated. Maybe a little faint."

Aggie shook her head and he felt her embarrassment, her disbelief and wonder. "I can't believe this. I just had a public orgy with a disembodied gargoyle."

"It is one for the books," Charlie said, feeling rather satisfied with himself. Aggie's eyes narrowed.

"You don't mean that literally, do you?'

"Of course not. I'm a gentleman."

"Right. That explains the complete lack of inhibitions."

"And I suppose I was doing it all by myself, completely uninvited?"

"No," she said, after a moment that stretched too long for comfort, during which he listened to her mind replay the events of the last several hours. "I suppose not."

Her agreement did not make him feel better; he could sense her embarrassment turning into shame, confusion, and he wished very much that she would not feel that way about what had just passed between them.

"The rules change when you're invisible," he told her. *And when you're next to the most beautiful intelligent woman you've ever met in your entire life.*

Charlie wanted to tell her that, too, but was afraid of what she would say. He had been taking liberties with her mind; curling deep inside it, trying to better understand her heart and soul. Understand, too, why he was becoming so enamored with her. Everything he saw only made his feelings intensify until all he could feel was an ache in his heart, a burn, like the insides of his chest were swimming through fire.

Not that there was anything he could do about it. Just take what he could, appreciate what time he had, and hold it dear. Because even if things were different and he truly had a chance of happiness with the woman beside him, one wrong move could end it all. Charlie already knew that he should tread lightly; Aggie had a heart of deep passion, but it scared her, what she felt. When Aggie loved, she loved with all her being, every fiber. But to let go like that, no matter what had just occurred between them—to throw herself on the mercy of a stranger—a strange creature, at that—would require time and patience and the continued example of his good devoted heart.

Because she had it, his heart. He could not imagine another person he would rather give it to, and this, after a long life spent alone, judging and finding want, always holding himself back from others. Love at first sight; he had thought it a fairy tale.

Not anymore.

Stupid. This will never work. You're locked in a cage half a world away. Your body will never be hers to hold. She will never see you in the flesh, and one day, when the witch grows tired of your dying, she will find some other use for you, and you won't ever see Agatha again. How dare you fall in love—now, of all times? How dare you want her to love you, knowing what you do? And even if by some miracle you could be together, you are both so different. You aren't even human. You have no idea if she would love your true face.

The odds were insurmountable, the risks unimaginable; but looking at Agatha as she started the car, listening to the hum of her thoughts as she settled down to the business of Emma—*We are going to save you, kid, just hold on, hold on, hold on*—made him want to leap headfirst and challenge it all.

What a sap, said a little voice. *Your brothers would laugh if they could see you now.*

Well, fine. He could live with that.

"Emma's in Darrington?" Aggie said, checking the map. "That's about a couple hours away."

"Do you have a plan for getting her out?"

"Nope," she said. "Though whatever I do will depend a lot on your ability to do some recon for me. Otherwise, I'll just have to walk up blind and get myself invited inside. Not impossible, but I prefer knowing what's waiting for me."

"Equipment, mostly. Cameras, lights. All in the living room."

Aggie frowned, backing out of the parking spot. "And no one questions that when they come over? If they're that respected in the area, they must socialize. Word of any weird goings-on gets around in small communities. Trust me."

"Firsthand experience?"

"Yup. When I was growing up, I couldn't get away with anything in my neighborhood. I kind of stood out."

"In a beautiful way, I suppose," he said, deciding to be bold.

Aggie glanced at him, following the direction of his voice. A smile tugged on the corner of her mouth. She liked that. He could hear it in her head. "Only my parents said that while I was growing up. Said it and meant it, that is."

"Why did they raise you in that town if it was so prejudiced?"

"My dad had a niche, and he thought we needed the money. Tough skins, that's us. He was the only lawyer in that area, and people didn't have much choice but to come to him for help. And he looked like what people in that area expected, so he didn't have much trouble with locals. One bit Navajo, and a whole lot of Scottish and French. My mother, on the other hand, was the dark one. Jamaican, Mexican and Irish." She smiled. "I need to marry someone Asian, and then my children can make the Census Bureau insane."

Charlie said nothing. He wondered if humans and gargoyles could make babies together. He wondered, too, if that would be right or fair to the child.

She wanted to know where he was from. Inside her head, she asked. She asked for much more, but there was only so much he could tell with the time they had. And words, ultimately, were meaningless.

"I spent my childhood in the country," he said quietly. "I was born in Maine, close to the border. It was very quiet back then, but—"

"Back then?" Aggie interrupted. "How old are you?"

He could see her imagining him as some ancient lumbering creature—replete with all the necessary accessories like white hair, wrinkles, and incontinence—and said, "Stop that. My kind age slower than humans, that's all. I'm only sixty."

"Only sixty?"

"Closer to thirty of your years, if that makes you feel better." And he knew immediately that it did.

Aggie chewed her bottom lip, which was very kiss-able, and oh so impossible to touch in the way that Charlie wanted. Trying to ignore her mouth, he said, "When I was a still child—or at least, a child as my people define it—I was sent into the city. Gargoyles need to learn integration at a young age. We're naturally solitary, but forcing ourselves into areas of high population enables us to suppress the urge to hide. It's better that way. In the city, people don't notice if you're a little . . . strange. It's free anonymity."

"Free loneliness, too."

"You know what it's like to have secrets, Agatha. Sometimes what you try to hide takes over your life. It becomes your life. Or in my case, it *was* my life, from the day I was born."

"Was?"

"Finding Emma shook things up. Changed my priorities. Or maybe just reawakened my true nature."

"Which was what?"

He wanted to smile. "Protecting others."

"You say that like it's something funny."

"Because it is, in a way. I never used to think about what I could do for others. Not really. I was too caught up in staying anonymous."

"Helping people is dangerous," Aggie agreed. "For anyone, it's dangerous. You open yourself up, physically and mentally."

"I suppose. I don't regret it, though. Not at all."

"You can't be faulted for nobility."

"Just as long as it doesn't expose us. Something I think you understand."

Aggie smiled. "It's the Dirk & Steele creed: Help others, no matter what, and keep the secret safe. All because it's a big bad world, and we're just too different to be left alone if anyone should find out the truth."

"How did they find you?"

"Don't you already know?"

Money, he thought, but said, "I like to hear you talk."

"Awfully friendly all of a sudden, aren't you?" Aggie had a sly glint in her eye.

"Something has come over me," he admitted. "I've turned into a wild beast."

A low laugh escaped her. "It was money. I was stupid and needed to pay for college. I thought I could play the lottery and get away with it. Problem is, I see multiple futures. The more time between the present and the future I'm trying to predict, the more variations there are, which meant I had to play the specific numbers almost minutes before they were announced. I won, too. Cashed in a cool million."

"But some questioned it."

"Yes. The investigating officials never could prove anything, but it got my name in the papers. About a week after that, I received a call from Roland." She shook her head. "I thought the man was on crack, but he knew things . . . things about me he couldn't, and then once he introduced me to the others and showed what they were all about . . ."

He saw her memories, shared her doubts and awe, and then, later, her love for all those people in her life who were friends, close as family.

"You're happy with them," he said, feeling wistful.

He was close to his brothers, but not like this. Never like this.

"Happier than I ever imagined I could be. I don't know what I would have done if I hadn't gotten hired. If I hadn't been pointed in a direction that helps people."

"You would still have done good," Charlie guessed.

"I don't know," Aggie said. "Really, I don't. Choices, Charlie. I would have made choices I'm not sure I would have been proud of down the line. The future allows for second chances, alternate paths, but once you fall into the present and the past, that's it. No going back."

It was not safe for Charlie to materialize, not with so many cars around, but he wished for at least the semblance of a physical form so that he could pretend to sit with her in this car, in the flesh. "My father once said that it's our inability to change the past that helps us make better futures."

"He's an optimist."

"Yeah, he was."

Aggie frowned. Charles heard the question coming, but there was no time to listen to it, no time because his heart tugged and he had run out of death. He said, "Agatha, I have to go," and for the first time he felt her own heart scatter toward him—her thoughts, her emotions, a trickle of something deep and powerful that Charlie was too afraid to call love but thought could be the beginning, the baby root, of some terrible wonderful affection. He held on to that feeling, to her heart, and he said, "I'll be back."

She said his name, but the car and her face and the world faded and he snapped back to the sandy floor in

the middle of his prison. The witch stood above him.
Her hair was a different color: burnished copper, framing milky skin. Green eyes this time, but still glittering,
hard and cold. She did not have her knife.

"You've been playing me for a fool," she said. "You
sly creature. You've been running high while I cut you
dead."

Charlie tried to sit up, but the witch placed one small
foot on his chest. Her strength was immense, impossible. He could not move her.

"No," she whispered, as her white robes billowed in
the windless room. "You will not be leaving here again
for quite some time."

"How did you find out?" he asked, because the game
was up, and there did not seem to be much point in pretending otherwise. His brothers watched.

"It occurred to me that no one would want to die as
much as you, simply for the peace of endless darkness.
So I searched for your soul, and did not find it where I
thought it should be. Instead, I discovered a very long
and winding trail." The witch traced his chest with her
toe, curling her foot around his bone plates, the wiry silver lines of his corded muscles. "Very long, very windy.
And I must say, you are peculiar. Saving a child from the
darkness? Pleasuring strange women from beyond the
grave?"

"You have to let me go back," he said. "Please. Just let
me help save the child. That's all I ask."

The witch shook her head. "The child is beyond saving. You don't realize, do you? Her captors are not entirely human."

Charlie grabbed her ankle and twisted. The witch danced backwards, smiling, hair glinting bright and hot. He scrabbled to his feet, stretching to his full height, wings arcing up and up, pulling on his tired, misused muscles. His claws dug into his palms and he said, "What do you mean, they're not human?"

"Poor gargoyle," she whispered, still smiling. "The blood of your kind must be growing thin to not recognize the scent of a demon."

His breath caught. "Impossible. They're gone."

For a moment he sensed a shiver of fear inside the witch's gaze. "Not all of them were shut behind the gate, my sweet. And those who remained . . . changed. They never left. They did as your kind did. Lived as human. Thinned their ranks. There are not many left, and they are weak now. So very weak. But a weak demon is still a demon, and you know how much they enjoy pain." She shook her head. "That mother and her son don't even realize what they are. All they have are urges, a desire for suffering. Depravity in its very worst form."

"And they choose to listen to that desire," Charlie said, feeling the echo of his conversation with Agatha ring dull inside his heart and head.

"They choose," agreed the witch. "We all choose, one way or another."

She passed backwards out of the circle drawn in the sand. Light flared around her feet and she said, "Be good, sweet Charlie. Dream of your little girl and your woman and your days in the sun. Dream of death."

"No, please," he cried, throwing himself after her.

The line flared white hot, and he cried out, blind, clutching his burning face.

The witch said nothing, but he heard the tinkle of her laughter as she left the cavern and shut the thick door behind her.

Charlie slumped to the ground. After a time, the burning in his cheeks subsided. His eyesight returned. He stared at himself, at his immense body, all his wasted strength—all while Agatha journeyed alone to save the life of a child who was being held captive by the descendents of real evil. The old enemy still walked.

You lied when you told Agatha there was no such thing as a creature born wrong.

Maybe, though at the time he did not believe excluding demons was such a stretch of the truth.

If Mrs. Kreer and Andrew are part demon, they're also part human. Don't let the witch wrap you up with words. And don't forget, too, that she could be lying.

Could be, might be. It didn't matter. He was stuck here, with no way to help Agatha or Emma.

He thought of the little girl, waiting for him in the darkness; the comfort she had taken from not being alone. And his rage—his unadulterated rage at not being able to protect her from abuse and degradation.

He thought of Agatha, too, going there without his help. She would make do without him—he knew that. She would find some way in.

Charlie stood and looked at his brothers. "I have to help them."

But the only way to leave was to die, and he had no weapons. Nothing but his own hands.

And his brothers' bodies. The edges of their wings were sharp.

It took Charlie some time to muster up his resolve. It was not easy.

And when he began killing himself, it only got worse.

CHAPTER FIVE

The winding drive from Seattle to Darrington went much faster than Aggie anticipated, but she blamed Charlie for that, because all she could think of—between preparing for her pseudo Rambo-like rescue of Emma—was his voice, his warmth, his touch.

Funny, but it was his voice that lingered heaviest in her heart. The sex he had given her—if that was what it could be called—had been past good, more than extraordinary, utterly beyond Aggie's scope of limited experience, given that she usually shut herself off before things could get too tight. Not enough trust, too much fear that her secrets would be discovered. But here, now? Her lack of inhibition was a total shock.

And yet, his voice. She missed his voice. She wanted desperately to talk with him, and not just because she needed to know more about the house Emma was being kept in, or the Kreers and their habits. She simply wished to hear him speak. To say anything.

You are so ridiculous, she chided herself. *Big tough strong woman, taken down by a ghost with a magic touch and a hot, hot, voice.*

Well, maybe she was being silly, but that didn't matter. Aggie missed him. The son of a bitch was growing on her. She just hadn't realized how much until his last disappearance. It bothered her, the way he left. It felt like it was against his will.

You don't know anything about him. Not really. All you're running on now is faith. Everything he's told you this far could be lies.

Maybe, but she did not believe that. Call it gut instinct, call it whatever you liked, but she trusted him. God help her, she even liked him. Maybe liked him a little more than she should. Maybe, even, that "like" was something stronger. Stronger than lust, stronger than anything she had ever felt before.

Oh, how she wanted to hear his voice.

Seattle had grown up and spread out during the years since Aggie had last been there; the suburban sprawl along I-5 as she traveled north was unrelenting, and even visions of the Cascade range on her right did little to alleviate the gray and steel and glitter of encroachment. But then she left the freeway, left behind malls and cookie cutter developments, and wended her way high and higher into a world of rock and forests. Darrington sat at the base of Whitehorse Mountain, surrounded by enough hiking trails and parks to make an outdoors-type weep for joy. Aggie thought it was all very pretty, but she kept recalling Emma locked in darkness, Emma before the camera, Emma being touched, and she had to roll down her window for some air, which was crisp, full with the clean tangy scent of wild things. Sparkling and pure.

Maybe there are gargoyles hiding up here.

Maybe shape-shifters, too. Maybe a whole host of creatures out of legend. The world fairly teemed with mystery.

But still, she wondered. Would it be possible for a gargoyle—whatever that was, since Charlie still had given her no description at all, save for *I'm not human*—to live as himself in a place like this? Few people, lots of places to hide. At most, an urban legend, able to come and go. It sounded ideal to Aggie.

Then again, given what little Charlie *had* said to her, being away from people would probably miss the point. If a gargoyle's true nature were one of protection, then the urge to be in areas where such a gift would be most necessary might be great indeed. Even if it was unconscious. Suppressed.

Her cell phone rang. It was Quinn.

"Roland got hold of me," he said without preamble. "I guess this is what you were going to talk about last night when you called."

"I told him not to get you involved," Aggie said, exasperated. "You need a break."

"So do you, Aggie. But you should have just come and told me. Better that than running off alone on some mission of mercy."

"You were occupied," she reminded him, "and besides, the circumstances are complicated. This isn't just some whim I'm acting on."

"It never is," Quinn said, and Aggie wondered how much she should say. She knew for certain that Quinn could be trusted with Charlie's secret, but that was not her call to make—not her secret, not her life. And frankly, she did not want the responsibility of being the one person to reveal the existence of a whole other race of supernatural beings—in addition to the ones currently sharing their office space at work. Though, really, if Charlie were fully aware of the existence of those golden-eyed shape-shifters, she wondered if the reverse were true—if Koni and Amiri and Rik knew all about gargoyles, and had simply never said a word.

That bothered her. It made her wonder if there wasn't some kind of supernatural union or club, whose members all swore secrecy. No one talked about each other unless forced to, everyone pretended he was the only weird creature in the world, and that way the whole crowd stayed nice and anonymous and faceless.

"There's a little girl in trouble," she said to Quinn. "Her name is Emma, and her kidnappers killed her mother. More child porn. Could be they're even part of the same ring. Their names are Kreer."

"Sickos of the world unite," Quinn said. "So, what's your plan? Have you alerted the police yet?"

"There's . . . been some indication that the police would be unwilling to go after these two, especially without hard evidence in hand. Apparently, the mother and son responsible for the abuse are . . . well-liked within the community."

She heard his brief snort of laughter. "So basically, you're going in there guns blazing to get the kid, and to hell with the Man."

"Kind of."

"You are so nuts, Aggie. If you don't keep the evidence intact, if they get a chance to destroy anything—"

"I know," she interrupted him. "I'll be writing you letters from prison."

"Oh, my heart. But don't worry, Aggie. I'll wait for you."

"Thanks a lot." Aggie saw a sign up ahead. DARRING-TON: 13 MILES.

"I'm almost there," she told him. "Any words of advice?"

"There's a small airport on the edge of town. It's called Gold Hill. You should go there first."

"Uh, yeah?"

"Yeah. I'll be waiting for you."

And he hung up the phone.

Quinn cut a very sleek and tiny figure at the edge of Darrington's municipal airport. Leather jacket, jeans, big silver belt buckle. He was not alone, which surprised Aggie. Amiri was with him, standing tall and lean and graceful, dark skin glowing with rich undertones. His short black hair was streaked blond. He wore a simple buttoned shirt and narrow fitting slacks. His eyes were golden. Like a cat.

Both men stood in the sun, just outside a very old and dusty café that had no sign or name, but which clearly served some kind of food. The tables outside were filled with men, as were the tables inside, pressed against the windows. Coffee and sandwiches, Aggie saw when she pulled up. Futures fanned before her; a chaotic dance of warm homes and arguments and television. She did not single anyone out. She did not want to know. All the men who had been staring at Quinn and Amiri suddenly turned their attention to her.

Ah, scrutiny. The blessing of being different. And a stranger.

"Maybe if we pretend we're circus performers they'll crack a smile," Aggie said, as both men climbed into her car. Quinn took the passenger seat; Amiri slid easily into the back. Both their immediate futures were simple, stable: no bullets or blood.

"I don't know," Quinn said, glancing back at the unblinking stony faces still watching them. "I don't think the circus would do all that well up here. I think the clowns might be too much of a shock."

"Speaking of shocks," Aggie said, and Quinn shrugged.

"Why fly commercial when Roland is willing to spring for a private jet? The plane is still here, by the way. I hope you didn't get a round-trip ticket."

"How the hell did he know I was going to Darrington?"

"You bought the ticket with the agency credit card, and the rental car company wrote down your destination for their mileage calculation. You figure it out."

"I was begging for an intervention, wasn't I?"

"Oh, yeah. Big time."

Aggie looked over her shoulder at Amiri, who was, as usual, quiet. "Hey," she said. "How did you get roped into this?"

A small smile touched his mouth. "You mean, how did someone as new as myself become assigned to a task of such importance? I am, as Roland has said, green. But practice makes perfect." His accent was buttery, pure Kenyan.

"I asked for him," Quinn said. "Having a shape-shifter around might come in handy."

"Oh, right. Because cheetahs are native to the forests of Washington."

"Who is to say they are not?" Amiri asked. Golden light momentarily spilled from his eyes, curling down his cheeks, which fuzzed with spotted fur before quickly receding into smooth skin. His smile widened. His teeth were sharp.

"Nice," Aggie said.

Quinn shook his head and pulled a piece of paper from his jacket pocket. It looked like something torn out of a telephone book. "After what you said to me about the Kreers, Amiri and I did a little poking around at the airport. Here's their address. We tried talking to the guys you saw—didn't mention the targets, so don't worry—but they weren't much for sharing. Old loggers minding their own business. Or acting like it, anyway."

"Those kind usually make the worst busibodies." Aggie parked at the side of the road and checked the address against the map. It was impossible to tell just how isolated the Kreers were. She wished Charlie was here; she needed to run a little reconnaissance. Maybe Amiri would be good for that. She had not worked much with the shape-shifter, but she had heard stories. He was fast and silent. Deadly. The reputation did not jibe with his schoolteacher personality, but hey—all of them had their masks.

Either way, you'll just have to make do. Charlie will be here when he can.

Right. Only, she still couldn't shake her worry that he was in trouble. If only he had been in some kind of pseudo-physical form that she could have seen; a reading of his future would have been easy. She would have known, maybe, what was going to happen to him. Of course, her ability to gauge Charlie's future had been spotty from the beginning. Every time she looked at him, all she saw was sex. Which was great, but kind of pathetic.

She poked the map with her finger. "Based on this, the Kreers live fairly close to town, right across the Sauk River."

"Let's do a drive-by, then," Quinn said.

The town itself was small and plain; Aggie did not guess there were many jobs around. It reminded her of growing up in Idaho, surrounded by enough natural beauty to shake a stick at, but not much in the way of money to decorate that stick. Tourism and construction seemed to be the main sources of income; that, and logging. Aggie also saw a lot of churches. The parking lots were full. Services. Sunday.

She wondered which one Mrs. Kreer and her son attended.

"What time is it?" Aggie asked.

"Not quite eleven," Amiri said.

Aggie gave the car a little more gas. "The Kreers go to church. It's Sunday. They just might be out of the house."

Quinn made a clicking sound with his tongue. "Won't be for long. Not unless they take a lunch out."

Aggie glanced at the men. "So, you guys feeling lucky? Or how about just crazy?"

"I believe crazy is part of the job," Amiri said dryly. "Or so I was warned."

"Speak for yourself," Quinn told him. "This work is the only sane thing I've ever done."

Which might be true for Aggie, as well, but she did not want to think too hard on it. She'd had a normal upbringing, a stable family, but none of that had ever been enough—until she found Dirk & Steele. A job she loved. An insane job, with insane risks. She would not trade it for the world.

They crossed the Sauk River and drove up a road that curled higher into the mountain, looming white and sharp above their heads—immense, cold, its stark beauty intensified by blue sky and glittering sun. Warmth; Aggie tried to feel it through the window on her face, but sunlight did not compare to Charlie.

Where are you?

Ten minutes of driving, and they passed the Kreer's long driveway, a gravel track that curved out of sight inside the trees. Their name was painted on the mailbox. Aggie drove another minute, then pulled over on the narrow shoulder. Amiri began unbuttoning his shirt.

Aggie and Quinn stepped out of the car, listening hard. "I think we're clear," she said. "Amiri?"

The shape-shifter pushed open the back door on the side near the woods. He was completely naked. Golden light streamed down the long lines of his body, and Aggie watched, breathless, as fur rippled from his torso, his hard thighs. Claws burst from his fingernails.

And then Amiri was gone, and a cheetah stood in his place. The cat twitched its tail, gave them a look that was pure man, and then slipped silently into the forest. Aggie watched him leave, her vision shifting, and saw his future: the edge of a clearing, a small two-story white house. Different angles of the house, different variations. She did not see a car, but that meant nothing. One of the Kreers could still be at home.

"I never get tired of that," Quinn said.

"Ditto," Aggie said absently, as the vision cut off. She thought of Charlie. Wondered what he looked like. He said he was ugly. She doubted that. Different was never ugly. She sighed, and felt Quinn look at her.

"Aggie," he said quietly. "Is there anything wrong?"

"What do you mean?"

He just waited, and Aggie shook her head. "Everything's fine."

"I don't believe that. You're not telling me everything about this case."

Well, at least he had waited until Amiri was gone to pin her down—for what good that did him. "I can't talk about it, Quinn. There are . . . elements involved."

"And?"

"And that's it. It's not my story to tell."

Quinn leaned back against the car. "It's a man."

"What?"

"There's a man involved."

"No."

"Yes."

Aggie gritted her teeth. "Just leave it alone, okay? I haven't held anything back from you that could endanger us."

"That's because you don't know jack shit. I can tell. All you've got is a situation, maybe a vision, and now an address. Someone put you up to this."

Aggie said nothing. It was the truth, and she could not lie to Quinn. She could, however, divert—and she was prepared to do just that when warmth spread down her neck and back, a fire that flowed right down into her lower stomach. Aggie shuddered. Quinn said, "Are you okay?"

She was more than okay. Charlie was back, and the joy and relief she felt in that made her woozy. She was becoming a total basket case, and all because of a man . . . gargoyle . . . whatever.

"I'm fine," she said, and then, inside her head, *Welcome back.*

Deep inside her ear, a whisper, as Charlie said, "I won't be for long."

Why? Are you in trouble?

He did not answer. Aggie threw her frustration at him, all her fear and worry, and he said, "It means a lot to me that you care."

Then give me the truth.

"I can't."

"Aggie," Quinn said, more insistent this time.

"Wait," she said, and to Charlie: *I need to tell Quinn about you. This won't work if I don't.*

A lot of things would not work if she could never tell her friends about him. She had enough secrets in her life.

The warmth around her body disappeared, and in its place ran a sense of longing, homesickness, a memory of heat and light and goodness wrapped tight around her soul. She missed him. She did not understand why she felt that loss so strongly, but she did not question it. The feeling was too elemental, as natural as breathing, the beat of her heart. She could not distrust something that felt as innate and instinctive as the desire to live.

And then, right in front of her, Charlie materialized: a large man-shaped body of moving shadows. No face, no defining features of any kind. Just darkness. Quinn jumped, gasping.

Thank you, Aggie thought, and touched her partner's shoulder.

"It's okay," she said. Quinn did not relax. His fingers twitched—a futile attempt at telekinesis, maybe. She did not think anything like that could work on Charlie. Her vision shifted; she saw a probable immediate future of calm acceptance, even a smile or two. She breathed easier. "Quinn, really. This is Charlie. He's the person I couldn't tell you about. He's not dangerous."

"Depends on who you talk to," Charlie said, and held out his shadowed hand. Quinn stared at it, and then, with a wild look at Aggie, reached out slowly to shake. He flinched when he touched Charlie, who said, "Sorry about the grip. I don't have much of one."

Quinn's fingers passed through Charlie. "But you're warm."

"Um, yes," he said.

"Okay." Quinn took back his hand. "This is weird."

Aggie raised her brow. "We're psychic detectives. We work with shape-shifters."

"It's still weird. And hey, did you tell him about us?"

"I'm a mind reader in this form," Charlie said. "She didn't have to tell me."

"So, what are you?" Quinn asked Charlie, and Aggie could see his fear drowning in rabid curiosity. "Are you a ghost? Something else? Are you . . . I don't know, astral-projecting?"

"Not quite," Charlie said. "Close, though. But, um, we should go. Now. The house is empty. Or it was. I went there first to check on Emma."

Aggie did not hesitate. She jumped into the car and Quinn crawled into the backseat, forgoing the passenger side for expedience. Aggie gunned the engine and peeled back onto the road, roaring at high speed until she hit the Kreer driveway and pulled hard on the wheel. Quinn yelped, sliding. The back tires churned gravel.

"Amiri?" Quinn said, trying to get his balance.

"He'll have to catch up. Shouldn't be difficult."

And it wasn't. Aggie caught glimpses of a golden body inside the trees as they neared the end of the driveway. Running, running, and . . .

—she saw Amiri, naked, standing beside their over-turned vehicle, struggling to pull her bleeding body through the window. Quinn lay very still on the ground nearby—

The probabilities were high, but she saw another varia-tion: Amiri running beside their vehicle as it sped across the grass.

The trees ended on the edge of the clearing. Beyond, a green meadow cut by the driveway, and beyond that, the house from her earlier vision. Memories of the future, colliding in her head. Danger, danger. She glanced down at the speedometer. Sixty miles an hour. She slammed on the brakes.

"Shit!" Quinn hit the back of her seat. "What happened?"

"Something bad if I didn't stop. Look at the driveway ahead of us. Do you see anything out of the ordinary?"

Quinn kneeled on the seat and peered over her shoul-der out the windshield. "No."

"Neither do I. That's the problem."

She turned her attention on Quinn. Less than a minute from now he was still fine. In all the variations, fine. Though in thirty percent of them he stood outside the car, looking down at the ground. Gazing at—

"The driveway is booby-trapped," Aggie said. "Spike sticks. Would have blown out our tires, and at the speed I was going . . ."

"Are you kidding?"

"I wish."

"What the fuck is this? I thought these people were well-respected. Don't they get company?"

"Maybe they leave them only when they're out of the house. In this area, I doubt they're alone in doing that. People take security into their own hands. Hell, when I was growing up, our next door neighbor rigged a trip-wire in front of his door and kept bear traps on the lawn. He didn't want the kids kicking soccer balls on his grass."

"I need to talk to you about your childhood." Quinn looked around. "Where's Charlie?"

"He's probably at the house with Emma. At least, I hope he is."

Quinn grunted. "You like him."

"Yes."

"Uh-huh. You see those spike sticks?"

"No." Aggie drove off the driveway into the meadow and cut a wide swathe through the thick grass. "And I'm not going to take the time looking for them."

"They'll know someone's been here when they get back. You're leaving tracks."

"What are they going to do? Call the police?"

"No, but I hope that's what we're planning on doing."

"As soon as we've got Emma out of that house, we'll park our asses and dial nine-one-one."

"This is a terrible plan."

"Yes," Aggie agreed.

Amiri burst out of the woods, racing ahead of them to the house—a golden spotted arrow, lean and precise; surreal, magical. Aggie soaked it in, refusing to take the moment for granted. She was practicing for Charlie.

The Kreer home looked very clean and simple. A

farmhouse. Very little decoration. Red geraniums poked up out of the ground, along with some ferns. Aggie parked the car. Quinn got out first. Aggie sat and watched him and Amiri, tasting the future.

Nothing bad, nothing dangerous. She let out her breath, slow.

Amiri did not change shape. He slipped up the front steps and sniffed the door. Aggie followed him. She did not go for her gun. No need, yet. She did, however, pull some latex gloves from her pocket and snap them on. She handed a pair to Quinn. If she had her way, this house was going to be crawling with cops in less than an hour, and she didn't want any of their prints getting confused with the Kreers.

The front door was locked. Quinn pulled a pick set from his pocket and got to work. It was an old mechanism; he tripped it within seconds and the door swung open. Aggie made the men wait before going in. She watched their bodies and in all the variations saw them moving free and alive through the darkened home.

They entered a long hall lined with framed photographs. A staircase was on their right, and to their left, a few steps away, a sliding door. Aggie pushed it open and saw cameras.

Warmth surrounded her body. Charlie materialized. Amiri laid back his ears and growled.

"He's a friend," she said to him. Then to Charlie, "Where's Emma?"

"Follow me," he said.

"Quinn," Aggie prompted, and watched him pull a tiny digital camera from his pocket.

"On it," he said, and began snapping pictures. Amiri stayed with him. His eyes glowed as he watched Aggie leave with Charlie.

"I missed you," Charlie said when they were away from the others.

Unexpected. Her breath caught. "I missed you, too."

"This might be the last time we get to see each other."

Aggie stumbled. "What?"

Charlie said nothing. They reached a door that had duct tape around its edges and a rolled towel pushed up against it on the floor.

"Emma is expecting us," he said. "I told her you were coming."

"Charlie."

He moved, wrapping his shadowy arms around her body. Warmth sank deep into her skin, flooding her mouth—like a kiss. And then it was gone and Charlie said, "No time. Go to her."

Aggie choked back her questions; her eyes felt hot, wet. She didn't know why she wanted to cry, but her heart was aching, throbbing. She unlocked the basement door and jerked it open, tape ripping away from the walls. Light flooded the basement, and in front of her, waiting on the steps, was a little girl, blonde and pale and delicate. Her eyes, though—her eyes were old. Piercing.

"Emma," Charlie said. "This is Agatha. She's going to help you."

Aggie reached out her hand and waited for the girl to come to her. She knew Emma would; the variations of all probable futures were quite certain on that, but Aggie did not want to push. The girl had been pushed enough by adults and strangers.

Emma studied her face with grave intent, and took Aggie's hand. Her skin was cool and damp, but Aggie drew her from the darkness and tried not to show her surprise when the child wrapped her arms around her hips and hugged her tight.

"Thank you," the child murmured, and Aggie bent down and picked her up.

She was lighter than she looked; frail, almost. Her breath whistled in Aggie's ear. She smelled like cement, mold, decay.

Charlie stood unmoving, watching. Featureless and smooth, like a warrior wrapped in black cloth, head to foot. Aggie pushed her mind and saw a room with sand and blood, sand and statues, bloody stone, with bits of flesh hanging in threads and chunks, draped on wings.

She swayed and Charlie said, "No, don't. I don't want you to see."

"Charlie?" Emma asked, and he reached out to touch her face. The little girl closed her eyes and buried her face against Aggie's neck.

Later, she said to him, and then remembered his words, his kiss. There would be no later.

Where's your body? Aggie asked him as she carried Emma away from the basement.

"Agatha." His voice was quiet, right in her ear. Maybe they were talking mind to mind.

You tell me, Charlie.

"There's nothing you can do."

You let me be the judge of that.

"No. I won't risk you getting hurt." She wanted to kill him for saying that, and he said, "I'm already dead."

Again, *not* what she wanted to hear.

Quinn was still in the living room. He had pulled some tapes from the shelves, and had a folder full of photographs spread on the table. Aggie glimpsed flesh in those, and looked away—she did not want Emma to see any of that. Amiri prowled around the room, tail lashing the air. The little girl stiffened when she saw him, and Aggie whispered, "It's okay. He's a good cat."

"Are you guys ready?" Aggie asked, and Quinn nodded. His face was hard, eyes too bright—

—and then a shift—Quinn screaming at her to run, run, get out—

"They're coming," Aggie said.

"They're already here," Charlie corrected. Aggie went to the window and peered outside. She saw Mrs. Kreer and her son opening the trunk of their car. Caught sight of a rifle.

"Armed?" Quinn asked, and Aggie thought of those tire tracks she had left in the tall grass.

"Oh, yeah."

Quinn shook his head. "These people are too hard-core. Most in this business are cowards. They run. They lay low. They don't fight. Not like this, anyway. So they see a car out there. Maybe we're not in it, but that's no call for violence. They can't know for certain we're inside their home or that we're here to bust them."

"Logic doesn't matter, Quinn. They have something big to lose, not to mention they're a lot crazier than your average insane person. Shooting someone isn't going to mean much." Not when they had already killed Emma's mother, and maybe others over the years.

"It's worse than that," Charlie added, in a hard voice that sent chills up her spine. "They're not entirely human."

Everyone turned to look at him. Emma scrunched tighter against Aggie.

"You want to run that past me again?" she asked, slow.

"They've got demon in them," he said, and it was suddenly hard to hear him because he got quiet, like the air was too heavy for words.

Emma shrank in Aggie's arms; Aggie wanted to shrivel up alongside her. "Charlie. What, exactly, does that mean for us?"

"I don't know," he said. "But it's bad. It also explains why I haven't been able to read their thoughts."

"Aw, hell." Quinn clicked the safety off his gun. "Aggie, go to the back of the house and call the police. Charlie and Amiri, go with her. I'll take care of this."

"Quinn—" she said, and went blind as she saw blood run from his heart, his throat—and in another future— and in another—another—

"They'll kill you," she hissed. "I see it. Come with us, right now."

"No," he said, and gave her a hard look. "Fate is just probabilities. I'll take my chances."

The porch steps creaked. Emma whimpered. Aggie

hugged her tight and turned down the hall to the kitchen. She felt Amiri at her back. Charlie appeared in front of her, a shadow running. She reached into her pocket for her cell phone, but before she could begin dialing, a gunshot rang out behind her. Charlie blinked out of sight.

Amiri growled, using his body to push Aggie against the wall. She listened hard; ahead of her, she heard a creak. Mouth dry, she set Emma gently on the floor and held her finger up to the girl's mouth. Emma nodded gravely. Aggie looked at Amiri, gesturing with her chin. The shape-shifter blinked once and leaned protectively against the little girl. Safe. The probabilities were safe. Aggie put away her phone and reached for her gun.

Charlie reappeared beside her. Bone and blood loomed around him, golden sand, a woman with red hair and red lips and a red dress . . .

There's someone in the kitchen, she told him. *Can you distract him?*

"I've tried that before," he whispered in her ear. "They don't see me."

Quinn?

"Alive. Tracking."

Taking his chance with fate. Something Aggie needed to do for herself.

She held up her gun and slinked down the hall toward the kitchen. Charlie disappeared, but she knew he was close. Warmth pushed against her ear and he said, "It's the mother. She has an ax. She's waiting by the entrance to the kitchen."

Perfect. Just great.

"You have bullets," Charlie said. "Shoot her and be done with it."

We can't kill them, Aggie said. *We do that and we'll just make trouble for ourselves with the law. Not to mention the Kreers might have useful information about other victims, maybe people in their network, if they have one. We have to—*

But whatever she was going to say died as a high screech cut the air and a body flung itself from the kitchen. Aggie cried out, squeezing off a round into the wall that did nothing to slow the old woman, who swung her whistling ax hard and fast. Details died; all Aggie could register was a blur made of pure fury, a mouth that flashed white and sharp, and she felt Amiri behind her, pushing Emma away as the child cried out a word that was high and sweet and not quite a scream. For a moment the air shimmered—Mrs. Kreer faltered—and Aggie took the chance offered and dove toward the old woman, rushing and rolling past her. She smelled mold, mustiness . . . and then the air cleared as she entered the kitchen, spinning on her feet.

"Come on," Aggie snarled, goading the old woman. "Come and get me."

Get me, get me. Only me and not the kid. Don't follow Emma.

Mrs. Kreer hesitated, glancing over her shoulder as the tip of Amiri's tail disappeared around the corner in the hall. She began to follow them and Aggie thought, *Fuck it all.* She aimed her gun at the old woman's leg and pulled the trigger, feeling a grim satisfaction as the bullet slammed through the meat of Mrs. Kreer's thigh, making her stagger, lean against the wall.

But the woman did not fall. She did not drop the ax.

"Oh, shit," Aggie muttered, as the old woman turned to face her. For the first time she was able to get a good look at her face. Mrs. Kreer appeared the same as Aggie remembered from her visions; clean and coiffed, with high pale cheeks and a small wrinkled mouth. She wore a black sweater over a white turtleneck. Long embroidered pants ended neatly above her ankles. Mrs. Kreer: ordinary woman, pillar and post and proud mother. Only her eyes gave her away. Aggie had never seen anything quite that cold or black.

"Don't move," Aggie said. "I will shoot you again."

But Mrs. Kreer moved and Aggie was not surprised, because that was what the future held in all its variations—fighting, the old woman fighting like her life depended on the kill—and when Mrs. Kreer brought down the ax, Aggie was ready. She leapt backward, probabilities spinning, calculating the future even as she danced across the kitchen floor, dodging the whirling steel of Mrs. Kreer's weapon. Her palm was sweaty around the gun, but she stayed patient, moving and moving and—

The future shifted; Aggie's foot hit the trail of blood dripping from the old woman's leg and the floor disappeared as she went up and up—

—and slammed into the ground so hard she stopped breathing.

Mrs. Kreer darted forward, but not before Aggie mustered enough strength to kick out with her feet, catching her in the gut. The old woman made a woofing sound, but collected herself faster than Aggie. Struggling to stand, Aggie saw—*wild eyes, swinging blades, screaming and yelling and blood everywhere, blood and meat*—but then a gunshot split the air outside the house, she heard a shout—Charlie—and the future changed as she felt his warmth surround her.

He materialized in front of Mrs. Kreer—shadows gathering, swarming like bats to make a body—but the woman showed no indication she saw him. Yet, when she lunged forward to attack Aggie, she passed through him and a curious thing happened. Mrs. Kreer swayed. She lost her balance. Her grip around the ax handle loosened. Aggie darted forward. Distracted or ill, the old woman could not defend herself quickly enough and Aggie slammed the butt of her gun against that graying head, dropping her to her knees and stunning her long enough to wrench the ax out of her hand. The old woman began to fight back, snarling, but Aggie hit her again in the head, knocking her flat on the ground and immediately stomping on that wounded leg, grinding her heel into the bullet hole, savoring the anger in her heart as she made Mrs. Kreer writhe.

"Agatha." Charlie appeared beside her. "Agatha, stop."

She did not want to, but she understood why she should. She eased up on the old woman, but only for a moment. Aggie reached into her pocket for plastic cuffs and tied the monstrous woman's hands behind her back. Did the same to her feet, arching her like David Yarns, hogtied, ready to be put on the spit and cooked and turned, cook and turned. No running for this one. No more hurting children.

Mrs. Kreer's future was done.

CHAPTER SIX

Quinn was alive. Despite all the variable futures that had him bleeding or hurt or screaming, he was alive. Lucky man. When he entered through the back door off the kitchen, Aggie had her back turned. All she heard was a creak, a step. Scary. She spun and almost shot him.

"Bang, bang," she said. She put down her gun, clicking the safety back on. "That scared me. You okay?'

"Better than I was three minutes ago. Kid is down. I got him tied up in the backyard."

"Tough?"

"Not really, though there was a moment or two." Quinn tapped his head. "Luckily for me, I have magic bullets."

Telekinetic bullets. Aggie smiled.

Beside her, Charlie drifted down to the ground and crouched over Mrs. Kreer. The woman's eyes were open, staring. Aggie did not like to look at that cold gaze; there was something alien about it, distant. It gave her the creeps, made her stomach turn. What could compel a person do such things to a child? It was inexplicable, and she thought about what Charlie had said. That Mrs. Kreer was part demon.

"Yes," he said softly. "I can see it in her now. I was not looking before. It's very weak, though. Just a trace. That would be enough, though, to influence her behavior."

"I thought you said those things were gone from the earth."

"I thought they were. Some . . . must have remained. Evolved, perhaps. I only recognize this much out of instinct."

Quinn stirred. "Are you talking about the 'D' word?"

"Yeah," Aggie said. "Though it's bullshit, giving them an excuse for all the things they did."

"No," Charlie said. "I'm not saying that."

"No?" Aggie wished he had a face. She wasn't even sure why he floated around in a human body. *Be a cloud,* she thought. *A bird.*

And then, *Don't leave me.*

"Aggie," he began, but she shook her head.

"You say Kreer and her boy have some demon in them? I'll buy it. But who's to say I don't have some demon in me, too? I might even have more than them. Maybe seeing the future isn't just some freak of nature, but a freak of some ancestor. But you don't see me out murdering and molesting."

Charlie stirred. "I believe we already had this conversation, and I'll admit I was wrong. Some choices are products of nothing but pure nature, Agatha. Maybe some people *are* born wrong."

Aggie wanted to disagree—wanted to so badly because it was principle, the building block of her life that fate was built upon variations, variables, all playing each other to mix new futures and ways of being. Choice, choosing well, creating a good life that was a product of small moments . . .

But to be faced with the possibility that destiny might be inescapable—that the future was already written in only one way, with one outcome—and to have that outcome be so dark and destructive . . .

It scared her. Because if people could be born whose only purpose was to hurt others, then what did that say for the future?

"That there are also those who are born to do good," Charlie said quietly.

A nice thought, but Aggie was not convinced. She did not want to be convinced of the alternative to choice, to free will. Aggie looked down upon the old woman, who stared at her, mouth pursed, a fine shudder racing through her body. Maybe she realized the shit she was in; maybe she was angry or scared or just plain cold. Aggie steeled herself and kneeled. Bent close.

"You look so ordinary," she whispered. "But you're rotten on the inside, and you *chose* to be that way. Maybe you *do* have some bad mojo in your blood, maybe you got a bigger darkness in your heart than some, but I won't let you rest your laurels on that. You dug your own grave, Mrs. Kreer. You buried your own heart."

"My son," said the old woman. "What have you done with him?"

"Not nearly enough," Quinn spoke up. "But I can change that, if you like."

Mrs. Kreer sucked in her breath, making a hissing sound that sent chills up Aggie's back.

"Right," she said, standing. "I need some air."

There was a scuffling sound from the hall; Amiri emerged from the shadows. Emma had her hand on his back, buried in his fur. Charlie appeared before them in an instant, blocking her view of Mrs. Kreer. Aggie joined him and swept the girl up in her arms. Carrying her down the hall and out the front door into the sunlight. Emma covered her eyes.

Aggie felt warmth on her back, another kind of sun, and Charlie said, "I need to go soon."

"You said that a while ago."

"And I've had far more time here than I should have. It won't last."

Aggie carried Emma down to the rental car and placed her in the backseat. Quinn joined them and said, "Amiri is standing guard on the big bad momma. I'm going to head out back and check on her spawn."

Aggie dug into her pocket and pulled out her phone. Tossed it to him. "Police still haven't been called. Be sure to warn them about the spike sticks."

"I'll take care of it," he said, and walked away, dialing as he went.

Charlie kneeled in front of Emma. He touched her small hands.

"You were very brave," he said to the girl. "I am so proud of you."

"My mommy," Emma said.

Charlie hesitated. Emma looked away. Aggie's eyes felt all hot again, but she swallowed down the ache and said, "I need to talk to Charlie for a minute, okay? We'll be right over there where you can see us."

Emma raised her gaze; old eyes, haunted eyes. She glanced at Charlie's shadow and said, "You're leaving."

"I don't have a choice," he said, and Aggie heard the pain in his voice, the hoarse hush.

"Okay," Emma said, and reached out to hug him. Her arms passed through his body, but Charlie wrapped her up in himself and she whispered, "I'll miss you."

"I'll miss you, too," he said. "You changed my life."

Emma began to cry. So did Aggie. Charlie pulled away, gliding fast over the meadow away from the car. Aggie stumbled after him, wiping her eyes.

"Charlie," she called after him. "Charlie, stop!"

He did, waiting for her to catch up, and though he was not solid, Aggie still pressed against his apparition, soaking in his heat, his presence, the comfort of knowing he was there. In all her life, she had never felt such a need to simply *be* with a person; but here she was, and her heart was breaking because—*I need to breathe, I need to eat, I need to love.*

"You'll find someone new," Charlie said, rough. "You'll forget me. You didn't know me long enough for anything else. We were barely friends."

"We could have been best friends," Aggie said, shaking. "I think, maybe, we already are."

His body seemed to contract in on itself—at first she thought he was going to disappear, but it was nothing; a shudder maybe. One to mirror her own. She wished she could see his real face . . . and then thought perhaps it did not matter. *This* was Charlie. The real him.

"Agatha," he whispered. "I wish things could be different."

"Tell me," she breathed. "Tell me why they aren't."

"I don't own myself," he said, and if there had been pain in his voice earlier, it was nothing compared to now: broken and hollow, dull and dead as stone. "I'm . . . locked up. My brothers, too. All of us kept, like animals."

Aggie thought of her future memory, the sand and the woman, and Charlie said, "Yes, her."

"Why? How?" How, in this modern world, with so many eyes, so many ears?

"How was Emma taken? And that boy you saved? The most terrible abuses happen in plain sight, and no one sees. Hearts go blind. Do you know why, Agatha? Because it takes courage to help others. More courage than anything, because it means opening yourself, dedicating yourself to something that is beyond your life. Easier to just . . . walk on by. Ignore and pretend. It's safer that way."

"You didn't do that."

"But I have. Maybe I will again. I hope not. I don't want to be that man anymore." He stopped, pressing her tight within himself. "That's not something you need to worry about. You, Agatha, are a champion. True blue. My huntress."

And you are my dark knight, she thought, *my mysterious companion.* She could not say the words out loud. They felt intimate, somehow. As though to say them in the air would be exposing a part of her that was raw. Thoughts, though . . . thoughts were still reality. And she meant them. She really did.

"Mysterious companion," Charlie echoed. "Dark knight. Maybe I'm not quite Batman material, but I like that. I like being that for you."

Her mouth curved. "And the woman who keeps you? You haven't told me why. Or how."

"Because she can. Because she wants something from my brothers. Their obedience, their pride, their strength to draw on in order to make herself more powerful."

"But you're here. You're able to dream your way out."

"No," Charlie said. "This—me, what you're looking at—is not a dream. It's my soul, Aggie. My spirit, my consciousness, whatever you want to name it. And the only way . . . the only way for me to separate my soul from my body is through death."

Understanding was slow. Her mind tasted the words, rolling them around, horror growing as she sounded out the concept in her mind. Death. His death. It was impossible.

"No," Charlie said. "Every time I came to see you or Emma, I had to die first."

"But when you left . . ."

"It was because my body came back to life, calling back my soul. My kind are hard to kill, Agatha. We . . . regenerate our vital organs. Call it a . . . a consequence of our early purpose, which was to battle creatures more powerful than ourselves. It gave us an edge."

"But if you have to die in order to be here, then how? Who does it?"

"The witch—the woman keeping me. She would . . . cut out my heart. All my vital organs. Doing it that way takes longer, so I could stay with you and Emma. But she found out. Got angry. To be here this time, I . . . had to do it myself."

Aggie choked. "Why? Why would you put yourself through that?"

"How could I not?" His hands passed over hers and warmth rolled up her arms into her chest, her heart. "Death really wasn't a high price to pay."

She couldn't talk. It was too much—Charlie dying, Charlie murdered.

Charlie killing himself.

Aggie shook her head, helpless, and Charlie said, "You don't have to find the words. I hear you."

He heard her. He heard everything. She wanted to say, *Don't go, please, we only just got started,* but it was no good begging him to stay. Instead, because she had to say something, anything to fill the silence inside her breaking heart, she whispered, "You're warm."

"Yes," he murmured. "I can be warm, even as a dream."

"You're no dream. Don't keep calling yourself that. You're real. You're more than idle fantasy."

She wondered if he smiled; the warmth around her body intensified. "My body is quite some distance away. I'm also dead. I think to call me anything but a dream—"

"Ghost. A big hulking scary ghost."

"Scary."

"Terrifying. My knees knock when you're around."

"I'll take that as a compliment."

"Yeah? You like that?"

"I do," he said, and then, softer, "Take care of yourself, Agatha. I wish I could be here to watch over you. Maybe . . . maybe I'll get another chance one day. Just to say hello."

It was the wistfulness in his voice that got her; the sense that he had already given up. Anger threaded through her gut; pure stubbornness. "I don't live on maybes and hellos, Charlie. Not this time, anyway. I'm making my own future."

"Agatha."

"No. Where's your body?"

"She'll kill you."

"She can try. And if you won't tell me, then I'll do it the hard way. You forget who I work for. I'll figure it out."

"Agatha."

"Charlie." Her voice broke on his name, and inside her heart she begged, she screamed, she threw her thoughts at him and raged. She refused to let him suffer; she refused it with all the power of her heart. Because it was wrong, because he deserved better, because *she* deserved better than to be given just a taste of some perfect dream, some possible mysterious future, and then have it snatched away like so much candy in the fist of a bully. No, absolutely not. She would not allow it. Short time together, maybe—but that was enough to know she wanted more, that she would do anything to get it, to see him safe. Killing himself, murder—that was torture, plain and simple. And he had endured it for her and Emma. The least she could do was return the favor.

Charlie touched her face, drawing near, wrapping his spirit so tight around her own that she thought she must be a caterpillar and he was the cocoon, and together they would merge and transform into something beautiful.

"Somewhere in Glasgow," he whispered. "But that's a fool talking. I'm crazy. Don't try."

"Then don't leave me."

"Agatha," he said again, and she felt his soul press upon her mouth, infusing her with radiance and fire.

And then he pulled away, far away, and she cried out, hands scrabbling the air.

She could not hold him.

When he opened his eyes the witch was there. She sat in the sand beside Charlie, cross-legged, covered in blood. His blood. The knife lay across her thighs.

"I should cut off your head now and be done with it," she said. "You are such a pain."

"You extended my death," he realized.

"I did," she said. "I was overcome by a moment of weakness. I saw the lengths you went to secure your own exit, and could not help but admire your dedication. Death by repeated gouging and impalement? And on your brothers, too. That is rather sick."

"Just a bit," Charlie admitted. "You didn't give me much choice."

"I suppose not. I also underestimated you. Which is why your brothers will be sleeping outside your prison from now on."

Charlie looked. She had already moved them. They crouched just beyond the circle in the sand. Their bodies were still stained from his blood.

The witch smiled. "Love makes such fools of men, human or not."

Charlie said nothing. Love had not made a fool of him. Love had given him everything. He had never imagined it could be that way, that he could be sustained and strengthened by his love for another, his compassion. But yes, truth. He loved. And if he never was able to see Agatha or Emma again, he had that much, the knowledge and the memory.

Agatha is coming for you.

She would never find him. Glasgow was a big city, and he had been deliberately vague. He could not lie to her—not when he wanted so badly to tell her the absolute truth—but he also could not risk her life for his. It wasn't worth it.

"You're thinking of that woman," said the witch. "I can see it on your face."

Charlie sighed. "What do you want?"

"So much," said the witch. "I'm having another guest tonight."

"Is this also someone who sees you as an asset?"

"Yes," she said. "And I want to impress her. I was thinking steak. Fresh meat." She raised her knife and turned it this way and that, so the light rolled off parts of the dirty blade.

"Don't get your hopes up," said the witch, raising her knife. "I'm not going to kill you."

"If only," Charlie said, and then braced himself. He wished he could fight. He hated being so helpless.

She cut him, deep.

If it had not been for Emma, Aggie might have remained sitting in that meadow until the cows came home; the sky went dark, and birds forgot to sing. As it was, she remembered that there was someone who needed her, someone whose pain was greater than hers, and she put her heart aside to return to the rental car and the little girl within.

"I saw him go," Emma said. Her eyes were red. Aggie wished she had a doll to give her. Something to hold on to. She ended up giving herself, sitting down on the seat beside her, wrapping a gentle arm around the child's narrow shoulders.

"I'm all alone," Emma said. "My mommy is gone."

And she began crying again, this time in earnest. Aggie wanted to march inside the house and put a bullet in Mrs. Kreer's head. Her son, too. Maybe more than bullets for him. She had not seem him in the flesh yet, but she remembered the hunger in his eyes and knew. Just . . . knew. It made her sick.

"Don't worry," Aggie promised. "I'll take care of you."

And she would, somehow. She did not know what that meant, only that saving one life was not enough, not if that life got dumped by the wayside and handed over to the system. Emma might be crying now, but that was good, healthy. The kid still had strength, still had . . . something more inside her that was not yet broken. Despite everything, despite all the hardship, Emma was still strong. Aggie could see that in her eyes.

And another reason to fight: Charlie loved the child. Aggie had to do right by him, too.

In the distance, she heard sirens. As Aggie and Emma waited for the police; the little girl continued to weep. The big girl wept, too, but she tried to keep it on the inside, where her heart was howling.

Amiri slunk out of the house. Aggie saw him and pushed his clothes out the back door, distracted Emma while he silently changed shape some distance away, and put them on. The little girl twitched when she saw his human face and body, but Amiri shocked Agatha by rolling up his sleeve and showing off his arm, which suddenly rippled golden with fur.

"I am a fairy tale," he said gently, and Emma nodded with grave understanding.

She got another surprise when the police arrived— the FBI was with them. In fact, there was more of a federal presence than a local one, and Aggie thought, *Roland, you are a devil.*

The cars stopped, surrounding them. Men and women piled out. Emma leaned against Aggie. An agent approached; a tall, spare man. Blond hair, nice face. She recognized him; he had been at the crash scene only yesterday—a lifetime distant. He was going to see a lot of very bad things in the next five minutes; the probabilities were quite high.

He glanced at Emma and Amiri, and then to Aggie said, "Ms. Durand? I'm Agent Warwick, with the FBI. Maybe you remember me. We got a tip that, uh, *you* had a tip. Related to the David Yarns case you assisted on yesterday afternoon."

"Assisted" was generous; Dirk & Steele's help on high profile cases like Yarns's was usually billed as a tip-off or private-citizen intervention—which didn't bother anyone at the agency, just as long as the job got done. The feds and local PD could have all the ego bolstering they wanted.

"Yes," she said to Warwick. "That's correct. We came out here on an investigation and discovered evidence of an abuse in progress. We . . . took the child out of the situation and, given what we saw, secured the perpetrators—a woman named Mrs. Kreer and her son, Andrew."

"And this is the child?" Warwick asked carefully. Emma gave him a long, level look that was far too old for her years.

"They kept me in the basement," she said. "They made me do things."

Which was really all the testimony anyone should need. Warwick swallowed hard, nodding. Aggie told him where to find Emma's kidnappers—as well as Quinn—and after a swift, "Stay here. We'll need to take your statements," Warwick jogged off and began coordinating their approach into the house.

"Efficient," Amiri commented. He sat in the grass, arms braced on his knees.

"Yeah," Aggie said. "Although I know who to blame for that."

Her phone rang. She answered it with a sigh and Roland said, "Perfect timing."

"You called the FBI?"

"The FBI called *me*. I only happened to mention you were out of the state, investigating another potential connection to David Yarns. And gee fucking whiz, they were more than happy to assist."

"Convenient. How did you even know where to send them? The exact address, I mean. You must have given them something more than just Darrington."

"Do you remember that I was going to send Max down to the precinct to attempt a surface scan of David's mind? Turns out there *was* a connection between your pervert of yesterday and your pervert of today. A big one."

"She's the boss," Aggie said softly, making the intuitive leap.

"Maybe, possibly. You'll need to tell me one day how you knew."

"Ghosts and angels," she murmured. "More mystery than you can shake a stick at."

Aggie disentangled herself from Emma, and with a quick, "I'll be right back," walked a very short distance away. Amiri inched closer to the girl. Aggie saw Emma place a tentative hand on his shoulder.

"Good kitty," she said.

"Roland," Aggie said. "We have to do something about Emma, the victim in this. She deserves better than an FBI social worker and foster care."

"Doesn't she have family?"

"Her mother's dead. I never talked to—I never talked about whether she had other people to take care of her. I've got a feeling, though, that she's pretty much alone."

"Shit. Aggie—"

"No," she said. "Find a way."

"For what? Do *you* want her?"

Aggie swallowed hard, thinking about the possibilities, what that would mean. She looked at the girl and saw the future fan out, and for a moment it was like seeing her own fate, her own probabilities; like last night in her home, being slammed with an image of this girl in need. Only now, the girl in her head still had need, but different. Just as important.

"I don't know," Aggie said, quiet. "But she needs something more than what the system can give her. I know it."

There was silence on the other end, and then, "Okay. I'll figure it out, make some calls. That's why we have those expensive lawyers, right? We'll make it happen. In some variation. But Emma will have to leave with the FBI today. That can't be helped."

"I know," Aggie said. "Thank you, Roland."

"Whatever. You and the boys, though . . . good work. Really fucking good work."

"Good boss."

"That's right," he said, and hung up.

Aggie went back to the car and snuggled up next to Emma. She thought about both their futures. Amiri sat still. Quinn trudged over from around the house and joined them.

He took one look at Aggie's face and said, "You okay?"

"No," she said. "But I will be. I need to go away after this."

Emma stirred. "Charlie."

"Yes."

"He's my ghost," Emma said. "My friend."

"He's mine, too," Aggie said. "But he's lost now, and I need to go find him. I need to do for him what he did for you. Take him away from the dark place."

"Can I come with you?" Emma asked.

Aggie shook her head. "You'll need to go with the police today, but that won't be for long. You'll have a better place to live. Safe, with good people."

"I'm scared," Emma said.

"I know." Aggie put a hand on the child, soothing, calming. "You have a right to be, but we'll take care of you. I promise." She gestured to her colleague, who had just appeared. "This, Emma, is my friend Quinn Dougal. He gets kind of cranky, but he's a good person."

"You're little," Emma said to him, with the simple honesty of the very young. "But you don't look like a kid."

"No," Quinn said kindly. "I'm a bit older than that. Humans just come in all sizes, that's all."

Emma still clutched Amiri's shoulder.

"What's your name?" she asked him, and he told her, and she liked that.

Time passed. The FBI and police took their statements, and then they took Mrs. Kreer and her son. And sometime after that, as the afternoon stretched into evening, they took Emma.

Before the child left, she reached out with her skinny arms and pulled Aggie in for a hug. Emma smelled better after being away from the basement—like sunlight and sweet grass—and when Aggie pulled back to look into her eyes she saw a hint of green that she had not noticed before. A flickering light that was pure and shot full of spring and leaf. Otherworldly, almost.

"You'll find him," Emma whispered, with a conviction that was quiet, more confident than her years. "You'll find Charlie."

"And when I do?" Aggie found herself asking, compelled by strength of the child's voice, the heartbreaking sincerity of her old, old gaze.

Emma brushed her fingers against the corners of Aggie's eyes, and for a moment the air seemed to shimmer, and the child said, "You'll see."

And that was the end of it. Aggie watched her go and felt like another piece of her heart was breaking. She had never realized she could feel so much for others in such a short amount of time. Charlie, Emma. There was something wrong with her. She needed to turn something off.

No, she told herself. *Don't you dare. Your isolation is over. All you need now is courage.*

"What are you going to do?" Quinn asked, coming up to stand beside her. He took her hand and held it.

"I'm going to find him," Aggie said, glancing down at her partner, wondering if she would ever be able to tell him the whole unbending truth. "One way or another."

Quinn and Amiri returned to California that evening on the private jet, but Aggie did not go with them. She drove back down to Seattle. She did a lot of thinking. She did a lot of listening to herself.

When she got to the airport, she bought a ticket to Scotland.

CHAPTER SEVEN

It took her a month to find him, and even then it was by accident.

Or not. Aggie was never quite certain.

From Seattle to Chicago, and from Chicago to Glasgow, a hop, skip, and a jump. She entered that city and saw that Charlie had been right: it was big. But if a gargoyle could die and leave his body to save a girl and fall in love, and if shape-shifters could walk the earth, changing from animal to man while psychics banded together under the auspices of a detective agency with a really cheesy name, then *anything* was possible. Anything at all.

She parked herself in a nice hotel on the edge of George Square, the heart of the city. People massed, the crowds ebbed and flowed, and from a bench she could watch faces and futures, seeking always blood and sand,

and a man who was not a man but something more than human.

She listened to the futures as she walked, too, which was how she spent most of her days. Up at the crack of dawn, and then down to the street where she would stay out until all hours—much to the chagrin of the hotel staff, who always said when she came back through the lobby, "Please, dear, it's not safe, this city isn't safe for young women at night." And Aggie knew this, but no place in the world was safe for anyone, and she kept on prowling, looking, searching.

There were endless paths in Glasgow; the buildings were old and the streets older, the architecture rich and fascinating. She went to Glasgow Cathedral and the Necropolis, hunting for witches amongst the holy and the dead; at the University of Glasgow she talked to historians, delved deep into libraries for clues on haunts and gargoyles, found legend, lore, wondered sometimes, too, if the men she spoke to were not gargoyles themselves, hiding in plain sight. She scanned the local newspapers for anything out of the ordinary—strange deaths, odd sightings, lights in the sky—and she sat in cafés and pubs and watched and watched and watched.

And even then, she got lucky. Or not.

A month after Aggie arrived in Glasgow, she found the witch sitting at an outdoor café behind the Gallery of Modern Art, sipping tea. She knew it was the witch because she recognized the face. Aggie, standing on the sidewalk, temporarily lost her mind. Froze up. She saw in her head a pleasant modern kitchen, something cooking in a pot. She did not see anyone who could be Charlie, but perhaps that was yet too far ahead in the future.

But there it was: *her*. Aggie did not know what to make of the witch. She was, by any definition, a lovely woman: thick brown hair, a delicate thin face punctuated by luscious red lips and two black eyes. A little doll. Given what Aggie knew of her, she was not that impressed.

Aggie waded past waiters and diners and sat down at the witch's table. The woman did not look at her right away; she read a book of poetry by Carl Sandburg. Aggie waited. She was patient. She watched the woman's shifting future.

The witch finished her tea. " 'Broken-face Gargoyles.' It's a very good poem. Have you ever read it?"

"No," Aggie said.

"Oh, you should. It's quite beautiful." The witch put down her book and looked Aggie in the eye. She had a powerful gaze, but Aggie remembered Mrs. Kreer, and this was not as bad.

"You smell like him," said the witch.

"That's some nose you've got," Aggie replied.

The witch's lips thinned. "I was referring to energies, darling. Although you *do* have an odor. Not bathing much lately, are you."

"I've been busy."

"Yes, I know. You're in love with an associate of mine."

"How interesting you know that. I've been looking for him."

"I know that, too. Would you like me to take you to him?"

"If I say yes, will I be writing my own death?"

"Oh," said the woman, and her red lips curled, just so, like petals. "I can think of something far more interesting than mere death.'

"That's good," Aggie said. "Let's go."

The witch lived in the Merchant City, a place where Aggie had spent quite some time. Apparently the wrong time, because she certainly had not seen anything that would indicate a witch keeping house with a captive gargoyle.

But there, at a warehouse Aggie remembered passing on at least three separate occasions, the witch pulled out a set of keys and said, *"Mi casa es su casa."*

"That's quite all right," Aggie said. "I think you have enough people in your home."

The witch smiled—*and her teeth are white and sharp, and the pot bubbles as she says, "Have a bite, you'll like this, since gargoyles are to your taste*—and a shift, a—*knife that she holds*—and—*blood*—and pushed open the door. Aggie, blinking, reading violence and sickness and death, followed her up the stairs.

The home was surprisingly mundane. The kitchen was dressed in steel and black and gray, with splashes of red tile; fruits and vegetables covered a long wood table. Something boiled on the stove. Aggie remembered *gargoyle,* and her stomach hurt.

"So," said the witch, as she put away her book and

purse. "Let's get down to business. I assume you've come to fetch Charlie."

"Yes," Aggie said, and the future spun yet more blood, more viscera; the knife in the witch's hand was long and sharp. The probabilities were high. Aggie was going to die very soon.

The witch made a humming sound. Aggie wondered just what the limits of her powers were, but she decided the woman was not a mind reader when she said, "I can't imagine what you plan to offer me—or even if Charlie would go with you. He has his brothers to think of, and I simply won't allow them to leave. It's a matter of pride."

"I don't know anything about his brothers," Aggie said, "but I do understand Charlie's loyalty."

"Yes, I suppose you do." The witch wandered to the stove. "Are you hungry? I think you might like this. Charlie . . . made it."

Aggie thought, *I am going to fucking rip you apart.* But instead she said, "No, thank you."

The witch smiled. She opened a drawer and picked up a knife, pressed the tip of it against her palm until she bled. She spoke a sharp word. Aggie felt the hairs on her body lift. Aggie saw in her head—*bullets hitting the witch's chest and falling harmlessly to the ground—the knife darting quick at her neck, blood spurting—her heart in the pot, cooked with gargoyle in a soup*—and variations of the same: Aggie fighting, Aggie screaming, Aggie being killed. The witch always deflecting her blows with a smile.

Except for one time. One precious variation.

"You're scared," said the witch. "I can see it on your face."

"Yes," Aggie said. "You scare me. Does that make you happy?"

"I suppose so, though it also disappoints me. I . . . studied you, when I discovered Charlie's fascination. Very tough woman. Macho, even. Take no prisoners. And you are different"—she tapped her head—"up here. All of your friends are different."

Aggie said nothing. The witch tilted her head. "I have been entertaining guests lately, people who are like you. They also work for an organization. For a time, I thought perhaps yours was one and the same."

Aggie buried her emotions, the conflict those words stirred in her. Only recently had the agents at Dirk & Steele discovered they were not alone. The other side— and there appeared to be several groups, all rivals—was dangerous. And if one of them was trying to recruit this woman, who was so patently cruel and powerful . . .

We're in deep shit. They're one step ahead of us, and we don't even know we're in a race.

"Where's Charlie?" Aggie asked. "I want to see him."

"A kiss before dying?"

Aggie did not answer. The future had suddenly gone dark inside her head. Book closed, probabilities lost. Her gift had copped out on her, and again, at the worst time.

Remember what you said? You're making your own future now.

Faith, then. Faith, and the memory of what she did have.

"Charlie," Aggie said again, and did not look at the knife.

The witch smiled. She pointed to a door set in the stone wall off the kitchen. Aggie waited for a moment, then walked to door. Glanced one more time at the witch, who stood watching like a perfect deadly little doll. The future lay quiet.

Aggie opened the door. She was not sure what to expect, she had caught only glimpses before, but what lay before her stole her breath.

The entire floor of the room was covered in sand. Inside the sand, a circle. Beyond the circle, three stone statues of winged creatures, and inside, at the center, curled in a ball was another body, this one made of flesh. Aggie saw wings and silver arms, long silver legs, and part of a hard stomach. The face was hidden, but she saw wild hair, silver and blue and black.

She stepped into the room, walked to the circle and stopped. Instinct. She did not think she would survive crossing that line in the sand.

"Charlie," she said, and her voice was loud. It echoed, though the room was not large.

The body stirred, uncurled. Red eyes peered at her from a face that was strong and bony and utterly inhuman.

But not ugly. Charlie had been so wrong.

"Agatha," he whispered, and it was odd, so odd, to hear his voice—that lovely gentle voice—come from a real face, a moving mouth. She wanted to touch that mouth; she wanted to press herself close and feel his warmth, his breath, his voice in her ear. No more illusion. Just flesh and blood.

Relief poured through her muscles; her knees trembled, but she did not fall down. She did not cry. She wanted to do both those things, but she felt the witch behind her and she could not afford weakness. She looked into Charlie's eyes and she tried to tell him, tried to make him understand what she felt, and he nodded, slowly. She saw the same message in his eyes—and *God,* it was good to see his eyes, no matter their color. It was good to see his face and not some shadow, some replica. The truth was so much more beautiful. A perfect accompaniment to a brave and lovely soul.

"So there is your gargoyle," said the witch. "Are you disappointed? Were you expecting a prince?"

Aggie smiled at Charlie. She did not bother answering. It was a waste of breath. Charlie's silver lips curved upward. He stood, slow, and his height was immense. He folded his wings around his body; they covered him like an iridescent cape made of silver skin and pink veins and light bone.

But there was terrible fear in his eyes. As much fear as love, and Aggie looked down, away, because she could not bear to see it. She turned to face the witch.

"What do I have to do?" she asked.

"No," said Charlie in a hard voice. "No bargains."

"He's right," said the witch. "I don't bargain. And I am going to kill you. I just wanted Charlie to see it with his own eyes. He's such a hopeful creature. I think he really did believe you would find him."

"He was right to believe," Aggie said, and she felt him stand directly behind her. She imagined his warmth spreading out through the circle against her back, embracing her body down to her soul.

The witch played with her knife. "If I was a better person, this would be the moment when I let you both go. I would change my ways and become good, and this would be my first act of redemption."

"It's not too late for that," Charlie said.

"I think it is," the witch said. And then, to Aggie: "I made a spell. You might have seen me do it. You cannot hurt me."

"I know," Aggie said. "I wasn't going to try."

The witch swayed close. "You have a gun in your pocket. You won't use it? Not a bullet, then? Not a fist in my face? No scratching and clawing to save yourself or the gargoyle you love?" She studied Aggie's face. "I didn't expect you to be a quitter. You're committing suicide."

Aggie thought about fighting, using her gun. Violence would be easy.

But it would also be the wrong choice. She had seen the bullets fall and her throat cut and her body eaten. No amount of fighting would save her from that. Nothing at all could do that.

You'll see, Emma had said, and it was true. The future had passed before her in all its infinite variations, spilling probability, and Aggie remembered. One time. One chance at life, and while she did not know why or how, it was still her only choice, an inexplicable leap of faith. And though it was terrible, terrifying, she made it.

Aggie looked at the witch and waited.

"Agatha," Charlie growled, desperate. "Don't, Agatha. Do something. Fight. *Run*."

The witch hesitated.

"What?" Agatha asked. "Are you changing your mind?"

"It's unnatural," came the reply. "What you're doing."

"No," Aggie said, and she glanced over her shoulder at Charlie. "Death really isn't a high price to pay."

"All right, then," said the witch—and plunged the knife into Aggie's chest.

She did it fast; there was no time to react. Aggie heard Charlie scream as she fell to her knees, and thought, *Oh, shit, that was the wrong choice.*

But as Aggie began to slump sideways, she gazed up to find the witch staring down in horror at her own pale chest—at the blood seeping between her own breasts, a mirror to Aggie's injury.

"Impossible," breathed the witch. "You cast nothing. There was nothing in you . . ."

Her voice trailed away and the woman staggered, falling clumsily to the ground beside Aggie, who watched with a numb sense of victory as her foe slumped on her elbows and then her side, gulping for air, fingers fluttering against the wound beside her heart. The witch's hair lost its luster, receding like coiled snakes to her scalp. Aggie saw gray. She saw a lot of other things, too—spinning lights, sparkling, as the pain hit and her body became one open nerve. The knife still jutted from her chest. Bad aim, though. It had missed her heart. Not that it mattered in the long run.

"How?" whispered the witch, her eyes rolling around and around in their sockets, unable to focus.

"Don't know," Aggie breathed, weakness flooding her limbs, trailing darkness through her mind. "But I think you're dying . . . and I just can't bring myself to feel sorry about that. You'll be gone and he'll be free. *I've seen it.* And that's all that matters to me."

Charlie still screamed. Aggie heard a beating sound, rough, like wings, like stone scraping, cracking, hammers slamming on rock, and it was terrible—those terrible sounds, violent and fierce like a tempest, like death—and Aggie, darkness fluttering in her eyes, thought, *Yes, even demons would be scared of that.*

Blood, everywhere. Hers and the witch's, mixing and soaking into the sand. Aggie stared at the witch, the dying woman, watching that blood pour from her body, and saw her make that final breath, the slow exhale.

Then Aggie closed her eyes and died.

CHAPTER EIGHT

It was a dream of light and warmth, a sickle-shaped sun inside her chest, glowing bright and brighter, burning her skin, and she heard a voice say her name gently, and then loud, louder and louder until she opened her eyes.

For a moment Aggie forgot herself and she almost became a fool. A screaming fool. But memory swept through her mind, stealing away the scream in her throat, and as her vision cleared and she focused on the four monstrous faces looming over her, relief and victory took the place of fear, and she wanted to weep for the joy it gave her.

She recognized only one of the gargoyles. Red eyes blinked inside a silver face ravaged by grief.

"Charlie," she whispered, but he did not say anything except to make a low noise, a gasping choke, and he buried his face against her shoulder and neck. Wings dragged over her body. She smelled of blood and sweat. Stone. Fire. Her chest hurt like hell.

"You're free," she breathed. "I guess it worked, then. Wow. That's good."

"Lady," said one of the gargoyles standing above her. "You got some brass knockers down there."

He was a darker shade of silver than Charlie, but his size was the same, as were his wings. His chest was shaped differently. More ridges. Same with his face, his jutting brow. The other two beside him were a little broader through the chest, somewhat shorter, but their faces were less bony. She wondered absently, shape-shifting powers aside, how any of them ever passed as human. That was some trick.

"Charlie," Aggie said again. She tried to move her arm to pat him on the back, but was too weak. "Charlie, are you okay?"

He shuddered and pulled himself just far enough away to stare into her eyes. "Do I *look* okay?"

"You're alive," she said, feeling stronger. "So yeah. You look pretty damn good."

Charlie groaned and squeezed shut his eyes. He rolled off her body, sprawling on his back in the sand. Aggie felt very small next to him. She looked down at her chest. The knife was gone. There was a hole in her shirt, lots of dried blood, and beneath all that, a scar.

"How?" she asked them.

"My brothers," Charlie said, unmoving. "It's why the witch wanted them."

"We're mages," said the one who had spoken to her first. "It's rare amongst our kind. The witch knew it.

She wanted to control us, siphon off our powers for her use alone."

"What about Charlie?"

"I was away from home," he said. "And I'm no mage."

"But the rest of you can bring people back to life? Is that what you did for me?"

The three looked at each other; Aggie was not sure she liked their expressions. Human or not, their faces were still an open book. A symptom of bad liars, she thought.

"Under the right circumstances," one of them said, "we can resurrect the recently dead."

"Uh-huh," she said. "But . . ."

"But everything has a price," said the other. He had green hair, Aggie noted.

"That doesn't sound good," she said. Charlie stirred beside her and propped himself up on his elbow. Gazed down at her with eyes that were exasperated, a mouth that curved with affection and a body that leaned so protectively over hers that Aggie felt like she was stretched beneath a great stone wall.

"I told you that gargoyles live longer than humans," he said. "I gave you part of that life. My life. So Aggie, the next time you croak, so will I. So please, don't go throwing yourself on any more knives. Or bullets. No more car chases, either."

"You'll be asking me to check into a nunnery next."

His brothers laughed out loud. Charlie gave them dirty looks. He climbed slowly to his feet and then said to her, "I'm going to move you now. Are you ready?"

"Yes," she said, and he very carefully scooped her up

into his arms. She looked down. The knife lay on the ground nearby. So did the witch.

"She aged," Aggie remarked. White hair, deep wrinkles, shriveled breasts and bony hips. Blood covered her.

"Everything before was an illusion."

Aggie did not feel much when she looked at her. Empty, maybe.

"How did you know?" Charlie asked. "How did you know that giving yourself up like that was the right thing to do?"

"Even we have no idea how you did it," said one of his brothers. "We have never seen a spell backfire in such a way."

"I saw the future," Aggie said. "There was only one variation where she died and Charlie was free, and that was the one I chose. I didn't think of the how or the why."

"But you knew you would have to die."

"I was going to die anyway, Charlie. I just didn't want it to go to waste."

Charlie sucked in a great deep breath. His brothers stood around, solemn. Aggie soaked in their bodies: wings and eyes and strong bony faces. Odd and beautiful.

She felt tired. Charlie said, "Sleep, Agatha. I'll be here when you wake up."

"Good," she murmured. "I missed you." And then, lulled by his movements, she fell into a sweet darkness.

Charlie did not lie. He was there when she opened her eyes. He stood at a window, wings draped over his shoulders. He looked like a gothic angel. The room was dark. Aggie lay on a wide bed and the sheets were cool and soft on her body. She was not wearing any clothes.

She did not say anything for some time. Just watched him.

Finally, though, she said, "You lied."

Charlie jumped, and it was nice knowing she could surprise someone like him. That he was twitchy, no matter how medieval he looked. He walked to the bed and sat gingerly beside her. The mattress groaned, as did the bed frame.

"I would never lie to you," he said.

"You said you were ugly."

A smile tugged on his lips. "I still think I'm ugly. By human standards, anyway."

"And by gargoyle?"

He shrugged, but his smile grew. Aggie laughed. Her chest did not hurt, but she winced anyway. Reflex. Charlie's smile died.

"You scared me to death," he whispered. "You shouldn't have done that."

"I didn't have a choice. I told you. I was going to die, anyway."

"Then you shouldn't have come to me. I was stupid to tell you where I was. You could have been killed. You *were* killed. Agatha . . . I had no future beyond death until I met you and Emma. And then . . . then you go and. . . ." He stopped.

"I'd do it again," she said softly. "Or do you regret killing yourself every time you came to me and Emma?"

"That's different, Agatha. I was able to come back to life."

Aggie sighed. "I'm sorry, Charlie."

He shook his head. "Don't be. I wouldn't want to live without you, anyway."

Her heart hurt hearing those words. Charlie looked quickly away, eyes downcast. He began to stand, but Aggie grabbed his hand. His skin was warm and leathery. He went very still when she touched him. She tried to see his future—*their* future—but her mind remained dark and quiet.

"Don't leave me," she said to him. Charlie sat down, though he still did not look at her. He turned her hand over in his large palm, tracing it gently with the tip of his finger. Aggie shivered.

"I am touching you," Charlie whispered. "I am touching your hand. Do you know what a miracle that is?"

"I think I do," Aggie said, smiling. "Would you like to touch more?"

Charlie froze. "Don't Aggie. Not unless you mean it."

"And why wouldn't I?"

He finally looked at her, red eyes blazing, but before he could say a word Aggie sat up fast and kissed him, pushing her mouth hard against his, burying herself into his body. Charlie shuddered, groaning, and she thought, *Maybe gargoyles don't kiss.* But then his tongue touched her tongue and he was so damn good at it that all those thoughts fell down dead and it was all she could do not to shout with joy as that kiss surged through her body, right down to her soul.

She broke off with a gasp, a burst of laughter, and Charlie's arm snaked hard and strong around her body as she clung to him.

"Are you real?" he murmured, burying his face in her neck. "Aggie, please."

"Please," she echoed, uncaring that his eyes were red or that his face was silver and his body was inhuman. She did not care, she did not care . . . because all she could think of was that voice, that spirit named Charlie that was here with her now, warm and strong and alive. "Please, Charlie. I love you."

"Aggie," he breathed, and it was enough to see the emotion in his eyes, to remember his sacrifices. It was more than enough to know that he felt the same.

Charlie lay them down on the bed and curled around her body. His wings draped and Aggie ran her fingers along the fine delicate skin, which was soft as silk, with a sheen to match. He shuddered.

"You hide these?" she asked him. "I want to see you fly."

"Later," he said, "And yes, I hide them. I make them smaller and fold them around my body. I look like a very large man in human clothes."

Aggie tried to imagine, but could not. *Time,* she told herself. *You have time for all of that.*

"Emma's safe," Aggie said to him. She pushed up so close their noses rubbed. "If she doesn't have any other family, my boss, Roland, is going to try and intervene with foster care."

"That would be good," Charlie said. His large hands moved in slow circles around her back. His strength felt new and different; inhuman, but with enough similarities that Aggie thought she would be able to find her way around his body. The idea—and his touch—made her breathless.

"I was thinking of taking her," Aggie managed, trying to remain coherent. "If she wants me."

"That's a hard job," he said. "Raising a child."

"I could use some help," she admitted, and then bit her bottom lip. Her heart, which had just been so full of joy, shriveled a little as she waited for him to say something.

Charlie wrapped his hands in her hair, kneading her scalp, hugging her tight against his body. She kicked off her sheet and draped a leg over his hip, drawing him near. Charlie did not have much in the way of pants on. She felt him, hard and hot and long, against her body.

"I would be honored," he breathed. "I can't imagine anything else I'd rather do with my life."

"Good," Aggie said, and kissed him.

He broke off after a minute and said, "Maybe we're moving too fast."

"Like hell," she said. "I want this."

"I'm not human. I don't even look human. You might change your mind."

"I might change my mind?" Aggie sat up. The sheet fell away; she did not miss the hungry way he stared at her breasts and it made her so hot she felt woozy. "Charlie, I *died* for you today. And now you think I'm going to run—change my mind—because of the way you *look?* Who the hell do you think I am?"

"Well," he stopped. "Never mind."

"Damn straight."

"I mean, I *could* make myself look more human."

"*No.*" She grabbed his face, pressing her palms against the rough bones pushing up through his skin. She savored the differences, the beauty of them. "I want you just the way you are. You don't scare me, Charlie. You won't ever scare me. And," Aggie added, trailing her hands low across his stomach, "I won't change my mind."

His breath caught. She watched his face—and he watched hers—as she reached down and touched him. There were some differences. Charlie had . . . ridges. Nothing that she thought would hurt her. On the contrary, her curiosity was piqued. She was also quite mesmerized by his size.

"When was the last time you had sex?" she asked.

He did not immediately answer; Aggie realized she still held him and that her thumbs were doing all kinds of interesting things. She did not stop. Simply, increased the pressure and got the rest of her fingers moving, too. Charlie sucked in his breath; his eyelids fluttered closed.

"Charlie," she said quietly. "When was the last time?"

"I don't remember," he muttered, and gasped as she used her nails. He grabbed her arms and said, "If you keep this up—"

"Just *you* keep it up," she said, laughing, and scooted down the bed.

Charlie's legs began trembling before she even put her mouth around him, and she raked her nails down the sides of his thighs at the same time she wrapped her lips around his hard jutting head. He cried out, grabbing her shoulders, and she stroked her tongue over the curious ridges, tasting them, feeling them in her mouth as she sucked and licked. The tips of his wings draped against her hands. She reached higher and fluttered her fingertips against the thin membrane. Charlie growled.

"You like that?" she asked, breathing against his shaft, rubbing her cheek against its immense swollen length.

"I like it too much," he whispered. "I won't last for you."

"You'll last," she said.

His hands relaxed around her arms. "Come back to me, Agatha."

She was not done with him, but she moved back up the bed because there was something in his voice she could not disobey—hunger, desire, all those words for pleasure—and this time it was her legs that quivered and she was sure if he kissed her she would explode. Sure enough, when he pressed his mouth upon her she did feel sparks fly, but Charlie caught her in his arms and held her tight against his body, one hand behind her head, the other cupping her tight against his hard hot length. His mouth tasted so damn good she wanted to curl up inside his body and purr.

"Oh," she breathed, when his mouth left her and traveled up her cheek, to her ear. "Oh, wow."

And then she was on her back and his hands were on her breasts, lower—his tongue, lower—and it was even better than she had imagined, better than the last spectacular time when all he had been was an apparition of pure warmth.

She felt the tip of him at the edge of her body, and

she did not wait for him to hesitate, just moved her hips, swallowing him in one quick thrust, and she said, "Wow. Just . . . hold on a minute."

He went very still. "Did I hurt you?"

"No, no . . . I just need to get used to you. You're . . . big."

Charlie buried his face against her neck, but it was no use. She felt his grin as he kissed her cheek. And then he began laughing. Which made him move in different ways, and that was good, too.

All of it, deliciously, wonderfully, good.

And at the end of the night, when the sky began to lighten beyond the window, Aggie curled up inside his massive arms, draped in his wings, and listened as he said, "I love you very much, Aggie. And it's not the sex talking."

"I know," she said. "Same to you."

He laughed, and then, quieter, said, "We don't know a thing about each other. Or at least, you don't know anything about me. My family, my kind. Doesn't that scare you?"

"No," she said, and it was true. Always, she had feared for her heart, for the unknown. All her life, she had seen what the future held for others, but never herself. And that had made her cautious. Too cautious, too afraid of choices, of taking the wrong step and falling down into an unwanted future.

Until now. She was not afraid now. Not with Charlie. And that in itself was miracle enough to take a chance on.

"The two of us together," Charlie whispered. "We are impossible, Agatha."

"It won't be easy," she admitted. "But we've come this far."

"And if we don't last?"

"I think we will. The probabilities are high."

"Is that what the future says?"

"That's what *I* say," she told him.

"Well," he said, "that's good enough for me."

And he kissed her.